Also by Debbie Burns

Summer by the River

YOU'RE
MY HOME

DEBBIE BURNS

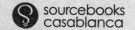

sourcebooks
casablanca

Published by Sourcebooks Casablanca, an imprint of Sourcebooks
P.O. Box 4410, Naperville, Illinois 60567-4410
(630) 961-3900
sourcebooks.com

Printed and bound in the United States of America.
OPM 10 9 8 7 6 5 4 3 2 1

For Jeni,
who, way back when, rode a horse across
town and knocked on my door,
and who introduced me to the
beauty of Lake Michigan

Chapter 1

IN THE DIM GLOW FROM THE NIGHT-LIGHT, RILEY crossed her old bedroom floor and dropped to her knees in front of the closet where she began rummaging through all the stuff she'd brought home with her deemed too essential to be stuck in storage. Finally, her fingers brushed the cardboard box she was searching for. Back in Atlanta, where she'd lived until two days ago, it was a quarter to six. Here in Missouri, it was an hour earlier, and not at all a desirable time to get out of bed. Especially for a girl with nowhere to go.

Thanks to Hercules, a big orange tabby cat with a long, spindly tail and the newest addition to her mom's cat menagerie, she was wide awake after several back-to-back pounce attacks. Apparently, he hadn't gotten the memo that cats in the Leighton household weren't allowed to disturb the sleeping.

On the bright side, there was no better time to head out for the jog she'd promised herself she'd get to today. With the heat wave hanging over two-thirds of the country, this was the coolest it would be today, and with as many breakups as she'd had over the last decade, Riley knew good and well she was nearing the end of her bounce-back window, the one at the end of which it became clear that pushing herself just a little harder wasn't going to fix all her broken and imperfect parts.

Box in hand, she sank to the floor and pulled out the brand-new, top-of-the-line running shoes that had nearly broke the bank. Some people went on benders after breakups. Some moped. Others hopped right back into the fray. Riley nearly always treated herself to a new pair of running shoes.

One of these days, her body would believe her "There's no better time like the present!" pep talks. She'd reconnect with the cross-country runner she'd been in high school, the one who could, a bit begrudgingly, complete a 5K on a Saturday morning and still make it to her volunteer job to walk dogs.

After tying on the shoes—walking in them really did feel like floating—Riley made her way downstairs. She spotted the soft glow of the light over the kitchen sink as she neared the landing and half expected to spy Tommy, her younger brother, who still lived at home. He had apartment-style digs in the basement and was a night owl. Instead, the coffee pot was brewing, and her mom was wiping down the counters as her other two cats circled her feet. She did a double take when she spied Riley walking in fully dressed. "Where on earth are you going so early?"

"Jogging." Riley recognized the irony in her single-word answer as she crossed to the sink for a drink of water. She was just over four weeks from turning thirty and could count on both hands the miles she'd managed to jog since track ended, but her mom didn't know that.

Brenda looked as if she were trying to bite back a comment, but temptation won. "Not to play mother to a girl who fled the nest at eighteen and hardly looked back, but it's dark out there. Careful not to trip on those uneven slabs of sidewalk."

"I will." While her mom was still in her pajamas, she didn't appear to have just rolled out of bed. "I didn't expect to see you up this early. Did Hercules wake you too?" Not that Brenda didn't have enough reason to be awake in the early-morning hours, even without a cat waking her up.

"No, he left me alone this morning. Seeing as you're up, I'm guessing he had plenty to entertain him."

"For the record, he's my least favorite of your cats."

"He's half-feral. Give him time; he'll be a sweetie soon enough."

Riley didn't agree but also didn't feel the need to argue the point. "So, what *are* you doing up? You feeling okay?" Maybe Riley had fled Atlanta on the heels of a breakup, but it was her mom's cancer diagnosis that had her heading home with the assuredness of a homing pigeon. If only for a little while.

Brenda smiled in that "I'm a mom and have everything under control" way of hers. "My sleepless early mornings started with menopause, not breast cancer, dear."

After drinking half the glass of water she'd poured, Riley set the glass on the back of the sink and nodded. "It's just that with radiation starting next week, no one would fault you if you're losing sleep over the thought of it."

"It's stage one, Riley. Well, it *was* stage one. Now that the lumpectomy's out of the way, it's probably not even that."

Riley knew better than to argue with her. Brenda Leighton was a go-getter who outpaced most go-getters. "They're getting really good at fighting breast cancer. At least, that's what I keep hearing. But I'm here if you want to talk about it." The declaration had her lips feeling a bit like rubber. Riley and her mom never talked about things. Not about anything real. Not anymore. Riley wondered if her mom missed their old talks as much as a part of her did—the part she worked hard to ignore.

Brenda's expression softened. "You know, I was thinking how it'd be nice to go get mani-pedis sometime. Like we used to."

You're going to have to get over all this

sometime. You might as well start with your mom.
"Yeah, that'd be nice."

"Great. It's a date."

Riley jutted her thumb toward the door. "Well, I'd better get out there before the sun comes up, seeing as it's going to be another scorcher." As she headed for the door, the cats followed, hoping for the chance to sneak outside. Riley shooed them off before stepping out into the silver-gray morning. Ever since she was little, her mom had been known around town for her dedication to the school PTO board, her award-winning Christmas cookies, and for the stray cats who found their way here.

Forgoing a calf stretch that would only give her more time to change her mind, Riley pushed off into a jog that was slow-paced enough a speed walker could pass her. Her new shoes clapped monotonously against the asphalt as her body acclimated to the early-morning strain. With the streetlights and hint of brightening sky in the east, she could make out the uneven slabs of sidewalk well enough not to worry about proving her mom right and tripping.

Two blocks in, her body announced it was time for a break, but she pushed on, weaving alongside streets ingrained in memory even though she'd all but avoided her hometown of Webster Groves since leaving for college. Quick trips in and out a couple times a year at holidays, that was it.

As Riley passed a quaint house on Portland Terrace, one with a delicate-looking concrete bench under a stately weeping willow, she remembered daydreaming of sitting there and reading a book every time she'd ridden past on her bike. After that, she jogged past two stately brick homes that were mirror images of one another, all the way down to the landscaping, matching rocking chairs, and ornate urns lining their porches, like matching rooks in a chess competition. They hadn't changed one bit.

At the end of block six, her legs protested their way to a walk, completely disregarding the mental pep talk they were being given.

Considering how hard she'd worked to get over him, Riley wished it wasn't Levi Duncan popping into mind again on this trip down memory lane. Ever since she'd decided to come home, he'd been a prominent fixture in her thoughts. Not that he'd ever been out of them for too long of a stretch at that. The part of her that didn't want to admit the truth knew that all the running away she'd been doing, hopping from job to job, city to city, guy to guy, had started with him.

"Nobody falls in love in their senior year of high school." Tightening her ponytail, she glanced around, half expecting someone out grabbing their morning paper to be witness to this outburst of doubt, but the stately yards she was walking past were empty, save a foraging bird or two.

Levi, with his amber-brown eyes that were mocking and playful and covering up a mess of hurt he didn't want anyone to see. Levi, with his athlete's physique and smooth-as-silk grin, who'd had close to half the senior class wishing they could call him theirs even though pinning him down had proven to be as impossible as carrying fistfuls of sand.

Just thinking of him filled her limbs with enough tension that she pushed off into a jog again. "We'd never have made it anyway." *Yeah, that's it, talk yourself down from that ledge of regret.*

Riley faltered a step even though the slabs of concrete underfoot were perfectly even. She might as well be standing at a stove, thinking of peeking under the lid of a boiling pot and knowing she'd be blasted in steam if she dared do so. She and Levi could never have made it—not with what they'd had going against them. End of story. Coming home didn't change that. Nor did pining about all the things she'd do differently if she could do them over again.

Despite protests from each one of her body parts, Riley powered through another three blocks before she spotted the High Grove Animal Shelter up ahead, partially blocked from view by the trees. She slowed to a walk to catch her breath again, dragging her forearm across her forehead to swipe away the beads of sweat lining it.

There it was—the one thing she'd missed over the years about her hometown as much as she'd missed Levi. Her mom's knack for acquiring cats had never left any room for a family dog. This led Riley here the day after her thirteenth birthday when she could finally enroll in the junior dog-walking program. Whenever life had served Riley an oversized bowl of lemons back then, this place had gotten her through.

She made her way down the gently sloping strip of grass between the sidewalk and the parking lot and crossed over to the building. It was still so early that the place was entirely dark, save a handful of floodlights both inside and out. None of the early-morning care staff or dog walkers had gotten here yet, so Riley felt comfortable peeking in the large front window. A familiar-looking silvery-gray cat was stretched out and dozing along the length of the windowsill. "Hey there, Trina." Riley resisted the urge to tap on the glass and wake the shelter's longtime three-legged feline resident. "Look at you, still going strong. You've got to be getting up there."

How long had it been since Riley had stopped by here last? Four or five years at least. Even by the dim light of a handful of interior floodlights, it was obvious some major remodeling had been done, and the open front room had a soft, inviting look about it. Riley promised herself she'd work in a real tour before taking off again, wherever it might be that she was headed next, depending on which of the résumés she was sending out resulted in her next job. Maybe she'd even see about walking a few dogs again too.

Stepping back, she caught a movement in her peripheral vision off to her left, one that was immediately followed by a shuffling in the darkness. Something was skulking in the shadows in the landscaping on the opposite side of the main door. Instantly, the fine hairs on her arms and back of her neck stood on end.

She wasn't alone out here.

Frozen in place, she struggled to make out what was lurking in the darkness between two wide-set exterior floodlights. Quite possibly she'd glanced straight into one of the lights for a second because she was seeing things. She was attempting to blink away her confusion when whatever she was staring at began to lumber upward. Every ounce of her yearned to bolt, but Riley stood frozen long enough to make out the shape of an animal—a giant animal—watching her in the darkness. A skinny pony, she first thought.

Another deep blink proved it wasn't a horse. It was a dog, one of the biggest she'd ever seen.

Riley's racing blood began to settle. Fifteen feet away, a pure bred—or mostly pure bred—Great Dane was silently staring her down. But what on earth was it doing out here and not inside? As soon as the thought crossed her mind, she realized the shelter would never leave a dog outside. This dog had either found its way here or had been dumped overnight.

"Hey, boy—or girl. Whichever you are." Without daring to step closer, she lifted a hand and made a kissing sound. Maybe the darkness made the canine seem bigger than life. "Want to come here?"

Its black tail pumping, the dog took what seemed to be a tentative step, rustling the bush behind it. After a second or two, it whined, a deep, pleading pitch. Out of all the dogs she'd walked and brushed during her volunteer years, she'd had almost zero interaction with Great Danes.

"You're tied, aren't you?"

It whined again, tail pumping harder.

Gentle giants, she'd heard, and hoped so. Suppressing the part of her that warned she'd had better ideas than approaching a stray dog who might very well outweigh her, she walked over. She kept her gaze down and her hand out while babbling softly about what a good dog it was. When she got close enough, and it pushed forward, pressing its big, strong muzzle against her hand, she believed her own proclamations.

The big dog sniffed her midsection and along her bra line before moving to her arms. Most dogs went for the crotch sniff. This one was too tall. Riley ran a hand over its smooth, solid head and along a silky ear. "It's disarming how big you are. You look like a dog, but you're entirely too big for one."

Its whiplike tail beat faster as Riley followed the long retractable leash to where it was wrapped securely around the base of a waist-high metal cutout cat silhouette in the landscaping. "I'm surprised you didn't pull that right out of the ground." Riley sank to her knees, and the big dog pressed in close, towering above her and sniffing the top of her head. The part of the leash wound around the base was a tangled mess. Every time she got a bit more untangled, she realized there was more to go.

She fiddled and tugged for several minutes as he whined—from this vantage point there was no doubt about his gender.

"It would be so much easier if I could unhook you, but I'm afraid you'll get away." It was getting lighter in the east, and she could see better with each passing minute. She was working out the last knot when she spotted a folded piece of paper in the mulch a few feet away, one that didn't look as if it had been lying around outside for very long.

After working the last bit of leash free and unwinding the handle through the final loop, she reached over and grabbed the paper. Aiming it toward the nearest floodlight, she read while the dog sniffed at it in her hands.

*This tears me up, but I lost my job and can't
afford to keep him, not the way he eats. I pray
you'll give Arlo the good home he deserves. I
guess you should know that he doesn't like loud
noises, raised voices, or being left alone. He'll be
three this November, and I doubt there ever was
a better dog.*

"Arlo, huh?" Still towering above her, Arlo
cocked his head and whipped his tail, whining
softly. "Oh, sweet baby, I'm so sorry, but it seems
you've got some changes coming your way."

He stepped in close enough that Riley pressed
her head against his thick chest as she smoothed
her hand along his side. She was still debating what
to do next when a pair of headlights pulling into the
parking lot caught her attention.

Arlo woofed a single woof that was fitting of
a dog his size, and Riley stood up, shifting the
leash handle from one hand to the other and folding the note. A handful of different "Oh, he's not
mine, I just found him out here" excuses raced
through her mind.

Even before the driver rolled down the window
of his pickup truck, alerting her that intakes weren't
allowed for another two hours and twenty minutes,
Riley realized this was one heck of a way to take
that first step back here that she'd promised herself
mere minutes ago.

Chapter 2

LEVI'S PHONE BUZZED IN THE DARKNESS. Dragging a hand over his face, one that hadn't seen a razor in days, he swiped it off the nightstand. Wincing from the glare of the screen, he held it out, extending his arm. Further away, the brightness was less piercing.

Staring at the screen hurt his head enough that he ignored all but one text, one that stood out among the rest. It was from Marcus, his best buddy from back home in St. Louis.

You'll never guess who showed up back in town.

That was it, no follow-up answer, just the statement. A face popped into mind, unsolicited, one that had Levi wincing internally even more than the glare of the screen did. He'd never admit to thinking about her, not this many years later, not even to Marcus, but even so, he found himself asking for confirmation.

Who?

Marcus had sent his text at one in the morning. Now, it was a quarter to seven. Levi didn't hold out hope of his buddy replying soon; no one in Levi's acquaintance cared less about the whereabouts of his phone than Marcus. But it didn't matter. It had to be her. Riley. Marcus wouldn't text him about anyone else like that.

With his skin suddenly too tight for his body, Levi dropped the phone on the nightstand, facing it screen side down. Spying the soft light slipping in from a crack in the drapes of the extended-stay hotel room he'd been at long enough that he had the itch to move on, he headed over and tugged them open. He stared out past the hotel property into the endless water that stretched in all directions beyond the soft, white sand and watched the gently rolling waves long enough that his breath began to match their rhythm.

It had been entirely too long since he'd been in the water, thanks to the mother of concussions curtailing his activities this last month—curtailing his activities the last thirty-five days, technically. Considering he'd practically been comatose those first four or five days after the accident, he was rounding it down to a month.

To hell with what the doctors said. His head wasn't going to heal any faster out of a wetsuit than in one. It was the opposite, he'd bet. Besides, swimming and diving weren't the same thing.

After throwing on his swim trunks and grabbing a towel, he headed out the sliding door barefoot. Leaving his bottom-floor hotel room's exterior entrance unlocked, he made his way down the sidewalk, across the dry, late-summer grass, and over the wide strip of beach. The fine, white sand under his feet melted some of the tension that had been mounting inside him.

For late August along the northern strip of Lake Michigan on the outskirts of Manistee, the summer tourists had mostly gone, and today, it was still early enough that the beach was largely deserted. Aside from an older man sitting in the sand, legs crossed, palms up, eyes closed, the only other beachgoers were those who were passing through, making use of the packed, wet sand at the water's edge. A woman jogged by, leash wadded in one hand, and an off-leash yellow Lab trotted alongside her, glancing Levi's direction for a second or two without losing a beat.

Witnessing their bond, a burst of anger sparked inside Levi. Who had time for dogs anymore anyway? Not him. He dug his feet deeper into the sand as he walked, the muscles in his calves and the back of his thighs welcoming a bit of exercise after too quiet of a month.

Even though Levi had used every trick in the book to forget about him, an image of Tank flashed into his mind uninvited. Glossy, chocolate fur, stocky but strong Lab body. Lively brown eyes reflecting a wisdom that went beyond his years and his species. Mouth gaping open in a wide grin, letting that pink-purple tongue loll out. That perpetual "what's next" expression on his face.

Levi had never been good at keeping track of dates and anniversaries, but now that he was deliberately trying not to, it was impossible to forget the last day he'd run his hand over the top of that boxy head or down those long, silky ears. Nearly seven months later, Levi still woke up most mornings braced to turn into his pillow so as not to get an up-close and personal whiff of dog breath in those early-morning hours as Tank made every effort to claim a chunk of Levi's morning before he headed out to work.

Dropping the bleached-white hotel towel on the sand just above the top of the swash, Levi headed for the water. The cool sting of the soft waves lapped up against his ankles, then his legs, as he made his way deeper in. Later, in the heat of the day and underneath a piercing sun, the chilly water would be more tolerable, but Levi welcomed the cold. He dove in when the water reached midthigh, savoring the way the brisk water cradled his body even though the ever-present pounding in his head crescendoed instantly.

Like most of his buddies from his Houston-based commercial diving school, Levi preferred the more buoyant, saline waves of the ocean to the calmer, freshwater ones he'd worked in the last several years. His old employer had reached out to him twice in the last year, hoping to entice him back, but Levi was done working on rigs. Up here along the shores of the Great Lakes, work was steady, which was more than he could say for his first seven years out of school spent as an offshore commercial diver. Out at sea, it was feast or famine, with no middle ground to come up for a breather during the on season and little to fill the void during the winter months that were too dangerous to work in the ocean.

Rather than surface, Levi remained submerged in the semiclear water, alongside the young sunfish, smallmouth bass, and walleye swimming close to check him out before darting away. With the water surrounding him, the text that had sent him out here didn't tear at him the same way. It was always like that. In the water was the only place his insides didn't feel like Mentos dropped in a bottle of Diet Coke when he thought about Riley.

It took a certain type of person to let people in—or dogs in, for that matter—and Levi had come to the realization he wasn't that person. He'd had the world's best dog and lost him years prematurely thanks to the bitch that was bone cancer. He'd fallen in love with the one person who'd not only understood him but who'd also understood all the things he never found a way to say. But then the cruel irony that was life had stepped in, and she'd shut him out and built up a barrier between them thicker than a castle wall. Impenetrable.

The only connections Levi had any interest in maintaining now were the ones he had with his buddies from work. He'd die for them, and they'd die for him, all without ever knowing much beyond the stuff that could be skimmed off the surface. And that was just fine.

It had been twelve years now since he'd been with Riley, and the women he'd been with since, the memories of them—their faces, bodies, and stories—faded till they were as dull as lake water. With Riley, little details didn't fade.

For that matter, neither did the scars.

He didn't care why she'd shown up back home, and he wasn't going to press Marcus to find out. Sure, he couldn't pretend that once or twice a year, in a particularly low moment, he didn't peruse her social media accounts. But that didn't mean anything. She was history, nothing more.

Liar.

The burning in his lungs and the sledgehammer pounding away at his skull from the inside forced him to the water's surface while his arms and legs itched to press on. It took only a few strokes to notice how much easier it was on his head to swim at the surface rather than underneath, so he stayed here, arching his arms and savoring the break of the water as the tips of his fingers pierced it.

Finally, he stopped and flipped onto his back, his body rocking with the gentle waves. He dragged a hand over his eyes, pulling in slow breaths while waiting for his vision to clear. The shoreline was a good hundred feet away, and he was double that distance down shore from his hotel.

He swam back lazily, pacing his strokes so that they were in rhythm with the pounding in his head, one stroke for every two throbs. By the time he'd retrieved his towel and made it back to his room, an hour had passed since he'd stepped out. As soon as he flipped on the shower to rinse off, there was a loud rap at the door, too loud for housekeeping. Shirtless and still in his trunks, Levi pulled it open without checking the peephole.

He blinked in surprise at the man standing there, at the wide shoulders taking up most of the breadth of the doorway, the buzz cut that was more gray at the temples than black, and the two jumbo-sized coffees in his hands.

"Gene." Levi's defenses pricked instantly. There could be no good reason his boss was standing in the hallway of his hotel on a Friday morning. No good reason at all. "I heard from the guys you were up this way. What's up?"

Gene was too quick to drop his gaze and glance down the hall toward the far exit. "I called. Last night and this morning. I wanted to catch you before I head out for Benton Harbor this afternoon.

Boyd gave me your room number when you didn't answer your phone."

Levi dragged a hand through his wet hair, his blond waves several shades darker after his swim. "Hang on. I was about to hop in the shower."

Gene followed him in without waiting for an invitation. There was a small couch and coffee table, but these extended-stay hotel rooms weren't for company. The only people Levi ever welcomed inside were dates, and even then, he preferred being a visitor to having one.

Gene was eyeing the messy bed covers and the bottle of scotch on the nightstand when Levi stepped back into the main room after shutting off the shower. He crossed the room and headed out the sliding door to the microsized patio with its wrought-iron table for two without asking if Gene wanted to join him. He dragged the far chair to the corner of the small slab of concrete, its metal feet scraping along the way.

Gene set Levi's coffee on the table and sank into the opposite chair, back and shoulders arrow straight and his own coffee in hand. His face carried the all-business expression he'd no doubt mastered long before walking away from his Navy career fifteen years ago and taking over this commercial diving business.

"Thanks." Levi lifted the cup in thanks before taking a cautious sip. Steam was steadily rising from the small hole in the lid. It was black; Gene wasn't the type to think of fixing it any other way, not that Levi cared for it another way either. "So, you showing up here. I know bad news when I see it."

Gene's lips pressed into a flat line, and he glanced over at the lake. "Knowing your dedication to the job, I figure you'll label it that, but I'm hoping you'll still think it over."

"Think what over?"

"Managing a crew. From above the water." His gaze was direct, somewhere between plea and command. "You've got ten-plus years' experience, and you know the water like no one I've ever met."

Levi sat forward in his chair. "For how long?"

Rather than answer, Gene waited him out for the space of several seconds. "Till you retire."

The weight of a thousand bricks pressed him into his chair. "You want me to send guys down on dives into water I'm not in? Into conditions I can't vouch for? Not a chance." Levi would be hard pressed to think of anything worse. "I need to be down there. It's the only way I work."

Gene cleared his throat. "I'm afraid you're going to have to find another way."

Levi locked his thumb and forefinger on opposite sides of his temple and squeezed hard. "Look, this isn't my first rodeo with a concussion. I'll get better. I'm getting better. I just need to get back in the water."

Gene's gaze lifted to take in Levi's wet hair. "By

the looks of it, you're doing that already, against doctor's orders."

"You know what I mean. That hypochondriac doctor needs to release me so I can get back to work."

"Levi…" Gene set his coffee down and rested his arms on the table, his fingers locking together. "Your doctor sent over her IME report yesterday. That's not going to happen." He cleared his throat. "It's *never* going to happen."

Levi pushed up from the table fast enough that the back feet of his chair bumped against the edge of the patio, and the chair tumbled over onto the grass. "That's a load of bullshit! I know what's good for me, better than she does." He dragged his hands through his hair and let out an exasperated grunt.

Looking back, he could see it now, the closed off way the doctor who'd been hired to run the Independent Medical Exam had been throughout her time with him. Nothing about the experience should've left him feeling hopeful to get back to work. "Look, if I need to take another month off, I'll do it. By then, I'll be good to go."

"That hit you took—Levi, you're lucky to be standing here, talking to me. You've been through the training enough times. You know the drill."

Levi knew the drill, but he wasn't about to say it.

When he kept silent, Gene continued. "With a moderate TBI like that, on top of mild concussions back in your football days, working as a commercial diver again would be iffy, at best. But you were unconscious right around the thirty-minute mark. Underwater, you're a high seizure risk now. No insurance company in the world's going to sign off on you going back in the water. Not for pay."

By the way Gene was eyeing him, Levi must have looked as if he were going to explode. He stood there, waiting, not giving an inch.

"Look, if this is a fight you really want to fight," Gene continued, "you can try fighting it in four or five years when you've had a good stretch with no symptoms and no seizures, but we both know how to do that math. You just hit thirty, man." Gene turned his hands up and splayed his fingers. "Commercial diving isn't a job for middle-aged men. And you don't need me to tell you that."

Levi righted his chair but remained standing. "I didn't do one thing wrong in that water."

"No one ever said you did." Gene's typically inexpressive face dropped in what could only be described as genuine empathy. "It may not seem like it right now, but this is a chance for you to explore something else. Something new. Even if you stick with not hiring your own lawyer to handle your case, you're going to walk away with a nice settlement. I'll make sure of that. Though no one'll blame you if you want your own representation."

"This report, I want to see it. My balance was

a little off, but how could it not have been? That Romberg test—nobody can balance like that."

"I guess I don't need to remind you that *you* used to be able to. Every physical, every year." Gene took a swig from his cup. "Look, the legal team is drawing up an offer. They'll have it to you by the end of the day. There'll be a copy of the medical report inside. Without a lawyer representing you, I feel compelled to say turn it down. They'll come back with something better."

"I'm not looking to make bank and sit on my ass, Gene."

"I know that. It's been a hard few years, Levi. Losing Carlos like that last October. Diver error or not didn't make it any easier on the team. It'd be good for them to see you find your way after this. It'll be good for me too. Heck, most importantly, it'll be good for you."

Levi shook his head, at a loss for words.

"How about shaking things up a bit? Maybe put a roof over your head that has a bit more permanence to it. Replace that bedside bottle of scotch in there with something breathing. Maybe another dog, maybe a woman. Maybe both."

"I had a dog, the best one in the world. I don't want another. As for women, they tend to wear out their welcome faster than it takes me to go through one of those bottles."

"Not all of them. Not the right ones." Gene stood

up with a nod. Man of few words that he was, he'd said his piece. "Think it through. Call me later, after you've seen the offer."

Levi followed him inside and over to the door. He knew he should thank him, should say more than, "I'll be seeing you," but nothing came.

He shut the door behind him, full of even more tension than before he'd headed out for the swim. His head was pounding every bit as hard too, but ripe, fresh anger was sharp enough to override it.

Bound up with tension, he crossed the room to the nightstand, reaching for the phone and ignoring the half-empty bottle next to it. Wouldn't he know it, Marcus had texted back, the single-word answer glaring at him.

Riley.

Chapter 3

ONCE RILEY EXPLAINED TO PATRICK—AN average-looking guy about her age with disheveled brown hair—that she was a former volunteer in town visiting and that she'd encountered the dog while jogging, he invited her inside. "Riley Leighton. You're on our roster, but you've been reallocated to the inactive list. A volunteer is a volunteer, though. If you'd like, you can come in and help get him settled."

"Are you kidding? I'd love to."

"He'll be our third Great Dane this summer, but the first with the fawn coat color. The breed hit number fifteen on the AKC popularity ranking last year, but they're expensive to care for."

"I can imagine." She offered him the note. "I found this near him. Apparently, it was the cost of his care that made him wind up here. His name's Arlo."

Now Riley remembered why Patrick was familiar. He managed the shelter's social media accounts, and she'd been paying attention to his posts. They were clean, sharp, and to the point. No extra fluff, good quality video, nice graphics. Considering as much time as Riley had spent studying successful posts, especially ones from nonprofits, she knew how to evaluate them. That detail-oriented spin they had seemed to fit his personality, with him remembering the coat colors of recent intakes as easily as he'd remembered her name from what had to be a lengthy list of volunteers.

Patrick directed her to head around back, then took off that direction in his truck. With what felt like glue sticking to the bottoms of her shoes, Riley smoothed a hand along the top of Arlo's head. The part of her that seemed to be perpetually five years old wanted to lock her arms around the dog and refuse to let anyone near him. As much as she loved the shelter, she didn't want to abandon this solemn-eyed dog here. Or anywhere.

Thoughts of what her mom would say if she showed up with him at home kicked her into gear. "Come on, buddy. There's no use dragging this out." There wasn't room for a Great Dane in the mix with Brenda's feral cat rescuing. Besides, Arlo's owner left him here with the intent of him ending up in the shelter's care, not in hers.

Taller than the thick-coated pony she'd led around last year at Naturally Green's employee picnic, Arlo plodded along willingly until they reached the steel door at the back of the building labeled "Intakes" where Patrick was waiting. Abruptly, Arlo planted his feet firmly in place and lifted his head, the whites of his eyes showing.

"Come on, buddy, let's go." Riley attempted to sound as reassuring as possible. "It'll be fine, I promise." It took a bit of pleading, but eventually he released that impressively imposing emergency brake and followed her inside to a small, sterile-looking quarantine room. "Good boy! Good dog, Arlo." She patted him reassuringly, and he pressed close against her.

Stainless-steel kennels flanked the room's two long sides, and an exam table and shelving were on the narrow wall opposite the door. Despite the soft lighting and melodic music playing over a set of speakers, Riley could imagine how traumatic it would likely be for an animal who'd been in a loving home to suddenly wind up here.

Perhaps it was the earliness of the hour, but none of the two dozen or so dogs and cats barked at the new arrival as they entered. This seemed odd until Riley realized they likely hadn't been here long enough to be territorial of their new digs. Out in the main kennels, it was a different story. The way Riley remembered it, when new dogs were introduced out there, it was louder than a bounce house packed with kindergarteners.

Arlo glanced up at Riley, cocking his head as a long, pitiful whine escaped. Trembling hard, he clung close enough that Riley needed to plant her feet to keep from getting bowled over. "Poor thing. He's terrified."

Patrick dropped an impressively thick set of keys into a side pocket of his cargo pants as he shut the exterior door. "Over ninety-five percent of intakes undergo high levels of trepidation when they first arrive."

Riley had never known anyone with a photographic memory, but by the way he was spouting out facts and figures, it seemed like a safe assumption that Patrick had one. "Oh yeah? I can see that."

"As an inactive volunteer living out of town, you're due for a tour. We've remodeled two-thirds of the building over the last two years. If another staff member is here by the time we're done with him, I'll request you be given one. I have six more items on my to-do list today than typical. Seven, including him, even though he isn't on it."

"That's a big to-do list, but yeah, sure. I'd love that."

There was only one kennel in the room large enough for a Great Dane, but it was taken by two yellow Labs who looked so much like matching bookends that Riley was betting they'd grown up together.

Clearly aware of the lack of suitable kennels, Patrick wasted no time hooking the two eager Labs up to leashes and walking them into the main part of the shelter.

Arlo relaxed enough in Patrick's absence to lean over and sniff two orange tabby cats in the nearest kennel. Riley wished like heck she had her phone to snap a picture. It would make a great Instagram post.

When Patrick returned a few minutes later without the dogs but with rubber gloves, disinfecting spray, a scrub brush, and a squeegee, Arlo glued himself to Riley's hip again.

"Where'd you take the Labs?"

"I moved them to one of the meet and greet rooms until someone gets here to take them outside for their morning break. They're finished with quarantine today. After Fidel gives them a temperament evaluation, they'll move to the main kennels with the adoptable dogs."

Riley was familiar enough with temperament evaluations to know they were conducted with both the dogs' and potential owners' best interests in mind. One of the things she'd always loved about High Grove was the way staff took care to match potential adopters with pets that would be a good fit in their homes. Good matches meant forever homes.

Arlo stayed pressed against her, still shivering and eyeing Patrick as if he might turn into a monster at any second. After Patrick set the supplies in front of the empty kennel, Riley took a leap. "I could clean it for you, since you have so much to do."

Patrick's face lifted in surprise. "Do you remember our three-step disinfection and cleaning process?"

"That I do! Mostly I walked dogs back in the day, but I've cleaned enough kennels here that I'm pretty sure it's burned into my brain forever."

"Good." He gave a little nod. "Then I'll do his intake."

After offering over an unhappy Arlo, Riley slipped on the rubber gloves and went to work. In addition to the supplies Patrick had brought in, there was a hose in the room and a large drain as well, essentials when it came to running a shelter.

A smile spread over her face as she went to work. Stepping out her front door forty-five minutes ago, she never would've believed she'd end up here, doing this like old times. And something about it felt more right than anything had in a long time.

"So, you're the social media person here, aren't you?" Riley said over her shoulder. "Your posts are great."

Patrick had lifted one of Arlo's ears but paused to look her way. "Yes, and no." Riley wasn't sure how to respond and was thankful when he continued. "I was, but I've been promoted to business manager. I'm continuing to oversee social media for the next forty-one days until our new marketing coordinator starts."

Riley released the hose handle as hope rose and fell in an instant. With all the résumés she'd sent out lately, how had she not seen that the shelter was hiring a marketing coordinator? *You didn't see it because you weren't looking for jobs in St. Louis, that's why.*

Working for High Grove would be a dream job, no question, but not only was there no way she was staying in St. Louis, she was also intent on keeping a low profile while in town. She knew way too many people around here—and way too many people knew her business—for anything else.

Still, this didn't stop her scheming. "You've hired someone already? It's a done deal?"

"Yes." Patrick raised his voice in the assumption that she'd not heard him over the spray of the hose. "He's finishing an internship with a shelter in Seattle, but he's signed the paperwork."

"But he's not starting for six weeks?"

That look again, like he wondered if she was hard of hearing. "He starts in forty-one days, so not quite."

Clearly Patrick dabbled in details, but Riley didn't mind. Maybe there was lemonade to be made out of missing this opportunity. Yesterday was her first full day home, and she'd sent off eleven résumés to all ends of the country. Now, she had nothing to do but wait. What better place to fill her time than High Grove, especially given the fact that her mom was doing so well?

Her mind raced as Patrick refocused on Arlo, using his thumb to lift the side of Arlo's floppy jowl to look at his pink-and-black gums and his massive molars and canines. Arlo craned his head away from Patrick and gave Riley a pleading look that made it clear he was much happier before the switch.

"I hope you don't mind my asking, but it sounds like you have your hands full." *Please, please, please, let them consider using a temp until they hire someone.* She couldn't think of anything she'd rather do to fill her time for however long she was home. In Atlanta, Riley had worked for a green lawn care company. In Chicago, an ad agency. In Memphis, a high-end sauce company. It was a long-held dream to switch over to the nonprofit world, animal shelters specifically, and nothing beat High Grove.

Patrick stopped working on Arlo's paperwork, making it clear he was not a multitasker. "With this intake?"

"Sorry, after this, I'll hold off any more questions until you're done with Arlo. With everything, I mean—your promotion and overseeing social media and all. I'm asking because I'm in town for a bit, and I'd love to make it back on your active volunteer list, walking dogs, cleaning cages, whatever. But social media, PR, grant writing, event organization—I'm betting I have experience with most everything on that job description, even without seeing it. I'd love to help with marketing too—if you're open to it, that is." Riley didn't know Patrick well enough to discern whether that look of concentration lining his face was a good or bad sign. "I'd be happy to show you some of my campaigns, my whole portfolio even, if that helps."

After a handful of seconds passed, he gave a little nod. "With luck, Megan will be here soon, and she can give you the tour."

"Megan?"

"Our director."

"Oh, that's right, Megan Anderson. I've not met her, but I've seen some of her interviews. She took over after Wesley retired."

"Yes, but she's a Williams now. For the last five and a half months. She's been married for longer than that. It took her a while to get around to changing her name. But if you're going to be helping with our social media campaigns, she'll want to meet you."

Riley sank back on her heels in front of the kennel, and Arlo whined like he wanted to join her. "That'd be great, Patrick." It was an indirect yes, but she'd take it. It was no doubt a sign of how imperfect her last few jobs had been, but she hadn't been this excited about something in a long time. "I'd love to be a part of this place again, even temporarily."

"For forty-one days?" The way he said it, it sounded like he wanted a bit more clarification on what she was offering.

"Most likely. I have some applications out in a few different cities, but you know how the interview process goes. Nothing's ever fast. I doubt I'll be hauling it out of St. Louis any sooner than that."

Patrick seemed to be thinking through this and eventually gave a nod. "Megan would appreciate having more time to work with me on some of what I'll be taking over for her while she's on maternity leave in November."

"Sounds like it could be a win-win then, huh?"

"Yes, it could. Assuming Megan thinks you have talent."

Riley was pretty sure her eyebrows shot up into her forehead. "Touché, Patrick."

As Patrick went back to his clipboard, Riley finished scrubbing down Arlo's kennel, each step of the routine coming back to her like she hadn't been away nearly as long as she had.

Prior to her arrival in St. Louis earlier this week, Riley had spent way too much time fixated on how all her old high school friends who'd stayed in town would react when they inevitably found out she was here. Considering the fiasco that was the end of senior year, Riley couldn't be blamed for a bit of worrying.

She'd not given any thought to the better parts of coming home, like hanging out with her brother again and reconnecting with this place. In the face of being here again, all that worrying she'd been doing seemed for nothing.

Riley hadn't wanted to cross her fingers—and toes—this much since she was eleven and hoping not to get picked last for the kickball games at recess again. She was home again, for a little while. She might as well roll up her sleeves and make the best of it.

Chapter 4

With Arlo's kennel ready and his exam finished, it was time to bid the gentle dog goodbye. "I wonder if he could use a potty break first." Not like she was delaying the inevitable much, was she? "I know he was outside, but with that leash so tangled up, he barely had room to move."

"That's true." Patrick directed her where to go but didn't join her. Not that Riley minded. She was too busy focusing on Arlo.

The doggie relief area for quarantined dogs was Astroturf and fairly small. A little way off, a larger one for the dogs who'd been cleared from quarantine was part gravel and part Astroturf. When Riley volunteered here, everyone had called it "The Island of Many Smells."

The sun had crested over the horizon, promising another scorcher, and beads of sweat dotted Riley's brow in no time. Days like today, those perfect Missouri fall days she'd been missing in the South seemed impossibly far away.

As Arlo sniffed about, Riley made a dozen promises that she'd be back to walk him. No matter what played out in regard to helping with marketing, she'd made up her mind about volunteering here again.

When she could no longer delay the inevitable, Riley coaxed Arlo through the quarantine door for a second time that morning. Patrick had stepped out of the room and been replaced by a woman scanning a chart. Recognizing her, Riley's pulse did a little skitter.

The woman's clear gray eyes brightened at the sight of them. "You must be Riley. I'm Megan, High Grove's director. Patrick's been telling me about you. Seems you two have really bonded, huh?" For a second, Riley thought Megan was referring to Patrick. "With him, I mean." She motioned toward Arlo.

Likely anticipating another exam, Arlo wedged himself closer to Riley.

"Oh, well, I rescued him from a tangled-up leash, I guess. Though for my part, he had me at hello, that's for sure."

"I bet. And judging by the way he's leaning into you for comfort in an unfamiliar situation, it's as much a sign of a good temperament as it is that he's been taken care of by whoever had him." Megan eyed the big dog more closely. "And what a good-looking Dane he is, healthy, well-fed, and in his prime."

"Yeah, he's a beautiful animal, that's for sure."

"I was just reading his chart and the note his

owner left. We'll have a look at the video feed later, but it probably won't show anything. At least whoever had him didn't hang on to him longer than they could afford to feed him. It probably goes without saying, but that isn't always the case, especially when it comes to dogs surrendered in secret like this."

Riley closed a hand over her heart. "I can imagine."

Megan stepped forward to shake Riley's hand. "Anyway, it's nice to meet you. Wesley was in charge when you volunteered, right?" Tall as Arlo was, it didn't take any effort for him to get in on the handshake action. He sniffed their joined hands before burrowing his nose underneath, earning some affection from two people instead of one.

"Yeah, he was. He retired while I was in Chicago. I got an invitation to his retirement party, but I couldn't make it. And now that I think of it, you and I may have been introduced a while back. I was in town for the holidays and helped with a fundraiser, but there were people here in droves, so I doubt you remember."

"Oh yeah? It's wonderful that you have a history here. We love it when our volunteers come back, even if it's only temporary." Megan clapped her hands together, looking from Riley to Arlo. "So, if it's been a few years, you're due for a tour. If you have twenty minutes, I can show you around. We've been blessed with some big grants and donations the last few years, and we've made some big improvements."

"I'd love a tour."

"Perfect. That'll give us a chance to talk about how you can get involved while you're in town. Patrick says you work in marketing, and you're interested in helping out here?"

"I do, and definitely. I'm between jobs at the moment, but I've worked in marketing the last eight years."

"Oh yeah?" Megan patted her stomach. "Well, heads up, we're hardly keeping above water, especially in terms of marketing. After a couple weeks of mandatory bed rest, I've cut back to part time for the next year thanks to a high-energy toddler and this one in the making." Spying Riley's look of concern, Megan waved her off. "Everything's progressing great, pregnancy-wise. I was just working too hard, here and at home. I'm saying all this because there's room for someone with an eye for marketing to step in and help. Especially with Patrick taking on some of my responsibilities. But fair warning not to take on more than you're comfortable with. Around here, you have to know your limits, as even I'm learning."

"It'd be my honor to help out in a bigger way while I'm in town. When I get back to my parents' house, I'll email you my portfolio, so you'll know what I can do." There was that nagging thought again, the reminder of how perfect this might've been had Riley been searching for jobs in St. Louis. *Which you weren't, remember?*

"That'd be great."

"And as far as biting off more than I can chew, I'm not worried about that. I came back because my mom's battling breast cancer and about to start radiation, but so far, she isn't slowing down a minute. I'm needed around the house less than I thought." Riley shifted as Arlo sank onto his haunches, his shoulder leaning heavily against her thigh. "I have some applications out in Kansas City and Phoenix and a few other places too, but nothing happens fast. With luck, I'll be able to help until your new hire starts."

"That'd be wonderful. Fall's such a busy time of year with all the special events going on, several here, and a handful elsewhere. I'll give you a list before you leave."

"Perfect."

Megan jutted her thumb toward the front of the building. "Ready for a tour?"

When Riley's hand came to rest atop Arlo's upper back, he gazed up at her with a trusting look that stabbed at her heart.

"This part's always hard," Megan said, sensing her hesitation. "But he'll get loads of attention, and you're welcome to spend as much time with him as you'd like when you're here."

Riley enveloped Arlo in a hug and mumbled that

she'd be back soon, then Megan opened his kennel and began beckoning him in. Thanks to his interest in the green-and-white knotted rope inside his new kennel, he stepped in easily but lifted his head in alarm when he was unleashed and the kennel door locked behind him.

One wistful look in Arlo's direction later, Riley followed Megan out of the room, and a single determined woof rang in her ears as the door shut behind her.

Riley took a breath. *This is the part of working in a shelter you've got to get used to.*

Megan put a hand on her shoulder. "It's hard, I know, but this part's over with before you know it. He'll be up there on adoption row in no time. And a purebred Dane like him, he'll have a slew of people wanting to bring him home."

"I bet. I'd be one of them if I had a place to keep him."

"So," Megan said, "normally we start up front, but since we're in the back, and you already have a good sense of the place, I'll switch it up. For starters, our break room across the way has been a popular spot for the volunteers and staff as of late with new appliances and updated seating."

When they stepped inside, the small room was considerably swankier than the worn couch, nicked table, and seen-better-days fridge Riley remembered. "Nice set up."

"It's a step up, isn't it? More than a few of us have dozed off on the new couch for twenty minutes or so when overnight emergencies arise. It's every bit as comfortable as it looks."

Riley walked over to check out an impressively sized new fridge that was decorated with magnets from all over the world. When Megan shared that Riley was welcome to bring lunch along and keep it in the fridge, Riley's heart lifted at the promise of a whole new level of inclusion. Most of her shifts when she was a teenager had been shorter ones after school or on Saturday mornings and hadn't been long enough to worry about food.

After a short tour of the dog-washing station, supply closet, and medical room, they headed through the main dog kennels toward the front of the building. Since Riley had last been here, the side of the building had been bumped out, and the kennels had been updated and expanded, but the dogs inside were just as noisy and excited as Riley remembered. From Chihuahua tiny to mastiff large, they were all shapes and sizes, and Riley was looking forward to getting to know Arlo's soon-to-be kennel mates.

After they headed through the double glass doors to the front, the sound of barking dogs dropped a decibel or two. "That's one thing that hasn't changed," Riley said with a laugh now that Megan could actually hear her.

"They're loudest before breakfast. Once they eat and get a short walk or a romp with other dogs in the play areas, it's much easier on the ears to walk through there."

"I bet."

"Patrick said you started as a Junior Dog Walker. Did you live nearby?"

"I did. I grew up right here in Webster, on Fairview."

Megan's face lifted. "I'm a few streets over on Park. For the last few years, anyway. I grew up a couple hours away from here in the country, but I'm excited for the chance my kids will have to go to school here. I swear, this town reminds me of a snow globe village."

Riley struggled not to drop Megan's gaze as a wave of anxious heat rushed over her. Of all the places she'd lived the last twelve years, she'd never been anywhere else where the most common question on meeting someone new was to ask where they'd gone to high school. If Megan didn't ask, it was only because she assumed Riley had gone to Webster, having grown up in the heart of town.

"Webster's beautiful, that's for sure." And it was. Picturesque. Quaint. Snow globe–like, as Megan had said. At least, until it wasn't. Until the snow globe burst into a hundred pieces, and the shards were digging into your palms, and all you could think to do was run, run, and never stop running.

Knowing more of a reply was needed, she went a route that hopefully wouldn't lead back to talk of high school. "The houses are some of my favorites I've seen anywhere, except maybe Savannah, Georgia. It was my favorite getaway when I lived in Atlanta."

Thankfully, this got Megan asking about what kind of work Riley had been doing in Atlanta, and Riley was more than happy to fill Megan in on her role at Naturally Green. Most of her time had been spent managing their social media accounts, designing marketing materials, tracking sales data, managing the CRM, and organizing a handful of special events for customers.

They continued talking shop as Megan showed Riley around the front half of the building. It housed an expanded gift shop with dozens of items tempting Riley to spend her last paycheck on, a small stage for training and dog yoga sessions, several adoption stations, and staff workstations. Best of all were the various cats and kittens along the back wall in cozy cat bungalows replete with hammocks and a massive floor-to-ceiling play area where three young cats were at play, chasing each other up and down the climbing material and dashing into hidey boxes. Riley wanted to get her hands on the furry litter of young kittens in one of the kennels, irresistible as they were with their big, blue eyes and tiny bodies. Not wanting to waylay the conversation at hand though, she contented herself with a quick petting of Trina, the resident cat she'd spied earlier, and Chance, the geriatric cairn terrier who'd been a puppy recovering from parvo back when she was volunteering. "He's as sweet as ever. Aren't you, Chancey boy? And no one ever adopted him, huh?"

"Oh, he could've been adopted a hundred times over, but Wesley wouldn't allow it. As for Chance, he's never let being blind stop him from being in the center of everything around here, and it wouldn't be the same without him."

"I bet," Riley said, scratching Chance's belly as his back leg raced in the air. "I don't imagine it's easy, but everything you do has got to be more rewarding in a place like this. It's been a dream of mine to switch over to the nonprofit world for a while now. I'm crossing my fingers this time I can find something that moves me the way this shelter does."

"Why am I suddenly wishing we met two weeks ago?" Megan asked with a soft laugh that made it clear the comment was rhetorical. "I'm hoping our new hire from Seattle will have your passion. He seems to, at least."

"That's good." *Is it though? Yes, it is. Don't be a dolt.*

"Yeah. I'm convinced this new position will be essential to helping us implement our new strategic plan. There's a lot of momentum building on keeping pets in homes, and we're trying to step into it. So far, we've put out a series of training videos targeting some of the behaviors that trouble new dog owners the most, but we'd love to get funding to send trainers into homes before owners get to that point of no turning back with the more challenging animals. I doubt most organizations have a big-picture goal that ultimately puts them out of business, but that's the dream—a home for every animal. If we reach it, we'll evolve, I'm sure."

After giving Chance's wiry scruff another scratch, Riley stood up. "It's an admirable end goal, no question."

"Some days it seems like pie in the sky, but the only way to get there is to try, right? We're also wanting to do more to help families through unexpected hardship. Take Arlo, for instance. Sometimes, when things like job loss or medical leave happen, a bit of support with feeding their pets can make all the difference in keeping animals in homes."

"I bet. And your new marketing coordinator gets to take this stuff on?" Riley did her best not to sound wistful.

"It's a lot, I know, on top of the day-to-day marketing for the shelter. All I can say is we think big around here."

It was ridiculous to want to drop to her knees and plead for a job that had already been promised to someone else, but that was exactly what Riley wanted to do. *And what would you do if you got it?*

Hide out indefinitely from all your old high school buddies, the ones who've stayed in town?

The truth was, had she come across this position in time, Riley would've gotten over the hurdles of moving home and done her best to land this job. "I know you haven't seen my portfolio yet, but I swear, almost every experience I've had will help me at least move the needle on some of this stuff for you."

"That's awesome. With all we want to accomplish, ever since I learned I needed to cut back my hours, I've been worried about losing momentum here. But I need to remember things have a way of working out just as they should."

Riley figured that was advice to remember. With luck, her next job wouldn't end with another portable storage rental and a new pair of running shoes.

Chapter 5

RILEY SAT CROSS-LEGGED ON THE COUCH IN HER parents' living room, her laptop on a cushioned lap desk she'd found in her closet dating back to middle school. The sweetest of her mom's cats, a little calico female, was on the back of the couch, attempting to nibble on Riley's hair.

On the opposite end of the couch, her brother Tommy was transfixed with a project of his own. With her dad out for his Saturday extended-length gym workout, Tommy had claimed the living room TV and had Bloomberg live streaming in the background as he worked on his laptop. In the basement, he had three oversize monitors, a giant screen TV, and four servers, but he came up here for a change of scenery.

"How'd you swing being off work on a Saturday?" For the last four years, Tommy had worked three blocks away at a local deli and market, his most successful job to date. When he was three, Tommy was diagnosed with autism spectrum disorder. Since customer service wasn't his strong suit, he mostly worked in the back room prepping food and unpacking new stock rather than up front making sandwiches.

Tommy looked up from his computer but stared off to the side rather than at her as he talked. "By putting in a notice that I was quitting."

"You're quitting?" Riley blinked. "How come? I thought you enjoyed it there."

"I wanted to quit because I make more not working than working. But when I told Margie, she pointed out some valid reasons to stay on, so I'm reducing my hours by half instead."

"Well, I'm glad you're not quitting. Those guys are like a second family to you, but what do you mean, you're making more not working than working? You're getting paid on time, right?" Tommy had been managing his own money since his first job at nineteen. Since he didn't drive and wasn't much into socializing, his money went far, and the last Riley heard, he had a lot more tucked into savings and retirement than she did.

Tommy held up a hand for silence as a new round of market projections filled the TV screen. Riley was about to give up waiting when he answered. "Yes. I get paychecks every other Thursday. Like always. I make more money with this." He pointed to his laptop screen. "Day trading."

"Oh yeah? Dad said you're getting better at it." From what her parents had shared, Tommy's first couple of days that had ended in losses rather than gains hadn't gone well, as was evidenced by a string of nuclear meltdowns, the first in over a year. Since then, Tommy had gotten better about accepting that financial loss was inevitable at times with this type of risk, and Riley suspected the quote on the framed chalkboard in the kitchen about learning more from losing than winning had been placed up there strategically by her mom. Brenda had a knack for finding quotes that mirrored whatever was occurring in the Leighton household and putting them up there for all to resonate with, and in impeccable handwriting too.

"Last month I earned more through this than I did all last year from the deli."

Riley's jaw dropped open an inch as a not-too-distant phone conversation came to mind in which Tommy shared he'd spent less than five grand of the twenty-four thousand he'd brought home last year. "That's a lot of money to earn in a month, Tommy."

"It is." Turning back to his laptop, he added, "But it's not as much as I'm going to make."

Riley humphed appreciatively. If one of the Leighton kids was going to end up wealthy, it was probably going to be Tommy. Riley's youngest brother, Nick, now twenty-three, was down in Miami after dropping out of college in his sophomore year. Despite numerous setbacks, he was pursuing his dream of being a DJ but working as a lifeguard and living with a pile of roommates to make ends meet. Not that Riley could say she was doing much better, financially, at least.

Sweeping her hair out of the cat's reach, Riley skimmed the last few sentences of Megan's email again. It had taken two days, but Megan had gotten back to her this morning. She'd been impressed enough with Riley's résumé and portfolio to offer something unexpected—a five-week paid internship starting on Tuesday. In addition to the day-to-day posts on the shelter's three social media outlets and some newsletter content, Riley would be overseeing the PR side of special events, including three in September that were being organized by separate organizations to benefit High Grove.

Upon reading Megan's email an hour ago, Riley had run around the main floor doing a victory dance. "If you're so excited about it," her dad had said after congratulating her, "what do you think of trying to turn it into something permanent?" Riley's mom had looked just as hopeful before Riley reminded them that someone had already been hired.

It touched her a bit unexpectedly, seeing how her parents would enjoy her being in town again. No matter how uncomfortable those waters had been for a while, love still flowed under the surface. In both directions.

Behind her, the cat was nibbling at her hair again, and she swept it out of reach once more. A mess of split ends due to ill-suited cat grooming wouldn't do. After waiting a solid thirty minutes after the email came in this morning so she didn't look too eager, Riley had accepted Megan's offer, saying how much she was looking forward to starting on Tuesday. Ever since, her mind had been racing with ideas for posts and mini–social media campaigns.

Wanting to be well prepared for her first day, Riley opened the links to the September events she'd be working on: Pins for Paws, a bowling night with proceeds benefiting High Grove; Purses and Pumps for Pooches, a fundraiser organized by a local women's group; and a friendraiser with a new dog boarding and training facility not far outside St. Louis County.

Clinking on the link to the dog boarding facility, Coleman's Boarding and Training, Riley perused the site. As far as small business websites went, it was a good one: a clean, readable font and crisp, vivid images with accompanying text that was ample without being inundating. At the bottom of the first page, an image of a guy in military gear squatting alongside an impressive German shepherd had her jaw falling open. "Hold the phone! Are you kidding me!"

Scrolling up, Riley scanned the tabs at the top of the main page. There was an About Marcus section. Clicking on it, Riley balled her hand into a fist to keep from refreshing a dozen times as it loaded.

Tommy glanced over. "Your phone? Where is it?"

"No. Sorry. It's just that a guy I know from high school runs a dog boarding and training facility, and the shelter's going to be doing a friendraiser with him late next month." *Actually, I'll be the one coordinating it with him. With Marcus. With Levi's best friend.* "Holy crap. I never should've come back here. I swear, everybody knows everybody in this town."

"Statistically speaking, it's like that in other small cities you've lived in too. As an out-of-towner, you just didn't know anyone."

Riley closed her eyes, unable to gaze another second at the pictures of Marcus working with dogs, a few but not all while decked out in military gear. "Probably, but that's how I like it."

"Why?" For the life of him, Tommy couldn't comprehend Riley's need to relocate every few years. He thrived on predictability.

An image of all the jeering faces at prom flashed into her mind, and Riley slammed her laptop closed hard enough to earn a disapproving look from her brother who knew exactly how to treat electronic equipment, and slamming laptops closed didn't make the cut. "I guess it's just in my blood." Tommy wasn't a fan of horror movies and wouldn't understand the *Carrie* reference that came to mind whenever she thought about prom night.

Letting out a breath, Riley stood up. "Well, happy fortune making, bro. I'm off to…" To what? It was a Saturday, and Riley didn't have a single plan for the rest of the day. "Find Mom," she added, knowing her brother didn't appreciate unfinished sentences.

"It can't be defined as a fortune, but I'm up $217 since I started."

"This week?"

"This morning."

"Of course, you are." In Atlanta, Riley's monthly budget had little more excess padding than that after paying for rent, groceries, her auto loan, insurance, and other bills. "Remember me when you're sailing on your private yacht next to Jeff Bezos."

As she headed out, she heard her brother mumbling to himself that he neither liked water nor figured it was possible he could forget her.

"Touché."

After hauling herself up the split staircase with leg and butt muscles screaming with every step after three morning jogs in a row, Riley found her mom upstairs working in the bedroom that had once been Tommy's but was now her sewing room.

Before heading in, Riley dropped off her laptop on her bedroom dresser. Hercules—or Devil Boy as she was calling him after another night of disturbed sleep from his territorial stalking—was napping on Riley's pillow and no doubt leaving behind a pile of fur. He raised one cautious eye and let out a guttural growl at the sight of her before kneading his claws into her pillow. "You really are my least favorite cat. Ever."

Considering he didn't lose a beat in his kneading, Riley suspected he wouldn't miss any sleep over this.

Riley opened the sewing-room door to find her mom working on a baby quilt, this one light blue with dark-blue and green lettering. Eli Alexander, born three days ago on August 25.

"You know better than to step in here barefoot," her mom warned, hardly glancing up from the sewing machine she'd invested nearly three grand in a few years ago when her blossoming embroidery business warranted the pricey upgrade. "I'd like to claim the floor is needle-free, but that's not something I'd be okay being proven wrong about."

Not wanting to push her luck, Riley planted herself against the wall after closing the door behind her. This was the one room in the house where Brenda didn't allow her cats to roam—stray cat hairs didn't make for satisfied customers who left good ratings.

Sinking to the floor, her leg muscles burned like fire, but Riley reminded herself that a little bit of morning torture could do wonders for her waistline. "How's it going? Getting lots of orders?"

"About as many as I care to handle. I have a feeling I'll need to stop accepting Christmas orders again this year by Black Friday, as busy as my August has been. How about you? Did you email the shelter director back?"

"Yep."

"Wonderful. You always loved it there. I hope it's exactly what you're wanting."

"Me too."

"And I'm not just saying that because it might keep you home another few weeks," her mom said with a smile. "You and your little brother got the traveling genes, it seems."

Aside from Riley, her little brother Nick, and a cousin or two, none of Riley's extended family had ventured out of the St. Louis area. In fact, about half of them were right here in Webster. Not many people Riley knew could head home on holidays to the same house they'd grown up in.

At fifty-six, Riley's mom still resembled the high schooler who'd been voted best smile and who'd boasted the best pom routine, though she was an inch or two shorter than she'd been back then, topping just over five foot three now. She had wide hips, mocha eyes, and short, dark curls that had been colored since before Riley was born.

Ever since Riley was little, whenever they were out in public together, people had commented that she must take after her dad, just in case Riley and her mom didn't know they didn't look much like mother and daughter. Riley was five-seven, blond, with greenish-hazel eyes. It was Tommy who'd taken after Brenda most, in looks, at least. In personality, they were as different as could be.

"So, what about Monday?" Riley asked. "Think you'll need a ride to radiation?"

"Nope, I'm good. Your dad's taking the day off.

We're going to breakfast afterward if you'd like to join us."

The fact that Riley was so quick to look down at her feet again was proof enough that she still had triggers when it came to her parents' relationship. It wasn't as if she wasn't happy they'd found their way back together after being on the cusp of divorce in Riley's senior year. No doubt it hadn't been easy to do so. Especially when there'd been infidelity.

Riley's parents' issues weren't hers, she reminded herself. *Maybe not, but they affected you just the same, didn't they?* "Thanks. I'll think about it."

Brenda folded a bit of fabric between her fingers. "Plans tonight?"

"Nope. I thought maybe we could have that game night you've been talking about. And Tommy can buy the pizza. Have you heard how he's killing it with that stock stuff he's doing?"

Glancing over her shoulder, Brenda gave her a sharp look. "You *have* told your friends you're here, haven't you? I can't believe you haven't hightailed it over to Lana's yet. She's your best friend, after all."

"She's my oldest friend, not my best friend, and no, I haven't called her yet. I haven't even been home a week yet, and besides, she's got a baby and toddler. I'm sure she's busy."

Lana also had a devoted husband who she'd fallen in love with during their junior year of high school, a guy named Grant who'd stuck by Lana's side even though they'd gone to separate colleges and who'd proposed to her upon their four-year college graduation. Lana was living out her happily ever after. It was hard enough being back here without that in Riley's face too.

"Not too busy for you, I'm sure. And if not Lana, who is your best friend, then?"

Riley shrugged. "I'm almost thirty, and I've got a dozen close friends in different cities. I think I'm old enough not to have to name a best one."

"Everyone needs a best friend, Riley. If I didn't have Julie, I'd go berserk." When Riley didn't say anything, she added, "You know, I see Lana's mom at yoga every Sunday afternoon. Lana could use the reach out. It's not easy, parenting little ones."

Riley wiggled upward to claim a straighter posture. Her mom was right about needing a best friend. Riley was dying to confide in someone about the prospect of working on the friendraiser with Marcus, or whoever from his organization was in charge of marketing and social media. She couldn't imagine seeing Marcus and not talking about Levi. It'd be no different than ignoring the elephant in the room. Still, Levi, high school, and the explosive end to both hadn't been topics open for discussion in over a decade.

Thoughts of Levi invariably led back to that last night they had together before everything fell apart. No matter how many times she thought about it—or tried not to think about it—it didn't change the fact that the night had ended so differently than it had begun.

How unfair not to be able to know that her best moment was about to unravel into her worst.

But none of this was something she could talk to her mom about.

She cleared her dry throat. "Yeah, maybe I'll give Lana a call."

Chapter 6

"THANKS AGAIN FOR COMING ALL THE WAY OUT here with me," Lana said as she parked her Enclave in the far side of the Purina Farms parking lot. "Grant puts up a fight when I try to drag him along, and my anxiety gets the best of me whenever I think of attempting this place alone with two kids under three."

"I can see why it would." Riley scoped the numerous barns and outbuildings stretching across the hilly countryside west of St. Louis. In the back seat, Jackson, Lana's oldest, was squirming in an attempt to wiggle his way free of his confining car seat. "But why won't Grant come out here? Because of the drive?" Riley could've done without Jackson continuously questioning "How long until we get there?" along the way, but he was a toddler, and a toddler's patience tended to be hard won.

Rolling her eyes playfully, Lana made air quotes. "Because the earthy smells in the barn make him nauseous."

"Huh. I haven't been here in forever, but I remember loving the smell of the hay in the loft."

"You know Grant. He's my oldest baby, that one."

Twisting in her seat, Lana tapped her son on the knee to get his attention. "Come on, Jackson, aren't you going to ask one more time when we're going to get here so I can give you the answer you want?"

Jackson wasn't listening. He was staring out the window and grunting as he fought with his seat belt, his chubby legs already in go mode. "I want to go now! I want to go now!" Rosie, his nine-month-old sister who was strapped in a rear-facing carrier, must've still been asleep, as she wasn't making a sound.

"In a minute, little bud. Hang tight while I get your stroller." Hopping out, Lana headed to the trunk, and Riley followed her. "I've come to realize it's good Grant and I didn't have any classes together before our junior year. I seriously don't think we'd have hooked up if I knew him before he'd matured a bit, and even *that* is giving him a bit of grace."

Riley laughed. "You two balance each other out well."

The heat and humidity pressed in, warring with the remnants of cool air still clinging to Riley's skin from the AC. Knowing it was likely to top out in the high nineties before tonight's storms rolled in, hopefully putting an end to the late-August heat wave, she'd worn cutoff jean shorts, flip-flops, and a sleeveless tank. She'd confined her thick hair in a ponytail that spilled out the back of her well-worn

Redbirds ball cap, hoping to tame the inevitable frizz that set in on days like today.

After sliding on a front-facing baby carrier and clipping it into place, Lana tugged on a sun hat. With her dry-fit khaki capris and her Chaco sandals, Lana looked like an advertisement for Eddie Bauer.

Next, Lana pulled out a collapsible stroller and packed the bottom with sippy cups, snacks, a few toys, and a diaper pack. "Grant says I have more gear than a soldier heading out on patrol."

"No comment." Riley laughed even as a weird sensation swirled inside her. No matter what she'd told her mom, Lana *was* her best friend, a best friend who'd entered the "other land" of motherhood without her. Not for the first time, Riley wondered what she'd been so busy doing the last decade or so that actually counted for something.

"What?" Lana asked. "That look. You're judging me, aren't you?"

"Definitely not judging. If you picked up on a look, it was envy. You—" Riley tucked her hands in her back pockets. "You just do this all so well."

"Do *what* so well? Remember to pack a million things? Not swear anymore?" Lana waggled her eyebrows. "Because I forget about half of what I mean to bring every time I go out, and when Jackson's out of earshot, I curse like an emo teenager just to get it out of my system. Oh, and at least once a day,

I shut myself in our walk-in pantry to stomp my feet and scream into an oversize oven mitt."

Riley snorted. "Well, kudos for making it look easy."

Lana pointed a finger her way as she headed to the driver's side passenger door where Rosie was beginning to stir. "I'll remind you of that when we're walking out of here with two red-faced, screaming kids. There's something synonymous with meltdowns and leaving." She lowered her voice to a whisper. "And Jackson's meltdowns are DEFCON 3, maybe 2—not kidding. I meant to tell you to wear running shoes. You may have to kick off those flip-flops if he takes off."

"You're not selling this."

"Just remember 'Stop your feet' is for emergencies only. It works too. Mostly."

"What about keeping him in the stroller?"

"Not a chance till he's tired."

No matter how challenging this proved to be, Riley's insides still melted into goo ten minutes and one bathroom trip/diaper change later when Jackson reached up and grabbed her hand. He had zero interest in the exhibits and attempted to plough past them to get to the bridge leading to the animal barn and hayloft play area, but he didn't want to go it alone. With his mom moving too slow while navigating the empty stroller and caring for his sister, he was content with Riley. "'Mere,

Mommy's friend, 'mere," he repeated over and over as he tugged her along.

"Go for it," Lana said. "We'll be right behind you."

The part of Riley wondering if this might've been her life now had things not fallen apart so terribly with Levi reared its head. The feelings she'd had for Levi, they'd carried a promise of transcending those raging teen hormones and leading to something much more permanent like with Grant and Lana.

No sense thinking about that now. He's forgotten you, even if you haven't forgotten him.

Jackson led her along a wood bridge on the far side of the exhibit hall. On the bridge's other side, they entered into the top level of the massive barn where his Stride Rite sandals squeaked to a stop in front of the child-height activity tables loaded with model-scale John Deere tractors. There were two kids, siblings, no doubt, at the second table, but Jackson had free rein of the first one for now. Uttering a sound a bit like an excited gorilla, he lost no time pushing the nearest tractor along the dry, whole-kernel corn covering the table, his face a mixture of joy and rapt attention.

"This is what you were in such a hurry to get to?" With nothing to distract her, Riley soaked in his perfect skin, round eyes, pudgy cheeks, and small but capable hands. Any last parts of her that hadn't turned to goo yet melted completely. "I guess you like tractors, huh?"

Jackson's eyes were a lighter brown that Lana's, and his wild brown locks were a mixture of both parents. The same went for Rosie, whose current phase of stranger shyness would no doubt keep her at arm's length today. Not that Riley minded. Babies were cute, but toddlers were more fun on outings like this.

"He gets that from his dad," Lana said, entering through the door from the bridge, pushing the stroller off to the side. "Except Grant only moves that fast when he smells barbeque."

Laughing, Riley sank onto her knees after brushing away a few stray kernels of corn from the wood plank loft floor. "I'm realizing how much I've missed you."

"Enough to turn that made-for-you internship at High Grove into something permanent?" Lana's tone was hopeful as she lifted Rosie from the carrier and sank onto her heels, plopping her wide-eyed with wonder daughter onto her knee in front of the table. "Because it would make my day to hear that. No, my year. It would make my year."

"I'm afraid that's not up to me. A guy's already been hired, remember?"

"Then don't mind me, but I'm going to be sending out all the good vibes that something better lands on his doorstep."

Riley held up a hand. "Please, I'm enough of a wreck committing to five weeks here."

Lana pursed her lips and took a few seconds to respond. "Is it really so bad, being back?"

"In my head it is." Riley's soft laugh turned serious. This wasn't something she and Lana had talked about in years. "I just don't want to be remembered only for what happened at prom. For something that wasn't even my fault." Catching Lana's look, she added, "And that includes by all the people who felt sorry for me."

"Do you really think anybody's thinking about our senior year of high school anymore? I'm certainly not."

"Not until they meet a classmate they haven't seen in twelve years. Then they are."

"And you know this, or could that be your anxiety talking?" Lana's voice was gentle and reassuring, which in its own way poked at a painful splinter that was never buried too far beneath the surface.

"It probably is, but that doesn't help any in the moment."

"What's going on?"

Riley folded forward a few seconds, resting her forehead on the edge of the play table. "Turns out one of the special events I'm going to be working on for the shelter is with Marcus—or someone who works for him, anyway. How humiliating is that?"

Lana's mouth dropped open in surprise. "Wow. I knew he was doing that stuff with dogs, but I never would've guessed that. But if it makes a difference…" She stopped to redirect Rosie, who'd swept up a tiny fistful of corn off the table and beelined it straight to her mouth. After extracting it, Lana redirected her to one of the tractors. "If it makes a difference, I really don't think it was Marcus who started the rumors."

Riley took a second to answer. "I don't see how it couldn't be. Levi swore he only told Marcus. I only told you."

"And I told no one." Lana's big mocha eyes were clear, reminding Riley that she wholeheartedly believed her.

"I know, Lana. And Marcus swore the same thing, yet I was the laughingstock of senior prom."

"That's not true. A lot of the kids were pissed when they realized what was happening. It was just…you know…"

"The popular kids?" Riley answered for her. Heat rushed to her cheeks. "The cheerleaders, the jocks, the prom court…that sort of thing?"

"Not to dismiss what happened, but when did we ever care what they think?"

"When they found out my dad was having sex with Levi's mom, and Levi and I became the brunt of a million 'keeping it in the family' jokes at our senior prom, that's when."

This right here was why Riley hated coming home. She loved Lana, but the easier thing to do was stay gone and keep all this behind her. "They made buttons. Who makes buttons on the fly like that? Prom was less than forty-eight hours after Levi and I walked in on our parents going at it, and yet prom was busting at the seams with the popular kids all wearing buttons. *Printed* buttons."

Riley's palms broke out in a sweat. Why did she suddenly feel eighteen again? Hadn't she worked hard to put all this behind her? Yet, here she was, reliving that moment of finally putting two and two together an hour or two into prom. Kids she didn't care about were being overly friendly. That's all she'd thought at first. No one could know what she was trying so desperately to put behind her and still enjoy this night with the unlikely guy she'd fallen quite hard for. Lana would never tell a soul. Neither would Marcus.

Then Courtney, with her minions trailing after her, planted herself smack-dab in front of Riley when Levi was off talking to a friend. "Hi Riley! Having fun?" Positioning herself so there was nothing for Riley to do but read the button in her perfect sleeveless gown—one that never should've been pierced with a pin—that read "Got Mom? Got Dad? Got popcorn. KIITF." Upon looking around, Riley had realized to her horror that dozens of kids were wearing them pinned on dresses and suit lapels.

Popcorn. As if Riley's worst moment—walking

upstairs from Levi's basement to find her dad in the process of undressing Levi's mom—was something to be watched on the big screen.

"Trevor's parents ran a print shop." Lana's voice was gentle. "Not that it wasn't in terrible form; it just wasn't that impossible to do."

"Do you know they printed T-shirts to wear under their gowns at graduation? A whole month later. Only Principal Torkinson threatened to suspend anyone wearing them."

On prom night, the buttons had been innocent enough to fly under the radar of the chaperones. Riley still remembered the searing pain of the moment, when she'd realized how many of her classmates were in on the prank to humiliate her. Realized how many of her classmates knew her dad was sleeping around. Levi's mom had been single. For all Riley had known, her parents had been happily married.

KIITF. Keeping it in the family. Riley had figured out what the initials stood for after Levi broke Trevor's nose as the Black Eyed Peas "I Gotta Feeling" boomed over the speakers, his knuckles swelling instantly as he swore under his breath.

"It isn't an excuse, but you know Courtney," Lana said gently. "She was never one to take things lying down, and Levi did break things off with her like two weeks before what she believed was the most important night of high school."

"Is she still in Arizona?"

"Yeah, I don't think she's ever coming back here. Her parents moved out of the area after their youngest graduated. It's not like she has a reason to."

"At least I won't be running into her. Marcus will be bad enough. I swear if he so much as brings up Levi's name…" Riley trailed off, sidetracked by the guilty look sweeping over her friend. "What? And don't say nothing, because I know that look, and it's anything but nothing."

Lana shrugged. "I was debating how best to bring this up, but it's not sounding like you've talked to Marcus recently, have you?"

"Not unless you consider more than a decade recently, no. Why?"

"It's just that Grant said Marcus wanted to tell you himself. He was going to call you."

"Well, he didn't. I doubt he even has my number."

"Grant gave it to him."

Whatever this was, it was big enough that Lana wasn't noticing Rosie had the entire back end of a tractor in her mouth. Riley extracted it and attempted to refocus Rosie's attention by rolling it across the corn. "Why on earth would Grant have given Marcus my number?"

Lana's shoulders practically tucked up against her ears. "I've been meaning to call you about it, but my days are so crazy. When I have a few minutes of downtime, I forget everything I need to do."

"Oh my God, did something happen to Levi?" Alarm flooded in. *Please no. Let Levi be okay.*

"He's okay. He's recovering."

Riley's limbs went rigid. "Recovering from what?"

"He was working up in Michigan, and there was an accident underwater, not his fault, but a coworker's. A bar or beam or something got loose and fell into the water and struck him. Knocked him out completely. Honestly, he almost died. They had to send people down to pull him up because his line was tangled or something."

The room began to spin. Abandoning the tractor, Riley leaned forward to brace her elbows on her knees. Teardrops splashing on the wood beams between her legs were the only way she realized Lana's words had triggered them. Sucking in a breath, she swiped a hand over her cheeks. "But he's okay, right?" She looked up, searching her best friend's face for the truth.

Lana pulled her into a one-armed hug, and Rosie grabbed the brim of Riley's cap firmly enough that she'd have pulled it off were it not for her ponytail going through the back. "He's okay. Marcus drove up there a couple days after it happened. He didn't stay long, but they're still close, as guys go, anyway. From what Marcus tells Grant, Levi's making great strides. It was a bad concussion, but he's going to be okay."

"Thank God. I don't know what I'd do if..."

Riley readjusted her cap. What would she have done? It's not like she had one iota of claim to him anymore. "I know he loves the water, but I *hate* his choice of career. You know it's one of the most dangerous jobs on the planet, right? Every time I think about it… I don't know, it just reminds me of how we don't fit. If I'd have married him, I'd have worried myself to death years ago."

After extracting the tractor from Rosie's mouth again, Lana pulled Rosie from the table, planting her on the wood floor between them, an action that immediately caused Rosie to start fussing. "You're right. Risk like that would be one of the hardest things for any spouse to take. The thing is, Riley…" Lana needed to raise her voice over Rosie's rapidly escalating fusses. "Have you ever thought that maybe had you two stayed together, Levi would've made a different career choice?"

Riley shook her head. "That's not fair. You can't put that on me."

"I'm not trying to put it on you; that's not what I meant. But think about it." She lifted Rosie into the air, bouncing her a bit. "The both of you have been running ever since senior year, him choosing that career and living out of hotels, you not letting anything stick, be it a job, a guy, or a home. You hardly even came back for summer break in college, interning like you did and working in Europe and all."

Riley swallowed. Her mouth was so damn dry.

She wanted to get up and leave, and not just leave Purina Farms. She didn't want to go home. She didn't want to see her parents. She didn't want to walk the streets of Webster that held a zillion memories.

She wanted to run. The only thing holding her back was that she had absolutely nowhere to go.

Chapter 7

LEVI PULLED OFF THE HIGHWAY AT A GAS STA-
tion after a little over four hours on the road. He'd
made it to the southern tip of the lake on the outskirts of Indiana Dunes National Park. He didn't
know what he was doing, going home.

"Yeah you do. You know exactly what you're
doing."

It was like his first boss out of diving school once
said back when he'd been working in the Gulf: "You
can lie to others and get away with it about half the
time. It's when you start lying to yourself that you
wind up food for the sharks."

He wanted to see her. Riley.

He got out of his truck, a Dodge Ram, to refuel,
and then headed inside, thirsty for something that
wasn't water and wasn't scotch, which he'd managed
to abstain from the last few nights after realizing
exactly how much he wanted to get drunk in the
wake of Gene's news. After deciding on a Mountain
Dew and a bag of Doritos—Levi wasn't doing himself any favors with his food choices—he headed
back to his truck, opened the tailgate, and hopped
up, savoring the hint of rain promised on the breeze.

Nothing was forcing his hand, even if he was overdue for a visit. He could head anywhere in the world for a few months, then head home for the holidays. His mom and little sister would be content with that. His mom had driven up to Traverse City when he was in the hospital, and she wasn't expecting him now.

He hadn't told anyone he was coming. He wouldn't be missed. It was Sunday and late August; there was work and school for them tomorrow.

How about Alaska, before it gets too cold? Or Yellowstone? You've always wanted to go there.

He pulled out his phone after taking a swig of Mountain Dew and opened the maps app. It was sixty hours to Anchorage. His head throbbed just thinking about that much driving. After four hours, it was already pounding worse than it had in days. Yellowstone, on the other hand, was only a little over twenty hours away. And he wasn't in any kind of hurry to make it there either. He could take a few days. The bulk of his stuff was in storage in Muskegon, but the back seat of his truck was packed with enough of his belongings that he'd be fine in a variety of weather conditions.

After chomping a few more Doritos, Levi intended to search for places to check out along the way but instead found himself pulling up Instagram and typing Riley's name in the search bar. His heartbeat thudded to a sprint to find that, less than an hour ago, she'd been tagged in a carousel post.

There were half a dozen pictures of her with Lana and her two kids, pictures taken earlier today at Purina Farms: a group selfie of her, Lana, and Lana's kids seated on concrete amphitheater steps, the four of them in various stages of smiling and frowning; one of Riley chasing barefoot after Lana's toddler, captioned "This little guy can move" and another of the group riding in the back of a tractor, a giant grin on the boy's face. There were a few of Riley with Lana's toddler on her lap seated on a stool next to a massive dairy cow as they attempted milking it. Both her and the kid's facial expressions were a riot. She looked…remarkable. Those cutoffs, those legs. That ball cap and that hair.

She's never going to want you. You're a has-been who can't even work your job.

Levi pressed his phone screen off and closed his eyes. What was the point of finding a way to end up in the same place as her in hopes of initiating a conversation he'd been playing out in his head for way too long? If there was something he wanted to say, he should've done that years ago. He needed to get over her already. It had been long enough.

Clearing his throat, he headed around to the driver's side and sat down, fueled enough by hurt and anger that he could ignore the headache for another few hours. Grabbing another few Doritos, he pulled up Yellowstone again to confirm all he needed to do from here was get back on I-94 and circle up around the bottom-west side of the lake to I-90, which he'd be on the bulk of the way. Over twelve hundred miles, in fact. A long but easy trip west. He wouldn't even need to navigate.

It was the right thing to do, not going home. Not right now. Not while Riley was there.

He got back on the highway, glad to have mostly empty roads on a late Sunday afternoon. He thumbed through his playlists and chose an alternative throwback one he'd not listened to in a while, tapping his thumb slowly on the side of the steering wheel along with the beat of "Black Hole Sun" by Soundgarden, hoping to drown out his thoughts.

"Replace that bottle of scotch with something breathing. What do you know anyway, Gene?" He huffed. "Last I checked, you were twice divorced, and you don't even like animals." He shifted straighter in his seat and turned up the dial. "Nope. No way. No dogs. No women."

Minutes later, when he realized he was humming along to "Scar Tissue" by the Red Hot Chili Peppers, he skipped to the next song. He didn't need anything hitting that close to home.

Ahead, the left lane was closed for construction, and an old Taurus was planted in the middle lane, its driver cruising along a good ten miles under the speed limit.

He switched to the empty right lane to pass and glanced over as he did. A big chocolate lab was alone in the back seat staring out the window. His mouth gaped open in a happy grin, and his pink tongue flailed out. The big dog looked right at Levi for a moment, and Levi let his foot off the gas. *Tank.* God, how he missed his dog.

The encounter left him just unsettled enough that he took the next exit on autopilot. He made it a good three miles down I-65 South toward Terre Haute before he realized what he'd done.

It took close to an extra hour going this way instead of taking I-55 straight to St. Louis, but I-65 was always his favorite route home.

Chapter 8

A THUNDERSTORM BLEW PAST AROUND DINNER as predicted, with lightning enough to thrill a crowd awaiting a firework show. With just a couple days until the calendar flipped to September, Riley crossed her fingers for an early fall. Sweaters, boots, pumpkins, apples, flavored hot coffees... She craved the works.

Wiped from toddler care and sore from her morning jog, she savored the solitude of a warm bath after the storm passed. With her eyes closed, she could just make out the flickering light from the four lit candles on the vanity. Scooting lower in the bathtub, she slipped underneath the surface, the water stinging her cheeks and eyelids for a second or two.

She remained submerged for the full extent of her indrawn breath, taunted by a vision of Levi, unconscious, hurt, and floating in the murky depths of Lake Michigan. She'd been the one to walk away from their relationship—run, more accurately—after prom. She'd never forgotten the hurt in his eyes when she told him she couldn't do it, that she needed space. Levi, who pretended never to need anyone but who needed her.

If he'd died in that water…

She'd given up any right to him; she knew that, but the deep ache seeping into her bones all afternoon told a bigger truth than anything else. She'd never stopped loving him. If he'd died in that water, she never would've forgiven herself for cutting him out the way she did, for zipping up a full body coat of armor and pretending that the beautiful thing that had blossomed between them hadn't been special at all.

Finally, she was forced to surface for a breath of air. What would he do if she texted him out of the blue after all this time? She could say she'd heard what had happened and was thinking about him. *That you're always thinking about him.*

She let the thought percolate, sliding her toe along the rim of the faucet and wiping water from her eyes. As much as a part of her wanted to find out how he was really doing, she wanted answers first. Marcus had been planning to call her but hadn't. Had Levi found out and stopped him? Did he hold that big of a grudge against her?

"Would you really be surprised if he did?" A frown curled down the sides of her mouth at the sound of her voice in the quiet room. *Please, please, please say he doesn't.*

Maybe it wasn't Levi she needed to call but Marcus. She had the perfect reason to reach out, given what she'd be doing at High Grove. And even though they hadn't exchanged more than a dozen words in high school, he'd remember her. Even if prom hadn't cemented her into the memory of everyone attending, Levi was his best friend.

After lifting the drain plug with her big toe, Riley hauled herself out with a yawn, toweled dry, and rubbed on some lotion before heading to her room, wrapped in a fluffy towel.

Half the credit was likely due to her day in the sun, but she slept through the night without waking up once, and, mercifully, was neither attacked in the wee morning hours by Hercules nor woken by the sound of his paw rattling her closed door.

———

Hearing her parents as they got ready to leave for her mom's first radiation appointment, Riley dragged herself out of bed at seven thirty.

"What, no jog today?" her dad teased as she trudged downstairs still in her pajamas. Keith Leighton had less body fat than the average twenty-year-old male and looked forward to his workouts the way little kids looked forward to cupcakes.

"I don't know, maybe. I'm trying to remember how long it takes to stop being in so much pain the next day."

"Give it a couple weeks. You'll start to love the burn."

"You're not selling it, you know. Burns hurt."

"Amen to that," Brenda said. She was filling two stainless-steel mugs with coffee. In looks, Riley took after her dad's side of the family, minus a bit of the padding she'd added in her late twenties thanks to a love of sweet iced tea in Atlanta and a hankering for too many fried foods. Yet, it was becoming more apparent that she took after her mom with her disinclination for anything faster than a steady walk.

"You two heading out?"

"Yep. If you change your mind and want to join us for breakfast later, give me a call."

"Where're you headed, the Boardwalk Cafe or The Clover and The Bee?" Both of Webster Grove's most popular breakfast stops had their merits, and Riley could just as easily be talked into a hearty plate of stone-ground grits with cheese and poached eggs as she could a loaded omelet and crispy hash browns.

"Depends on whichever has less of a wait when I'm finished at the hospital. How about we text you?" Brenda finished stirring in her husband's creamer—two rounded scoops—and handed off his favorite mug as he squeezed her shoulder in thanks.

Not for the first time, Riley wondered how the conversation—or conversations—had played out in which they'd decided to stay together and give their marriage another chance. They'd had twelve years of morning coffees and shoulder squeezes to get past that rough patch in their marriage. Apparently, it was only Riley who'd never put the matter to rest.

Maybe it'd be easier if you spent a bit more time around them.

"How about I let you know? There's some stuff I'd like to get done today, since I'll be working all week starting tomorrow, but about your appointment—I hope it goes well."

"I have no reason to believe it won't, and there's no need to worry, Riley. With my faith and with advances in medicine, it's practically like another step in menopause."

Last Riley had checked, cancer was still cancer, but she bit back her comment. Her mom's confidence was audible in her tone and visible in her eyes. Her lumpectomy happened while Riley was serving out her two-week notice in Atlanta. From what her dad had shared, Brenda's only setback from surgery had been a few days of extra rest spent with a handful of naps broken up by binging Netflix and catching up on her reading pile.

After her parents headed out in her dad's Audi, Riley changed into shorts, a T-shirt, and her new running shoes and headed out for a walk this morning, not a run. Twenty minutes into it, a glance at her phone confirmed it was nearly eight thirty and an acceptable time to call a mother with two young kids. Lana answered on the third ring but, at the sound of the wailing baby in the background, Riley lifted the phone away from her ear and switched it to speaker.

Maybe there was no good time to call a mother with young kids. "Now's probably not a good time, huh?" Whatever had Rosie so upset, she was really letting her mom know it.

"No, it's fine. Just another day in the life."

"Well, I'll make it quick. I was thinking about our talk yesterday. I think I'll go ahead and call Marcus, if you'll text me his number."

"About Levi? That's great, and of course! I was hoping you'd reach out since Marcus didn't."

"Yeah, I was thinking I'll start with the friend-raiser, then work up to that. I just wasn't sure if you wanted to give Grant a heads up, since he said Marcus was going to call and didn't."

"No, his workdays are crazy, and I know he won't care. Besides, they're guys. Communication's not their strong suit. He and Marcus will probably only talk basketball or golf next time they get together." Rosie's angry wails abruptly petered into silence and were replaced by the sound of the heavier, shallower breathing of a baby. "I could hardly hear you, so I gave her my phone." Lana had switched to speaker. "If she starts drooling on it, fair warning, I'm gonna have to take it away, and they'll be h-e-double-hockey-sticks to pay. She's teething and really fighting her morning nap."

"Morning nap? It's eight thirty."

"I know. She was up at six and had a crappy night's sleep."

"Sounds like a rough morning. I can let you go."

"No, not yet. Be my lifeline another few seconds, will you? I already visited the pantry this morning—and that usually doesn't happen until the witching hour, if you want to know."

Riley bit her lip to keep from giggling. Her friend's tribulations weren't funny, not really, but her delivery was spot on. "Hang in there."

"I'm trying. So, you don't start at the shelter till tomorrow, right?" Riley heard a shuffling, and Rosie erupted into a fresh set of wailing as her mom gently instructed that phones weren't for chewing on. "How about swinging by tonight after these two are out for the night?" Lana said, switching to her no-nonsense voice. "Around 8:00?"

"Sure, I can do that."

"I'll see if I can schedule us late-night pedicures. I'd give just about anything for someone to rub my calves and feet right about now." Lana needed to raise her voice loud enough over Rosie's wails that a woman working in her front landscaping stopped to look in Riley's direction. Riley flipped her phone off speaker and still managed to hear her friend just fine without putting the receiver to her ear. "I know a place that's open late. Grant will be here, and if we can't get an appointment, we can walk the neighborhood—or drink, yeah, that one. I'll pump extra today in case we do."

"Sure, sounds good. Let me know if you need me to bring anything."

"Gossip. Bring gossip," Lana raised her voice even louder over what must have been a scuffle for the phone. "AKA, call Marcus!"

Riley was in the middle of saying she'd meant wine when the line went dead and seconds later the ding from Lana's text of Marcus's contact info was loud enough to be jarring.

She finished the remaining few blocks home with a nervous anticipation setting in. As she walked up her driveway, Riley studied her century-old Craftsman-style childhood home, taking notice of what she normally breezed past. With its overhanging eaves and gabled roof, there was a quaint, welcoming air about it that promised cozy reading nooks and the smell of fresh-baked cookies inside. Whether or not her parents' marital dysfunction had created its share of havoc in Riley's world, they had built a lifetime together and worked hard for this home. They'd done a remarkable job maintaining it for over two and a half decades. If it was any indication of the strength of their marriage now, they were doing just fine.

After letting herself in using the code on the side door, she headed straight for the kitchen and fished out the pitcher of tea from the fridge. Her mom's tea was green and unsweetened, not the sugar-loaded Luzianne home brew she'd acquired a hankering for in Georgia, but it went better with her new diet and exercise regimen, so she poured a large glass and did her best to appreciate its mildly bitter but clean taste.

Pulling out her phone, Riley hovered over Marcus's phone number. *If Levi wanted you to know how he was doing, then Marcus would've called.*

Bravery waning, Riley pressed on Marcus's number before she changed her mind. After the fourth ring, a message played indicating that the voice mailbox for Coleman's Boarding and Training was full and couldn't take any more messages. Her shoulders sank. Now she'd have to call back and risk seeming overly eager when his number showed up twice on his caller ID.

Pulling up his website, she skimmed through the "About Marcus" section once more. She never would've guessed Levi's closest friend would end up running a dog training and boarding facility, but likely there was a reason he and Levi had bonded so well back in high school. Neither of them had been good at sitting still. They'd played sports on the same teams all year long: football, wrestling, and baseball.

Marcus's choice to enlist in the Marines right out of senior year hadn't raised any eyebrows, especially after his girlfriend of two years broke up with him on the guise that, after accepting a generous scholarship from Cornell, she didn't think she could make a long-distance relationship work.

She and Levi would've been different, had everything not imploded. Riley had always been certain of that. *How so, considering you never even officially started dating?*

After getting partnered up in their Early Childhood Education class when there hadn't been enough robotic babies to go around, they'd gotten to know one another while being knee-deep in the main class project—the successful care of a demanding interactive newborn. That nightmare of an experience had morphed into their finding one reason after another to be in each other's company the second semester of senior year, an unofficial and somewhat flirtatious friendship forming as they spent more and more time together, studying and just hanging out, before she'd eventually found her way into his bed.

Remembering what that led to, Riley refocused on Marcus's website. The bottom of every page was highlighted with a message reading "Not sure if we're right for you? Come check us out!" The hours were listed at the bottom of each page. Riley clicked her tongue. It was open until 5:00 p.m. A quick check on Maps showed it was just a half hour from here.

"So, it's gossip you want tonight, huh, Lana?" Riley took a breath and released it slowly. "Call me crazy, but I guess I know what I'm doing today."

Chapter 9

"DUDE, IT'S ELEVEN O'CLOCK ALREADY. AREN'T you going to get up?"

Levi jerked awake when something soft and fluffy thwacked against his head. "What the hell?" He cleared his throat, sweeping off what turned out to be a decorative throw pillow that had seen better days. Bright light pouring in from the open doorway had him wincing and turning away.

By the time Levi rolled into St. Louis last night, it had been closing in on midnight. Not wanting to disturb his mom and sister, he'd given Marcus a call. They'd stayed up till the sky began to lighten, talking and drinking the last of Marcus's rum. "I could," he said, rolling over onto his back, "but sleep's nice too."

"If my ass is managing on two hours of sleep, you can manage on six, concussion or no concussion. And I could use your help with one of the dogs, seeing as you're here. He's a crazy one, let me tell you."

"Oh yeah?"

"You'll see. And in case you're wondering what smells so good, I made lunch. It'll be ready in fifteen minutes."

After Marcus took off, leaving the door open behind him, Levi stretched out on the twin daybed. From end to end, it was a bit short for his six-foot-one frame, and he rested the backs of his ankles on the side arm at the bottom. Levi had crashed in Marcus's spare bedroom, one of only two bedrooms in the twelve-hundred-square-foot ranch nestled in the corner of ten green and rolling acres that Marcus had bought a couple years ago not far outside the St. Louis County line.

As the smell from the oven reached his nose, Levi knew what was for lunch. Granted he'd hadn't stayed with Marcus for a few years, but the last he'd seen, his buddy knew how to make three meals that weren't on a grill, and one of them was a loaded breakfast casserole in which the oven did most of the work. Considering the loaded part was hashbrowns, sausage, cheese, and eggs, Levi had no complaints.

He lingered another minute or two, then headed for the bathroom before joining Marcus in the kitchen where he was pulling a glass pan from the oven. "I was hoping that's what I was smelling."

"You know it. How'd you manage in that Barbie-doll bed?"

"No complaints. Thanks again for letting me crash here."

"Yeah, man. Anytime. You know I mean that... Except for when I've got a girl over. Though busy as things have been, the odds are in your favor of having your pick of nights. Speaking of which, if you're in town long enough, we need to get the group together, the ones who're still here, that is."

Agreeing, Levi helped himself to a glass of water. Through the window over the sink, he spotted a girl in the distance walking a dog. She was in a field behind the three exercise paddocks up near the main house, another ranch, a basementless one that had been gutted before having thirty kennels and concrete flooring installed. With her long ponytail and slender frame, she looked young, maybe eighteen or twenty at most. "How many people did you say you have working for you now?"

"Six, but they're part time—I'm not making enough yet to offer benefits—and three of them only work evening shifts. And just a heads up, five of them are girls. Knowing how the female sex radiates toward you, they'll start giving you googly eyes within five minutes of you heading out there today, but they're off limits."

Levi grinned. "Oh yeah. Why's that? You growing a harem?"

Marcus rolled his eyes. "You know I cut and burn easily enough when there's just one chick in the picture, so I'll take that for what it is—sarcasm." Marcus's lopsided grin tended to be the only playful part of his demeanor. The rest of him, honed over eight-plus years in the military, spoke business. "It's because not a damn one is old enough to even step foot in a bar yet, except for Cindy, but she's married with kids."

Levi chugged the full glass of water even though it hit his stomach like a brick. "Then I'm insulted you felt the need to warn me."

"You'll see. Most of them don't look their age." Marcus grabbed two plates from the overhead cabinet and a large serving spoon from a ceramic pitcher on the counter. "Get 'em around a puppy, and they act it though."

Levi smiled at that last part. "Well, no matter who's testing the waters, I ain't biting."

"Because you've got someone else in mind?"

Marcus's cocked eyebrow was an added dig Levi didn't much appreciate.

"Look, man," Marcus continued, "I get you not being able to work anymore threw a big wrench in things, and that you were overdue for a visit like you said, but it's me. Let's be real here. You didn't want me calling her to tell her what happened, and I didn't. Then I sent you that text telling you she was here, and a couple days later, here you are."

"I wasn't even thinking about that text."

Marcus cocked his head. "You know I'm always one to call bullshit when I see it."

Levi headed for the table, choosing the seat on the far side, looking in. "What's your point exactly? Because I know you won't let this rest until you make it."

"You two actually being in the same vicinity—it's like Halley's Comet circled around again or something. You don't talk about her unless you're drunker than shit, and then when you finally start, you won't shut up. If you ask me, you either need to let her know you're still in love with her or get her out of your system once and for all."

Marcus was blowing a bellows at a pile of embers that needed to be left untouched. Fighting the urge to tell him so—and no doubt prove him right in the process—Levi dragged a hand through his hair. "Whatever, man. I appreciate the concern, but I've got this."

Marcus plunked a plate loaded with steaming casserole and a half-full bottle of 24-ounce hot sauce on the table in front of him with no fanfare.

"Thanks for the food." If there was anything better than melted cheese and sausage after a few too many shots of rum, Levi didn't know it.

"I couldn't put you to work on an empty stomach, could I?" After loading up a plate for himself, Marcus sat down on the opposite side of the table and doused his serving in enough hot sauce to make anyone sweat. "Look, I get you don't want to talk about it," he said after taking a bite and not seeming to notice the heat. "So, I'll give it a rest, but my vote is you find a way to meet up with her while you're here. Tell her how you feel. If it doesn't work out, it wasn't meant to be."

"Your vote?" Levi said, forcing a grin he didn't feel. "So, my love life's a democracy?"

Marcus cocked an eyebrow. "What can I say? You'd make a pathetic king. In that arena, anyway."

Considering how not eager Levi was to pursue this, thankfully, Marcus wasn't much for talking as he ate. After finishing about half of what was on his plate, Levi took a drink. "So, this crazy dog. What is it you want me to do?"

Marcus paused before taking another bite. "Mostly to serve as a distraction as I'm working with him. He's energetic enough to take these lightweights working for me off their feet. He's a registered border collie, but he's big for his size and exceptionally hyper. They're trying to get him focused on agility in hopes of having an outlet for that energy, but he's got the attention span of a senile basset hound."

Levi grinned. "Sounds fun."

"That's debatable, but he's growing on me, I guess, and his people have money to spend. They drop him off for daycare three days a week and pay for all the extras."

"Like training?"

"Yeah, that, and longer walks; supervised, small-session play; weekly baths. Practically everything I offer."

"Sounds pricey."

"It ain't cheap. They're spending close to a grand

a month right now—and that's when he isn't staying overnight when they're traveling."

"Sounds like a pretty good gig you've got going here." Levi nodded toward the window at the sink. "From what I could see, the property's great. Nice find." Last night, this far out from city lights, it had been too dark to take in much at all.

"It is great. Good land. Not much more than a half hour from downtown. No complaints."

Levi got up and helped himself to another scoop of casserole but stood at the counter to finish it. "You glad you decided to get out?"

Marcus joined him at the counter and poked his fork straight into the casserole for another bite of his own. He knew what Levi was talking about without having to clarify it. He'd done eight years of service in the Marines. For years to come, it would be the biggest thing in his life, retired or not. "I don't know if glad's the right answer. It was time, I guess. Still wound as tight as an old clock, you might say."

"Some things, I bet, are hard to let go." Even though he was talking about Marcus, slipping into a dive suit and submerging into the deep, gray quiet was something he bet he'd be dreaming about twenty years from now.

"Yeah, they are." Marcus dropped his plate in the sink next to a small pile of dirty dishes.

"You cooked; I'll clean."

"I was hoping you'd say that." Marcus clapped

him on the shoulder after glancing at his watch. "Come out when you're done. I'll be up in one of the paddocks working the dogs."

After Marcus headed out, Levi loaded the dishwasher and started it, then hunted through drawers until he located the Saran Wrap. Levi slipped the leftover casserole in the fridge, noticing how it was crowded with mostly eaten takeout in to-go containers, Heineken and Budweiser, a loaf of bread, a few packs of lunchmeat, a pound of ground beef, a carton of eggs, and four different flavors of hot sauce, but not a piece of fruit or vegetable to be found.

While wiping down the counters, he called his mom. When she didn't pick up—her workdays tended to be packed—he left a message that he was in town and would stop by tonight. After tossing down a couple Advil in hopes of quelling the not-so-dull headache hanging around after the long drive followed by a night of drinking, Levi helped himself to the last of the coffee in the pot. It had gone cold, and while he liked it better hot, Levi poured it over a glass filled with ice before heading outside, drink in hand.

The sun was high overhead in a mostly cloudless sky. It was hot out but not scorching, no doubt thanks to the blast of storms last night that had slowed his progress along the drive here. Even the notorious late-August St. Louis humidity had let off enough that Levi was looking forward to spending a few hours outdoors with Marcus and the dogs.

Maybe Marcus's house was a bit dated, but his buddy had been downplaying what a good piece of land he'd grabbed in purchasing this place. For the hilly area it was nestled in, the bulk of the property was relatively flat and usable, bordering a two-lane road in front and a combination of forest and farmland in back. Ahead, up by the house-turned-boarding-facility, were the three wrought-iron paddocks Levi had seen from the kitchen window. Each was maybe a quarter acre in size and partially shaded by a handful of towering trees lining a long gravel driveway splitting the length of the property.

Marcus was working alone in the furthest paddock with a youngish-looking German shepherd that seemed to have a decent amount of sense about it, judging by the way it was cuing off of Marcus's gestures. The other two paddocks had a handful of dogs in each, most of which were romping in play while a few were more aloof and hanging back.

As he passed by, Levi exchanged hellos with two of Marcus's staff who were standing near one another but in separate paddocks, looking after the dogs. They were young; Marcus was right. Too young to tempt Levi, not that he had any interest in being tempted, anyway.

After taking a swig of coffee, Levi rested his arms atop the chest-high fence railing of the last paddock. "What's the deal with that one?"

Marcus held up a finger, continuing to hold the

sitting-at-attention dog's gaze with his own. After close to a half a minute had passed, Marcus gave a nod and said, "Good boy." He leaned down to give the shepherd a hearty pat on the shoulder.

When given a verbal release, the shepherd took off, galloping over to Levi. After sniffing him thoroughly through the fence, he took off to check out the dogs in the nearest paddock.

"Not a thing's wrong with him, 'cept he's young," Marcus said, walking over. "And his owners are a bit impatient."

"I'm guessing you installed these yourself?" Levi said with a nod toward the row of paddocks.

"Yep."

"Why circular? Bet they were a bear to install."

"That they were, but for some of these dogs, being boarded has their anxiety off the charts. Better not to have any corners to get trapped in in the event a scuffle breaks out."

"Makes sense."

"Hey, I know you aren't going to need it with the settlement that's got to be coming your way after that accident, but if you're interested in work, I've got it in spades. Maybe you could stick around for a while." Marcus nodded toward the glass in Levi's hand. "The coffee's no better than what you've been getting, living out of hotels for so long, but it does the trick, and there's an empty room I could be talked into letting you claim for awhile."

Levi looked away, contemplating a response, and his attention was caught by a squat-looking bulldog sprawled out in the shade, lazily watching the dogs in the other two paddocks. Surprised as he was to find a dog here roaming free, unattended, he held off asking about it to address Marcus's offer. "Thanks, man, but after losing Tank, I'm pretty much done with dogs. For a while, anyway."

"I've got most of the help I need with the dogs—hell, I think most of these girls would stick around even if I didn't pay them. What I need is help with groundskeeping and maintenance. Knowing the hard-on you had for shop class, you'd appreciate the tool barn." He jutted a finger toward the detached garage behind the main house. "I know it's a garage, but the girls call it a barn, and the name stuck. Most of what's in there was passed along from my uncle. There's even a Select Series Deere for mowing the grass. I worked it into the sale of this place."

Marcus had taken quite a bit on, converting this place from a residence to a boarding and training facility. As Levi looked around more critically, a few things stood out that hadn't before, like landscaping that needed attention and gutters that needed cleaning. Aside from a wide path skirting the driveway from the road to the house that had a manicured look about it, the grass elsewhere on the property hadn't been cut in a month or more.

Under the remarkable blue hue of the sky today, everything looked green and inviting, surprisingly so for this time of year when summer had finally released most of its scorching breath. Maybe it was because he'd planted himself in the shade of a towering oak and the heat had relented, but it was easy to picture himself hauling in some of those suitcases from his trunk and staying awhile. Maybe even stringing up a hammock between two of these trees after hours when things got quiet.

The idea of losing himself in work here while he figured out—really figured out—what he wanted to do next sent a wave of peace over him the likes of which he hadn't felt in months.

He dragged a hand down his face, over his mouth and chin. "I could help you out for a week or so, if you need it. But don't hold your breath for anything longer than that. I have no intention of getting comfortable."

Marcus gave him a skeptical look before turning back to whistle at the shepherd. "Come, Duke," he said, clapping his hand against his thigh. The lean and leggy young dog bolted across the yard and came to an easy stop a few feet from him, ready to do whatever it was he'd been called to do.

"What's that look about?" The hair on the back of Levi's neck riled at not even hearing a "thanks" in response to his answer.

"Nothing, except the last thing you've been

doing since you took off is getting comfortable. I know better than to hope for that now."

As much as he wanted to disagree, Levi knew better than to lie to someone who quite possibly knew him better than he knew himself.

———

Twenty minutes later, Levi was in the back paddock with Marcus and the hyper border collie, his coffee finished, and his headache all but vanished. Marcus hadn't been kidding about the dog's energy level. The thing didn't stop moving. Even on a leash, Jax pranced and circled about, too hyper to listen to direction.

"Maybe they need to lay off giving him shots of 5-hour Energy," Levi suggested with a chuckle, shoving his hands in his back pockets as Jax tore like a racehorse around the paddock, and with the intensity of a dog who believed doing so would take him somewhere.

"Usually, he calms down after about twenty circles. Then I can get him to start listening." Marcus tossed Levi a tennis ball from a backpack at his feet as Jax sprinted the circular fence line, too busy to notice. "Keep this out of sight, will you? After I start working with him, when I tell you to, start tossing it in the air a bit. It'll be a challenge, but I want to see if I can keep his attention on me."

The three staff currently working had all stopped to watch, making it clear this dog had a reputation. Even the bulldog had moved shade trees to the one closest to this paddock and was observing Jax with what appeared to be bemused interest, judging from its classic bulldog smile.

The black-and-white border collie was big and striking, though he was too antsy to be winning any best-in-shows for some time coming. He was, though, beyond any doubt, built to run.

After what must've been close to the twenty circles Marcus had predicted, the dog stopped running and darted over to check out Levi, not nearly as winded as Levi would've guessed. He offered the back of one hand for a sniff, but Jax dashed out of arm's reach as if worried Levi would try to catch him. He barked once and wagged his tail, his mouth open in a pant.

On the opposite side of the paddock, Marcus whistled. Jax bounded over, his fluffy black tail sticking out behind him in excitement. Staring intently at Marcus, he barked a few times. "Yeah, yeah, no treats till you do some work." Marcus held his hand out in the signal for sit. "Jax, sit."

Jax barked and wagged his tail hopefully as he circled Marcus, but when Marcus didn't give in, he reluctantly sank onto his haunches and was rewarded with both hearty praise and a treat. Over the next few minutes, Marcus practiced all the basic commands including sit, down, stay, come, and leave-it.

"Go ahead and start tossing that ball in the air," Marcus instructed without looking away from Jax, who was still lying down—but uncomfortably so—after being given the stay command. "But don't give it to him if he comes for it, which he will when he spots it. Tennis balls are a close second to running in Jax's world. The goal is to get him refocused on me once he notices it."

Suspecting this refocusing thing would be harder to do for Jax than most dogs, Levi started throwing the ball in the air and catching it, not that high at first but throwing higher as he went. Jax didn't notice, zeroed in on Marcus as he was and with his back to Levi as he waited to be released from his half-lying, half-crouched position and awaiting his next treat.

Levi began throwing the ball higher and higher. The ball had just left his hand, his highest throw yet, when he glanced over and spotted Marcus's jaw dropping in surprise at something outside the paddock. "What the hell?" Marcus's soft exclamation was barely audible, but it got Levi's attention just the same.

The throw was high enough that Levi had time to follow Marcus's gaze. The world couldn't have stopped moving faster if a comet had struck. Impossible as it was, Riley Leighton was standing underneath the oak tree next to the bulldog, staring at Levi like she was seeing a ghost.

Levi caught the ball on autopilot, an impressive feat considering he only saw its return out of the corner of his eye. Every ounce of adrenaline in his body flooded his system, leaving him frozen in place and sucking the breath from his lungs in a microsecond.

Riley was here. Thirty feet away. Riley, who he'd not seen in nearly twelve years.

Like a bolt of lightning crashing down on him, the crushing feeling in his chest made it clear that he still loved her just as much as when she'd walked away.

Riley was here. In the flesh.

Thirty feet away.

Still holding the ball in the exact position he'd caught it, Levi didn't notice Jax charging his direction until the lithe dog had sprung into the air, launching himself at Levi. As fast as Jax was moving, his front feet pummeled against Levi's chest with the force of a sandbag shot from a catapult. Not braced for it, Levi went flailing backward like a domino. In midair, Jax chomped down on the ball and attempted to spring off Levi's chest with his back feet.

Levi's left hand and arm took some of the force out of the fall, then his ass hit the ground with a smack, followed by his right elbow, sending a jarring pain up his neck and into his head, hard enough that he was instantly seeing stars.

Jax hit the ground immediately afterward, half on top of Levi, half off him—without losing his grip on the ball. Hardly fazed, the dog popped up onto all fours and shook himself off before taking off at a run.

The fall had knocked the wind out of Levi. He was attempting to suck in a full breath as Riley's voice, the same, caring tone he'd be able to precisely recall on his deathbed even if he never heard it again, rolled across the yard, making it clear Levi wasn't seeing things.

"Oh my God, Levi, please tell me you're okay!"

Chapter 10

RILEY COULD KICK HERSELF FOR STANDING there gawking like an idiot when she spotted Levi on the other side of the fence, but a part of her hadn't believed what she was seeing. It was forever going to be one of those moments she'd give just about anything to undo. Levi was here in St. Louis, when Lana had told her he was up in Michigan recovering.

To add to her confusion, her brain had been busy trying to match up *old* Levi—the one who'd stuck around so prominently in her memory all these years—to *now* Levi. She'd fallen in love with a boy, and even though she'd seen a handful of his few-and-far-between social media posts over the years, she'd always imagined eighteen-year-old Levi whenever she thought of him. But the Levi standing in the training area was a thirty-year-old man.

At eighteen, he'd been tall and thin, and the guy that half the senior class fantasized about spending Seven Minutes in Heaven with. As it turned out, time and his choice of such a physical career had been good to him, really good. And clearly there still wasn't a high ball he couldn't catch—even when he was hardly paying attention. *Now* Levi could kick *old* Levi's ass and hand it to him in a Chinese food take-out box.

Now Levi wasn't going to care that Riley was sorry for walking away or that she'd never really gotten over him.

So, there she'd been, dumbstruck and frozen in place, wondering if she could back away without anyone seeing her when suddenly everyone was staring at her—and a forty-something pound border collie with Ninja skills pummeled right into him. A handful of seconds stretched out like an eternity as she stared, transfixed, waiting for a sign that he was okay, then Marcus was kneeling over him, and Levi was waving him away.

Levi rolled onto his side and pushed up into a sitting position, looking Riley's way again.

Get in your car and go. You don't have to explain yourself. Marcus has got this.

Riley's palms were sweating, and her breathing had gone shallow. So much so, her fingertips were growing numb and tingly. The tan-and-white bulldog at her feet who made wheezy sounds as she breathed wagged her nubbin of a tail and barked up at Riley like a medical-response dog letting her owner know something was off.

A not-so-quiet whisper reached Riley's ears from one of the teens ten feet away who'd been watching the training in the dog pen. "Who's that, and what's she doing here?"

Inside the pen, the border collie was circling the enclosure at an easy lope, the tennis ball in its mouth, clearly oblivious to its faux pas.

"Want me to get some ice?" one of the teens called over to Marcus.

"Yeah, will you?"

Levi waved a hand dismissively. "I'm fine. I don't need ice."

After exchanging a split-second look with her coworker, the girl took off in the direction of the house. Clearly, at this place of business, Marcus's wishes trumped Levi's.

Marcus looked over at Riley again. "Be right with you, Riley," he called before giving Levi another once-over. "How about we get you to that bench out there in the shade, and you can sit a couple minutes? Let that head of yours settle."

Riley didn't have to turn around to know Marcus was talking about the bench a few feet behind her. *Because that wouldn't be awkward.*

Levi got up on his feet with a litheness that surprised her after a jarring like he'd just taken. It seemed impossible that he wouldn't at the very least be battling a bit of whiplash the next couple days.

Riley was just starting to breathe normally again when she noticed the way Levi's hands clenched into fists as he looked back and forth between her and Marcus. His shoulders rounded like he was about to step into a very different sort of ring than the one he was in. "I told you not to call her. *You promised you wouldn't!*"

The words carried the thirty feet that separated them like he was standing right next to her, delivering a slap on the face she'd not been prepared for. That tone of his, could he be more put off by the sight of her? Riley didn't think so. Even though it hardly seemed possible, her cheeks flamed several degrees hotter than they already were.

Clearly Marcus hadn't called her because Levi had stopped him from doing so.

Of course. It made perfect sense. Levi was never going to forgive her. He didn't want anything to do with her. Why should he?

The bulldog was staring up at her intently and whined, fully aware that this new person to her space was in a state of frozen distress.

Marcus and Levi were exchanging rapid-fire words, but Riley's ears were pounding too loudly to discern them. "You promised you wouldn't" rang in her ears. He might've well have said "How could you?"

There was no saving face here, not a chance. Turning away, she strode back to where she'd parked her car in front of the main house in one of three marked visitor parking spots. There was no getting past this—no getting past an impulsive decision she made twelve years ago when her world was imploding.

It was a minor miracle that she was able to hold back the tears attempting to rush in, but even so, her nose betrayed her and began dripping like a faucet. At least her legs were obeying her. She was walking fast enough to leave those speed walkers who circled Lenox Square mall in Atlanta in the early mornings in the dust. Even the bulldog gave up following her and retreated into the shade after they hit a patch of full sun.

"Hey, Riley! Hold up a minute!"

Her ears were pounding hard enough that she couldn't be certain, but she'd put her money on it being Marcus, not Levi, who was coming after her. She didn't turn around to check.

She made it to her car, dropped her phone and keys onto the seat next to her, and pressed on the ignition with a shaky hand and finger. As soon as her seatbelt was buckled, she whipped into reverse, hurriedly checking her rearview mirror to make sure her pursuer was far enough away that she didn't have to worry about backing into him.

Her backup warning buzzed loudly just as she was hitting the breaks to flip into drive, but she didn't reach a complete stop fast enough. Her rear bumper smacked into something with a thwack.

"Crap on a stick!" It wasn't like she drove a big boat and had an excuse. Hers was a tiny Mini

Cooper. She popped open her door and leaned out just enough to see that she'd backed into a flagpole at the edge of the grass. It was still standing—thank goodness—but it was leaning like the Tower of Pisa. Weren't flagpoles supposed to be set in concrete?

Both Marcus and Levi were headed her way, Marcus leading and Levi trailing a bit further behind. Both had looks of obvious surprise on their faces.

Yes, thank you very much, she really did nearly take out Marcus's flagpole.

However humiliating it would've been facing them a few minutes ago, doing so now was even worse. If she'd done any real damage, she'd pay for it, but she wasn't about to deal with that right this humiliating second. She'd send money through Lana. Slamming her door shut again, she drove off down the driveway, not daring to look behind her—not that she could see much anyway with the tears flooding her eyes.

Tempted as she was to plow through the automatic gate at the entrance of the property, Riley drummed her fingers against the steering wheel as it chugged open at a snail's pace. "You're an idiot, running away like this."

Wasn't this what she always did, run away and not look back?

Maybe so, but Levi couldn't have been more clear that he didn't want her here. She was doing them all a favor. "Thank God for small cars." She slipped her car through a narrow space as the gate was still opening. As she was pulling onto the two-lane road boarding the property, a movement along the fence line caught her eye.

Riley sucked in a breath. Levi had just scaled the fence and was jogging across a narrow strip of grass onto the road. It was risk running him over or stop. "Could this *be* more awkward?" Riley muttered as she pulled over to the narrow shoulder and turned on her hazard lights. *Probably no, it couldn't.*

The driver's-side window motor whined as she opened it, and Levi came around to the driver's-side door. Her Mini had never felt so undersized as it did with him looming over her, clasping his hands on the top rim of her door.

"What the hell, Riley?" He was shaking his head, but there was a half smile on his face, making him seem more taken aback than accusatory. "You don't have to run off like this."

Despite the half-playful look on his face—or maybe in part because of it—Riley's anger flared. "It couldn't have been more clear back there that I was the last person you wanted to look over and see."

"Not true. I could name a few dozen on the spot I'd like to see a whole lot less than you," he said with a grin. "Besides, there's a difference between expecting and wanting, last I checked." Levi tapped on the rim of her door with his thumb. "But all the same, if I came off like an ass, I'm sorry."

He was just a little winded from his run and a few strands of hair were out of place, but it was his eyes that got her. The rest of him might've aged—in a good way—but all that Levi-ness was right there in those liquid-amber eyes, just the same as the day she'd ended things with him. Looking into them made her want to both sob and climb through the open window and plant a kiss on those remarkable lips all at the same time. *How about keeping it together in front of him, huh?* Riley cleared her throat. "That fall back there, was it bad for your concussion?"

That half smile curled into a bigger one. "I'll live."

A pickup truck passing on the other side of road slowed to stop, and the driver asked if they needed help, but Levi waved him on with a thanks.

"I'd, uh, better get moving."

Levi nodded toward the property. "Want to turn around and come back?"

"I would, but I'm late."

"You just got here."

"I know, but I was just stopping by to, uh..."

"Check the place out?"

"Sort of. I tried calling Marcus earlier. He's hosting a friendraiser here at the end of September, and I'm doing some temp work for High Grove starting tomorrow. It turns out that event is on my list." Riley knew Levi would remember the shelter. He'd gone with her there to walk dogs a few times when they'd been floating in the friend zone and too afraid to take it further.

"Oh yeah? I don't really know what a friendraiser is, but good for you."

"It's like a fundraiser but without the money-raising end of things." Riley rubbed her lips together. "I'm glad you're okay. I heard... I heard it was really bad."

"It wasn't good, I guess, but thanks. Things are getting better every day."

"That's good." Riley closed her hands around the steering wheel. "I didn't know you were here."

"No one really did. But it seems we'll be seeing more of each other."

"You're staying then?"

Levi raised an eyebrow. "For a little while. A month, it seems. If Marcus is having an event here in a month, he'll need some help getting ready."

Riley's face felt weird, like it was a little rubbery. Never in a million years would she have expected this. "Oh yeah?"

"Yeah."

A sedan zoomed past after switching to the open incoming lane to give them a wide berth. "I should go. But, uh, tell Marcus I'll call him. And about that flagpole—this backup camera is on the frits." Total lie, and she wasn't even saving face. "He and I can talk about the damage when I call him."

"The pole's fine. If you want some help popping out that bumper, give me a call." One eyebrow cocked slightly. "My number's the same, if you're wondering."

There went the hope her bumper was unscathed. "Thanks. Mine too."

"Good to know. Well, drive safe, and good seeing you, Riley Leighton."

That smile. Dear God, did she ever have a chance?

Levi stepped back, and Riley gave him a little nod before driving away. While a part of her still wanted to bury her head in the sand and never step foot here again, another part wanted to pump her fists and do cartwheels. She just wasn't sure which part she should be listening to more.

Chapter 11

"It's a good thing you ran after her, as big of an idiot as you were back there."

As much as Levi didn't want to hear it, his best friend was right. He'd caught the look on Riley's face just before she fled, and it nearly brought him to his knees. There were a million things he could've said upon looking over and seeing her, and not one of them included the cutting way he'd barked at Marcus for proposedly contacting her.

He'd hardly admitted it even to himself, but for a long time now, he'd been harboring hope of getting in the same space with her again, to have a chance to see for himself if she was one hundred percent over him. Wouldn't you know, when he'd gotten it, he'd acted like an ass.

Even with as much time having passed since they'd been in one another's lives, he could tell when she wasn't being entirely truthful just now, they way she'd dropped his gaze at first when saying that friendraiser was the reason she was here. Maybe Marcus knew more than he was letting on. "So, you really didn't call her to tell her I was here? Or shoot off a text or send a message through Grant and Lana?"

"I told you I wouldn't, and I didn't." Marcus was bent over, shoving a rock in the ground at the base of the flagpole in an attempt to straighten it. "Good thing for that bumper of hers that I haven't gotten around to securing this in cement yet."

"She knew about the concussion," Levi added. "If it wasn't you who told her, it was Lana. They were together yesterday. As for why Riley showed up here, she said she came by to talk to you about some event you're hosting at the end of September. She's going to be doing some work for High Grove, and a part of that entails helping with their part of it."

"Oh yeah? Small world. And you found out all that in two minutes?" Marcus stood upright again and wiped his hand on the outer thigh of his jeans. "That was a productive hop over the fence. And here I figured she came to see about boarding a dog."

"She doesn't have a dog. She's never had a dog. That I've seen anyway."

"Not that you're paying any attention anymore, right?"

Ignoring the look Marcus was giving him, Levi opted not to offer that he checked her social media posts enough to know she tagged shelter dog pictures with #someday at least a few times a year.

Marcus humphed into Levi's silence. "So, she knew about your concussion, huh? If that's the case, whatever she told you about her reason for showing up here out of the blue, I bet you a million bucks it was because she wanted a report from as close to the horse's mouth as she thought she could get—yours truly, of course."

A dozen different emotions swirled through Levi, not the least of which was hope that his friend was right.

Marcus stared at him a beat or two longer than usual as Levi failed to come up with a response. "I take it you made up for that Grinch-like greeting of yours just now with an apology?"

Levi thought back on the words that had been exchanged at that tiny car of hers, and a bit of doubt creeped in. "In the world of apologies, it might've been lacking, but it seemed like she accepted it."

The bulldog walked up and sprawled out on the grass between them, making Levi wondered how often she was here to be as comfortable as she was.

"Look, I know you're gonna say you've been over her for over a decade now, but take my advice and don't screw this up."

"I went after her, didn't I?" When Marcus didn't seem appeased, he added. "Exactly what is it you're suggesting I do?"

Marcus raised an eyebrow. "Maybe you give me more than just a couple days here and, in addition whatever maintenance you want to help with, you organize this event with her. Just might be the white flag to finally heal some wounded egos and give the two most stubborn people I've ever met a way to really start talking again." Levi was wondering if he should admit that he'd already told Riley he'd be staying on for a month, or if it were better to let Marcus think it was all his idea when his buddy added, "Think about it before you turn it down. Maybe it'll come with a bonus for taking on so much here."

Levi clapped him on the shoulder. "Considering I'm not about to take any sort of pay for helping you out, I hope it's either you investing in a spare bed that's not hobbit sized or, dare I say it, expanding your index of dinners by another few."

Marcus huffed as he headed down the driveway toward the kennels. "I find myself hard pressed to believe you've amassed any better cooking skills than me, living out of hotels as you've been. But anytime you want to hop in and cook, go for it. Besides, what's this hating on my cooking? I'm betting when you leave here, you'll be calling me Emeril."

Levi caught himself smiling, one of the few real smiles that brushed his lips since before the accident. The thought of hanging around here made more sense than he'd ever have guessed when falling asleep just before dawn this morning. On top of it all, Riley was home. Maybe not to stay, but for a while, at least.

Quite possibly only a fool would be hopeful about the prospect of fixing things with her, as long as it had been, but a fool's hope was more hope than he'd had in a long time.

Still sprawled out in the shade next to him, the world's friendliest bulldog looked up at him and pumped her corkscrew tail as if bidding him welcome all over again.

Chapter 12

IF RILEY HAD LEARNED TO DO ONE THING WELL over the last ten years, it was to dive into a new job. Even so, being at High Grove was like slipping into a favorite pair of yoga pants. Most of the staff had turned over since she'd last been an active volunteer, but since she'd been following the shelter's social media posts for so long, most of the new faces were familiar.

Tess and Fidel both wore the dual hats of operations staff and head trainers. Tess promised to be the more outgoing of the two, as Riley would've guessed from the posts she'd seen. Fidel's welcome was little more than a curt nod, though he seemed friendly enough with his coworkers that Riley was betting he would warm up when he got to know her better. Kelsey coordinated the volunteers and wore a dozen other hats as well; both she and Tess could have side jobs on the neighborhood welcome committee. They'd even gone in on a small bouquet of flowers for Riley's desk, a workplace-welcome first.

In Riley's first real moment of downtime a few hours into the day, she flattened her palms against her new desk and drummed her heels rapid fire underneath her as quietly as she was able since her new workstation didn't exactly come with a lot of privacy. She was getting paid to work here. This was going to take some getting used to.

Her desk was in the main area of the shelter toward the back, not far from the cat kennels and a towering kitty play area known as the Cat-a-Climb. Riley could think of worse things to have in her direct line of sight than a tower full of playful felines.

The next desk over belonged to Kelsey. Tess's desk was directly in front of Riley's, but Riley had a feeling Tess wasn't at it much. At the moment, she was out back with Fidel, working with the dogs who were ready to move out of quarantine today, determining their sociability. This was something Riley had always loved about the shelter, the way every animal undergoing the adoption process ended up with an ideal placement plan for adoption.

Riley was perusing a detailed analysis Patrick had put together of the last six months of social media posts when Kelsey came back to her desk, dog in tow. It was a toy-sized, Chihuahua-mix with long, wiry hair and a longer face than most Chihuahuas. Riley had spotted the little thing this morning during what was sure to become her favorite part of the day—the first thirty minutes when everyone pitched in to feed, water, and move the first round of dogs into any of four pens for exercise and play while their kennels were being cleaned.

Which dogs were placed in which pens with which dogs was Patrick's responsibility. The better she got to know him, the more Riley admired his photographic memory.

Another job perk Riley was excited about was the twice-a-day dog-walking breaks that were encouraged for office staff. Riley knew exactly who her first dog would be to walk today—Arlo. Man, had she been missing him.

Before starting this morning, she'd gotten here a few minutes early for a much-needed Arlo hug, borrowing her face into that silky smooth fur and locking her arms around his neck—even if his massive size had her doing a double take when he first stepped out of his kennel to greet her. After moving up to adoption row yesterday, he was much more accessible for hugs like this throughout the day.

"Is that a Chihuahua-mix?" she asked as Kelsey carried the little dog like a clutch over to her desk.

"Yeah, we think she's a wire chiwoxy." Kelsey grinned as she said it. "In case you're not yet up to speed on the dozens upon dozens of Chihuahua mixes out there, that one's a wirehaired terrier and Chihuahua mix."

"Yeah, that's definitely not my forte. I've heard of chiweenies before, but not chiwoxies. My dream dogs are all over forty pounds, which is why I've never had one, having lived in condos and apartments with pet size limits the last decade."

"I hear you there, but the little ones are adorable too. And working here, you'll learn the popular mixed-Chihuahua breeds, for sure. Sometimes, when they come in, it's like, really, what were you thinking crossing those two breeds? And how'd you accomplish it?"

Riley snorted softly, thinking of a boxer/ Chihuahua mix who'd once come through here years ago that she'd adored. "I bet."

"But as I've said before and will say again, I think I could get rich creating a designer Chihuahua-mix board game." As Kelsey sat down at her desk and moved her mouse to wake up her computer, she settled the small dog onto her lap. "In case Megan hasn't told you yet, you're welcome to bring dogs up to hang out and nap by your desk during the week when there isn't a ton going on adoption-wise. During the weekends, it's too crazy in here for it, but Mondays through Thursdays are a safe bet for a desk companion." As if she knew the routine, the little chiwoxy circled a couple times, then curled up in a ball as close to Kelsey as she could get and tucked her nose underneath her tail.

"Oh yeah? How sweet."

"Good for the soul, for sure." Kelsey gave the little dog a scratch on top of her head. "We've actually gotten a few of the long shots adopted this way. The key is picking ones who can settle down. The ones who can't, especially the really anxious ones, it's better to stick to walking them."

Riley's thoughts immediately ran to whether Arlo could fit up here. Lying down, his long legs and big body would take up most of the open floor space between her desk and the adoption counter in front of the cat kennels, creating a trip hazard for would-be adopters. The truth was, unsettled as he still was by this change of life circumstance, there was zero chance he'd settle down and doze the way the little creature on Kelsey's lap was doing.

"Oh, and fair warning, the policy doesn't apply to cats," Kelsey added. "Aside from Trina, we've not had any real success getting them comfortable outside of their kennels. They almost always bolt when something scares them, and chaos ensues."

"I could see that."

As Kelsey turned to her computer, Riley went back to comparing the results of some of Patrick's campaigns to the actual posts. For someone without a marketing degree, he'd done an impressive job developing a CRM and analyzing what worked and what didn't. Ideas for several new posts danced through her mind, and she began jotting them down.

The constant murmur of would-be adopters, playful kittens romping about in the activity center, and the muted barking of dogs behind the insulated walls leading to the back was enjoyable, especially after her last job. There, she'd effectively worked alone in an office the size of a broom closet and had a handful of notoriously stuck-in-their-ways lawn care technicians ogling her every time she stepped into the break room to fill up her water.

"Well, I'd better get this girl back to her kennel," Kelsey said sometime later, lifting the chiwoxy up to plant a kiss on her nose. The pint-sized pup licked the tip of Kelsey's nose in return. "I'll be training a few new volunteers for the next forty-five minutes or so." Kelsey stood up and tucked the dog under her arm like a clutch again. "I know there's a lot to learn, but remember, you aren't bolted to your desk. Some of us find we have to set a timer to remember to get away from our computers a bit."

"I bet. The way I see it, that's one of the best perks—" Riley stopped midsentence, her attention caught by someone walking in the main door. Clearly, her shock was visible because Kelsey turned to see what she was looking at. *Who* she was looking at, more accurately. Levi was here at High Grove. Bearing gifts of food and drink, judging by the paper bag and to-go coffee cup in his hands.

Riley gulped. There'd be no hopping in her car and fleeing this time. Levi paused just inside the door to scan the main room, his gaze landing on her. A hint of a smile turned up the corners of his mouth, leaving her no doubt he'd come to see her.

Chance was nearby sniffing the shoes of a potential adopter and scuttled over for a sniff. Levi sank onto his heels, switching both the bag and cup to the same hand to give the dog a good scratch of the ears as Chance's back leg thumped in unison.

"Well, Chance approves, so it's safe to assume your visitor's a good guy. Chance's first impressions are never wrong," Kelsey murmured with a smile. "And if he's surprising you with lunch on your first day, well, then we know it for sure."

Riley wanted to correct Kelsey's faux pas—the assumption that Levi was someone of unquestionable significance in her life—before it went any further, but Levi was on the move, striding over. "Hey Riley, how's the first day going?" He winked as he said it, that hint of a grin widening into a full-fledged one.

A dozen responses popped into mind, none of which would help this ease back into an ordinary first day on the job. She was still struggling to come up with a reply when Kelsey stuck out her hand after shifting the chiwoxy in her arms.

"I'm Kelsey." Riley's new coworker had clearly bought his unspoken assertion that theirs was a relationship that warranted popping in like this. "I can't tell you how excited we are to have her on board—even if it's just for a little while."

After setting the coffee on Riley's desk, Levi shook Kelsey's outstretched hand. "Levi Duncan. Nice to meet you."

The enticing smell of what promised to be a delicious mocha reached Riley's nose, disorienting

her further. Levi leaned the side of his hip against
the front of her desk, his waist at her eye level, and
an easy grin on his face. It occurred to her that,
eons ago, she'd been up close and personal with
the body part creating the slight bulge underneath
the zipper of his jeans. *Really? Your first day at work,
and you're thinking about Levi's penis?*

"I work with Marcus Coleman over at Coleman
Boarding and Training," he continued, directing
his words to Kelsey in a voice deep and rich as
molasses. "You all are staffing a tent at our upcoming friendraiser. Riley and I go way back, but when
she mentioned yesterday about helping out here,
it got Marcus thinking about some mutual collab-
oration we might do beforehand, and he wants me
to pick her brain. If now isn't a good time, I can get
on your calendar and come back."

As Riley stared dumbfounded, Kelsey looked
between them. It was unlikely she'd pick up on the
mischievousness in Levi's easy grin. Odds were,
she'd been too distracted by those thick lashes
and brows that were window treatments for those
gentle amber-brown eyes Riley had fallen in love
with. "What a coincidence," Kelsey said. "I was
just reminding her not to stay planted at her desk
too long. Here, we're big on brainstorming while
we walk dogs, if you two are in the mood for that.
There are benches in the shade out back too, if you
want a bit of peace and quiet."

Levi raised an eyebrow. "Both sound good to me. Up to you, Riley. Oh, and I got your favorite, white chocolate lavender mocha." He nodded to the untouched coffee on her desk as he dropped the bag next to it. "And this is that stuffed croissant you're crazy about."

"Webster Groves Garden Cafe?" Kelsey clasped a hand over her stomach. "That's my favorite coffee stop in Webster—in all of St. Louis, actually."

"Oh, yeah?" Levi asked. "Riley's too. What's your poison, and I'll pick it up next time I stop by."

Next time he stops by? Warmth rushed into Riley's cheeks.

"How sweet, but I'd better not answer that." Kelsey smiled good-naturedly. "I'm struggling to be good on this new diet, which is why I'd better not stick around smelling it or I'll cave and run there at lunch." Giving Riley a pointed look, she added, "Kidding, not kidding, but I do have to run. I'll catch you later, and nice to meet you, Levi."

And then there were two.

Riley busied herself closing the notebook on her desk. *Well, there goes a microsecond.* She was struggling with the fact that Levi remembered her favorite mocha—twelve years later—and it was stirring up a wash of memories of them sitting at a booth doing homework, their calves touching under the table.

"I know I should've called, given that it's your first day. I'm fully prepared to grovel," he said into her silence. "In here, or outdoors on a bench. Hell, I'll grovel while walking a couple dogs, if that's your preference."

Riley quirked her lips, doing her darndest to hold back a smile. Deny it as she might, her heart was doing a little dance. Unable to pretend to be busy with her notebook any longer, she met his gaze, and her darned lips betrayed her by breaking into a full-on smile. "Don't."

"Don't what?"

"Be you." His dark-blond hair was faded from the summer sun at the tips, and his medium complexion had a sun-kissed look, highlighting the whiteness of his teeth. Then there were those arms and that build. Perhaps one day he'd tire of his risky underwater diving career and make a living modeling watches or cologne. No, that wasn't Levi. Most mornings, Riley was betting he hardly took the time to look in the mirror.

"If there was any chance I could be anybody else, you'd think I'd have figured it out by now."

Giving a shake of her head, Riley said nothing.

"Well then, looks like I'll resort to groveling." Hiking his jeans, he started to sink onto his knees.

"Levi, don't!" Riley bolted from her chair. "Not on my first day please, besides, you already apologized for that less-than-fuzzy greeting of yours yesterday."

"Yeah, but it was kind of half-assed, don't you think?"

Riley snorted. "Dogs, let's walk dogs." Levi was one for drawing an audience even without trying.

She picked up the coffee to bring it with her but set it back down. She wasn't in the space for that much multitasking right now. As soon as she was through the kennel doors, she was at a quandary. Arlo was awake and tucked awkwardly into as much of a ball as a Great Dane can get at the corner of his new kennel. Spotting her, he woofed and lumbered onto all fours. This soft spot she had for Arlo, if it wasn't private, it was an inner-circle thing. And Levi wasn't an inner-circle member. Not anymore.

"How about we take that Dane?" Levi suggested. He was close enough behind her that she could feel his breath. "That's one impressive looking animal."

Of course he was drawn to Arlo. Of course he was. "You're picking up any messes then, right? Because he's also a very *large* animal, if you haven't noticed." Putting Arlo off for later now seemed completely unconscionable. A dozen other dogs were whining or barking, also wanting attention, but it was those chocolatey-brown and hopeful eyes of his and the gently wagging tail that spoke volumes to her.

"Yeah, I got his six." Levi grinned, unaware of how close to home he'd hit with his choice of dogs, and so quickly too. There were nearly fifty others at the taking, spread out in differently sized kennels along the length of both sides of the main room. "Assuming you've got bags. I don't do scoopers."

A soft snort escaped her. This was the Levi she'd first fallen for. Master of perfectly timed levity. Charming nearly to a fault. The Levi who'd later toppled her completely, that was the Levi he tried not to show the world, compassionate and wounded and covering it up with a smile or a joke.

"Then I'll walk this girl." She nodded toward a corgi/beagle mix, Bonnie, a senior dog with some bladder issues who'd been here for over a month.

"Kind of like old times, huh?"

Whatever he wanted by coming here, Riley wasn't sure she was ready for it. "That was a lifetime ago." The first time Levi had joined her here, they'd been uneasy partners forced to work together. By the last time, the flirting but not flirting was thick and heavy—the constant touching of arms and accidental brushing of hands and fingers— innocent and not innocent at the same time.

Riley grabbed two leashes and in just minutes, Levi was following her out the back door with Arlo trailing just behind him while Bonnie led the way. Was it her imagination, or was Arlo staring at her like she was betraying him by walking another dog? *Sorry, buddy. You're going to have to build up trust with other people anyway, seeing as I can't keep you.*

A blast of warm air greeted them, even this side

of the cool front. "How about we stick to the shade so they don't get overheated?" she asked.

"Yeah, sure. Good thing we're in Webster, where most of the trees predate the invention of cars."

Sticking to tree-lined streets meant they were best off keeping to the residential side of Webster, rather than heading downtown toward the college and restaurants where they'd be in more open sun.

It had been cold the last time they'd walked dogs together, just days before everything fell to pieces, and Riley had been underdressed enough for Levi to offer her his leather motorcycle jacket. When she'd refused to take it for worry of him being cold instead of her, he'd draped it over both of them. The dogs they'd been walking that day, Lab mixes, were like bookends and hadn't minded the forced proximity one bit. Her hip had ground lightly against Levi's outer thigh as they'd walked, and she'd been emboldened enough to slip her arm underneath his coat, locking it around his side. She'd lost her words entirely those first few minutes as she soaked in the feel of him, lean and lithe. Her whole body turned to rubber at the thought of exploring him. Not just exploring him. She'd wanted to hold on and never let go.

Riley Leighton, you are doing yourself zero favors with this.

As they headed around the side of the building to the sidewalks out front, Riley cleared her throat.

"So, if I can be right to the point, what're you doing here, really?"

Wagging her tail, Bonnie led the way despite some obvious stiffness in the hips. Arlo, on the other hand, sandwiched himself between Levi and Riley.

"Same thing you went to Marcus's to do yesterday. Talking friendraisers—or hoping to." His sly grin had her wanting to elbow him and kiss him at the same time. It was the perfect answer. She couldn't call him on it without calling attention to her poorly fabricated excuse for showing up at Marcus's.

Considering how long she'd been wanting to be in the same place with him, Riley figured she'd better not look a gift horse in the mouth. "We can do that, but as you know it's my first day. I'm still getting a handle on what I'll be doing this month."

"I can imagine, and really I just wanted to drop off that coffee and get on your calendar. Seeing as you aren't here long, I figured I might as well make the most of it."

Riley switched Bonnie's leash to the opposite hand. Levi was here. Walking her favorite dog. Telling her he wanted to make the most of the short time they were here. "Yeah, okay. I'm sure there's a lot we can do to play up the event. I have a Pins for Pups bowling event next week that I'm taking over advertising, but I think Marcus's open house would be fun to help plan." All the knowledge and experience Riley had gotten over the last eight years of working in marketing, and all that was coming out was that it would be fun? "Did you have anything specific in mind?"

That right eyebrow of his raised an inch. "Me, or Marcus? Because that's two different answers."

Riley knew better than to acknowledge banter. Of any sort.

"You're the marketing wiz," he added, having picked up on her look. "Everything I know how to do with much confidence is under the water. Well, mostly everything." That sly grin again.

"Yet here you are, in St. Louis, working for Marcus." It was supposed to be a declaration, but it came out sounding more like a question.

"Yeah, well, getting told you can never dive again kind of puts a damper on things."

Riley stopped walking midstep. Bonnie wasn't having it and attempted to press against her leash with the exuberance of a husky on a mission, only with a lot less power. "Lana didn't tell me that part." Riley shook her head. "How bad was it, Levi? Lana said you could've died." She realized she was showing her cards, but she no longer cared, not in the face of that declaration. Maybe it was what he needed because, for the first time since he'd walked in, that hint of a smile disappeared, and she was suddenly face-to-face with the Levi he tried to keep hidden from the world.

"What can I say? It was worker error, a new guy.

Dropped some beams off the boat and was too afraid of getting reprimanded to get on the radio. So I've been told, at least. I was forty feet down, welding, and didn't even see it coming. The last thing I remember about that day was when I was on the boat, putting on my gear."

"They found you when you were unconscious?" Now that she was looking for them, she could see the dark circles under those remarkable eyes. She'd been too transfixed by his gentle, playful gaze to look anywhere else.

"Yeah, thanks to the tether not breaking. Still took 'em a while to haul me up. Best they can tell, I was unconscious right about thirty minutes, which on top of a few prior concussions is a death sentence as far as a career in commercial diving goes."

Riley worked the loop of the leash in a circle around her wrist as Bonnie tugged on the other end. Her stomach knotted at the thought of Levi floating unconscious in the murky depths of Lake Michigan. "Levi…"

That playful smile returned, but this time she could tell the effort he was making to keep it there. He took off walking again even though, of the two dogs, Arlo was perfectly content to stand in the shade of a towering maple near the parking lot entrance. "It had to end sometime. I only know a couple guys who lasted in the career much beyond thirty-five anyway."

She knew better than to say she was glad he was done, even though being done would keep him safe. Safer, at least. This was Levi, with a list of previously broken bones longer than she had fingers and toes to count them with. More so, she'd heard his stories, knew how escaping to the water had been his only grace those summers he spent with his father, knew what it must mean to him not to be able to dive.

They'd reached the sidewalk, and even though it was a tight fit, Levi waited for her to fall into step alongside him. "I'm so sorry." They were small and insignificant words compared to the well of compassion inside her.

"I don't need your sympathy, Riley. Things are what they are."

It hit her all at once, the immensity of what it would've done to her if he'd died with so much unsaid, at least on her part. She stopped in her tracks, her hands going cold. She was going to have to say it, all of it. Own that she'd been so very wrong to cut him out the way she had. Own how both prom and her parents' untraditional ways had cut her to the quick just when she was beginning to let go and trust the biggest feeling she'd ever experienced. Own that ever since, she'd been running and running and running.

Levi stopped two steps ahead of her, waiting, studying her. As if picking up on her turmoil, Arlo circled back and pressed in, nearly knocking her over with his affectionate doggie hugs—his head burrowing into her stomach, forcing her to take a step back or be knocked over by his exuberance.

Levi locked a hand around her elbow even though she would've been able to get her balance without his help. "You okay?"

At his unsolicited touch, all those things she needed to say fought their way even further down her throat. Some part of her didn't ever want to be vulnerable again. Losing him once had sucked the wind from her sails. Losing him twice... She swallowed hard. "Yeah, I'm fine. It's just, how long are you here?"

"Today, or in St. Louis?"

At the far reach of her leash, Bonnie had dropped into what looked like four-wheel drive and was doing her best to get Riley into motion again. Clearly, she was a fan of walks. "In St. Louis. How long are you going to be home?"

He dropped her gaze even before they started walking again. "I haven't worked that out yet."

Despite the big rivers converging here, there were no sizeable bodies of water in St. Louis. Levi was out of his element here. He always had been. There were little odds he'd stay. *You're not staying either, remember?*

"Long enough to plan this little friendraiser with you. Long enough for that, for sure," he added into her silence.

The last weekend in September was just under

a month from now. She had a handful of weeks to find both the words and the courage to say all the things she needed to say. She felt herself nodding in agreement. "Okay."

"Okay." He mimicked the resolution in her tone, and that playful smile was back in full force. "I was hoping you'd say that with a bit more conviction, but I'll take what I can get." He nudged her with his elbow. This touching thing seemed to be starting faster this time. "It's been a while since we've worked on a project together, hasn't it? And to be clear, I've got no complaints about this one not coming with two extraordinarily long weekends with a cranky robot baby."

She shook her head, suppressing a laugh. Despite the physical changes, he was still very much Levi. "Dogs are way better than cranky robot babies, I'll give you that."

━━━━━━━━

Levi paused next to Riley's desk before heading out the door. The two desks flanking it were empty, extending their privacy another minute or so. It had been a leap, showing up at her job like this, but he had no regrets. Last night, he'd been itching to call or show up at her parents' doorstep, eager to deliver a much-needed apology. Yet, he hadn't been able to escape the feeling that she'd have hung up or been quick to point him toward the door.

As it was, judging by those first couple minutes today, she'd been close to doing that here in front of her new coworkers.

"Hey, I think I may have forgotten to thank you for the mocha," she said, taking a seat and moving her mouse to get her computer out of sleep mode. "You know, in the throes of wishing you'd disappear."

Levi grinned. "That's alright. I figured I had a ways to go to make up for being the world's biggest prick when I first saw you yesterday."

He'd dropped his voice considerably at the last part, but she still put a finger to her lips over the hint of a smile that was forming. "Language, please. Give me a few days to make an impression, at least."

"Before they realize you hang out with derelicts?"

Before putting away the dogs, she'd agreed to sit down with him next week and talk more about ways they might be able to draw more people in. "Let's see," she said, ignoring this last bit as she pulled up her work calendar. "I have the bowling event Friday, and you said earlier that you're out of town with your family Labor Day weekend, so how about early next week?"

"Sounds good, and send me the link to that bowling thing. I bet I can get a team going. Marcus is looking for an excuse to get some guys together."

As soon as he said it, Riley's jaw dropped open an inch. "That is unless you'd rather I didn't."

"No, it's just…" Her cheeks turned light pink. "By guys, you mean guys from high school?"

"Last I checked, I didn't go to college. Neither did Marcus." Then it hit him. Riley had been anything but interested in connecting with her high school classmates ever since prom weekend. Could he be more obtuse? "If it helps, I haven't seen most of those guys in years either."

"Yeah, but the last time *I* saw them…" Shifting in her seat, she tucked a lock of that golden hair he wanted to lose his hands in behind her ear.

"I know, Riley. But what better way to show anyone who might still be thinking about that that you couldn't give a shit? Pardon my French."

After a handful of seconds, Riley nodded. "'When in Rome,' right? I'll text you the link."

"Perfect. I'd say I'm looking forward to impressing you with my strike zone, but bowling is another thing I haven't done since high school."

She smiled. "If you're not winning, you can always drop some money on raffle tickets, seeing as it's for a good cause." She waved her hand around the room before turning her attention to her calendar again. "As for talking about the friendraiser, how about late in the afternoon Monday or anytime Wednesday after, say, ten o'clock?"

"Late Monday works. How about five?"

"I get off at five. I was thinking three or three thirty. At the end of the day, the staff pitches in with feedings and moving dogs in and whatnot."

"The way I see it, five works perfectly then. You know I'm no good at brainstorming on an empty stomach." As Riley's eyes went round, he was quick to add, "Pick you up here, or do you need to run home first?"

Her cheeks reddened just a touch. "Are you asking me to dinner?"

He shrugged, summoning all the indifference he could muster. "That's usually what I call a meal eaten around that time, unless I really sleep in, then it's a late lunch. Seeing how Marcus's got a list of chores longer than Walt Whitman's *Leaves of Grass*, I won't be doing much sleeping in."

"I don't—I don't know. Monday night's…" She shook her head. "Sorry, that *Leaves of Grass* comment threw me, but I'm not sure that's a good idea."

"There's a lot to be said for eating out on a Monday night. Less choices due to some closures, I'll give you that, but way less crowds." He knew perfectly well she was trying to back out of dinner and keep this meeting here at what was likely feeling like a safe place now that they survived twenty minutes together. But he had other ideas.

Riley gave him an incredulous look. "I know you know what I'm talking about."

"*Leaves of Grass*? Because I thought we were talking about dinner."

Fighting back a smile, she ran her tongue over her top lip, and Levi's salivary glands awakened instantly. What would he give to lean over the desk and kiss her the way he had the last time she'd been in his arms? Now that the thought was there, he could think of a lot of things he'd give to do it.

"Fine," she said. "Dinner on Monday. Something casual." She motioned downward toward her clothes. "Since I'll be in jeans and a shelter T-shirt. And ending by six or six thirty since we're leaving here at five."

He tapped his finger on top of her desk. "Sure thing. It's a date, Riley Leighton."

"No. No, it isn't. It's an off-property meeting that doesn't interfere with my work schedule."

"With food."

She pressed her lips together hard for a second, but the smile broke out anyway. "With food." She glanced across the room toward the main adoption counter. "I don't think I have anything in my budget to pay for business dinners, so let's plan on splitting the bill. Since it's business, I mean."

He dipped his head. "See you Monday, Riley." He'd argue the details with her when the time came. Until then, she could call it what she wished, and if Levi had any say in things, by the end of the night, she'd be singing a different tune entirely.

Chapter 13

By Thursday afternoon, Riley was starting to feel like a part of the crew. In addition to helping out with the dogs twice a day, she'd created her first series of social media posts for the shelter, a few of which were getting a slew of likes and comments, and she'd gotten a good handle on the three events she would be overseeing, the first of which was tomorrow. Talk about trial by fire! At least she wouldn't be alone with this one. There were several participating teams of volunteers and staff, Kelsey and her fiancé were working the silent auction, and Tess and Patrick would be outside with several adoptable dogs.

After getting Megan's consent, she was also in the process of lining up a range of community events over the next several months, ones her replacement would eventually get to oversee—a thought that was a bit bubble-bursting.

Picking up her phone, Riley checked her most recent post of a video clip she'd taken this morning of a corgi mix, a four-year-old with a teddy-bear cuteness to her, right after she'd been adopted. A rush of happiness swept over her to spy nearly eight hundred likes on Instagram Reels and almost double that on TikTok. Her hottest post so far.

She'd filmed the short-legged pupper from behind as she was trotting out the front door and being guided to her new owner's Corolla. While the sweet girl had been too tentative to hop into the back seat on her own, she'd planted her front feet on the door jam and whined. The video ended with the endearing dog shooting a backward glance back at the camera with what looked like the perfect doggie grin. Riley had tagged it #GoingHome.

As she was setting down her phone, it buzzed with a new message, this one from Levi. He'd started texting her on Tuesday night. His initial text in over a decade had been nothing more than a close-up of the friendly, lolling-tongued bulldog who'd been wandering around loose Monday. There were no words, just the picture. The image was more playful than flattering—not surprising seeing as bulldogs were more ugly-cute than cute—but there was something charismatic about the dog anyway. Maybe it was the way the light caught her lively black-brown eyes.

It had served as a conversation starter, and they'd been texting a few times a day since. Riley had replied with "Selfie?" and from there they'd gotten into a discussion about the merits of bulldogs. It turned out that one was homeless. Her owners had gone on a two-week vacation that stretched into almost three before Marcus began attempts to get ahold of them. The only cell number they'd left had been invalid, and the preapproved credit card on file had been shut down as well. Since then, she— Lola—had become Marcus's unofficial company mascot, and she was great at helping calm nervous dogs who were new to being boarded.

Riley opened Levi's latest text to find a snapshot of today's corgi post, followed by a comment of "Nice one." She bit her lip, but the smile broke out anyway. So, Levi was following the shelter's posts now, and he wasn't afraid to let her know it.

Thanks! Though it was all her. That grin... priceless!

Yeah, the expression was good, but it's that fluffy corgi butt that does it. That thing's like a feather duster.

Riley's grin spread across her face. Maybe it shouldn't make her as happy as it did, but there was no denying she lit up inside whenever she spotted Levi's name on her phone screen. After a quick image search and debating between a backpack and a rug, both featuring over-the-top cartoon images of fluffy corgi butts, she took a screenshot of the rug and sent it, then followed up with a short clarifier.

Who knew there was a market for over-the-top fluffy corgi butts?

Knowing his texts came randomly, she was getting ready to slip her phone into her pocket and head to the kennels to help with the four-thirty feeding when her phone buzzed with a reply.

Yeah, I don't want to see that after some dirty boots have been wiped on it.

She responded with the green "yuck" emoji, to which he replied that he'd see her tomorrow and had followed it with an emoji bowling ball and pins.

Maybe they weren't the most romantic of texts, but this was Levi. He'd never been much of a romantic or, at least, not one to own that sensitive interior he pretended so hard not to have.

Even though a part of her wanted to tamp it down, hope welled inside her. After a lot of years of not knowing, she knew what she wanted. Levi. On a platter. In the rain. In a car. On a bed. *Yes, please, on a bed.* She had more questions than answers as to how the two of them might be able to actually make it work long term, but being face-to-face with him had proven one thing. She wanted him. Unequivocally.

Enough to brave the murky waters of past mistakes and make amends for the hurt she'd caused him? Almost, kind of, sort of. If she lost him a second time around, she'd probably crawl into a hole and never come out.

As she headed through the double doors into the kennels, she spotted Arlo's empty spot and figured someone had taken him out for a walk. She didn't think it was her imagination that the world's biggest teddy bear was beginning to relax a bit more. He even seemed to be warming up to some of the other staff members as well. Hopefully, he was enjoying his time outside with whoever he was with.

To the excitement of nearly every canine in the place, Patrick was in the middle of feeding, and the kennels were anything but quiet. "Who first, Patrick?" She projected loudly to be heard. When he looked her way dubiously, Riley realized he needed clarification. "I meant, which dogs need to come in first, or next, if I'm not the first to step in to help?"

He glanced up toward the ceiling for a second in thought. "How about Betty and Wilma?"

"Sounds good." He was referring to the book-end pair of Labs that had left quarantine when Arlo arrived, and who would hopefully be placed together, considering how bonded they were. As Riley headed out toward the outdoor play areas, she spotted them romping in the largest pen with a young dalmatian named Dora. While the Labs were far from calm, Dora was acting like she'd had one too many energy drinks whenever she was awake, bounding around them in circles.

A lovable senior greyhound named George was in the pen too. Rather than interacting with the energetic bunch, he was off at the far end, sniffing along the fence line.

Watching the romping dogs, Riley began doubting her ability to herd the Labs into the small, sectioned-off area by the gate for safe leashing without Dora slipping in too.

"Want some help?" someone called. "Patrick sent me up to grab the other two."

Riley turned to see Tess approaching. "That I do. I was just wondering how I was going to do this."

"How about you try it alone first, and I'll step in if you need a hand. Remember, it's 90 percent presence and 10 percent stature." Considering Tess was a good fifty pounds lighter than Fidel, the other head trainer, Riley figured she knew what she was talking about. "When you believe you're in charge, they tend to believe it too."

Draping two of the leashes hanging by the entrance over her shoulder, Riley stepped into the main part of the pen. George noticed her immediately and ambled over, gray faced and stiff in the hips but with an air that said he knew the ropes. Riley smoothed a hand over his sleek forehead. "Sweet boy, Tess is taking you in for your dinner in a minute, once I get the wild ones under control." The three remaining dogs were circling so tightly about, they looked like a school of fish in predator-evade mode. Considering they'd been in the pen a good half hour, their energy levels were surprising.

Straightening her shoulders, Riley headed toward the group and gave an overhand clap. *How can you be commanding when they don't even see you?* "Come on, guys, let's go."

Still focused on Dora, Wilma swung wide and nearly knocked Riley off her feet. Whipping around, surprised, Wilma stepped in for a sniff of Riley's pockets. Using the opportunity, Riley made quick work of grabbing her collar and hooking on the leash.

Wilma's sister was quicker to notice her missing playmate than she was to notice the human who'd joined their group. She stopped playing and zoomed over. When she stepped in for a sniff of her sister, Riley was able to snap the second leash on to her as well. Both dogs were panting heartily. No doubt with this much exercise, they'd sleep well tonight—and cuddled together, as inseparable as they were.

With her playmates captured, Dora beelined for the water fountain for a drink, enabling Riley an easy pass at herding the Labs out through the first exit gate. "Well, that was easier than anticipated."

Tess laughed as she stepped inside for George and Dora. "You did great. You walked in with authority but without being intimidating, which is more important for some of these guys than others."

Riley herded Wilma and Betty out through both sets of doors but waited for Tess to hook up the other two. "So, how's day three going?" Tess asked over her shoulder. "Feeling overwhelmed yet? Because that's easy to do."

"Nope, not at all. I've been walking home on a cloud every day, if you want the truth. It's my dream job, mostly marketing, with just the right amount of play," she added with a nod toward the dogs.

"That's the case for most of us." George was the first on a leash, but Dora trotted over when Tess sank into a squat and was easy to hook as well.

Riley adjusted Betty and Wilma's leashes so that one was in each hand as they started down the sloping hillside. After getting the dogs settled, Dora and George in separate kennels, and the Labs in their shared, oversized one, Riley and Tess headed out for the next round of dogs. As they stepped out the back door, Riley spotted Arlo in the company of Fidel and a woman she'd not yet met rounding the corner of the building.

Spotting her as well, Arlo lifted his head and wagged his tail hopefully. Maybe it shouldn't warm Riley's heart to see how he was still so bonded with her, but it did anyway. Back when she was a volunteer, she'd had her favorites and had been equally sad and happy when they'd been adopted, but with Arlo, it just felt different.

Riley had just spotted the excited look on the woman's face when they got within hearing range of their conversation.

"We'll have to do a home visit after you fill out

an application," Fidel was saying, "but based on everything you've said, I can't see why you two wouldn't be a good fit."

Riley's pulse burst into a sprint. *No, no. Please no. Not Arlo. Not yet.*

"Is Arlo being adopted?" Tess grinned widely, oblivious to Riley's inner turmoil. Surprising all of them, Arlo burst forward, yanking the leash clear out of the woman's hand and nearly jerking her to the ground in the process. He beelined for Riley, whining and pressing against her in that way of his that nearly knocked her onto her bottom every time.

"Well, he's got some pull, doesn't he? Come here, boy." The woman jogged after Arlo expectantly. She was older than Riley by a decade most likely, solidly built, and dressed in medical attire. Once they got used to each other, there would be no reason to think she'd have any less trouble handling Arlo than Riley would.

With everything inside her screaming not to, Riley offered over the leash to the woman's outstretched hand. Was it her imagination, or did Arlo glance up at her like she was a traitor?

"I'll be more ready for that next time." The woman leaned over and began doling out affection that Arlo neither rejected nor reciprocated. Instead, he stared at Riley, the hair above those expressive brown eyes knitting into peaks. "It seems he's made a buddy here, hasn't he?"

"Riley was the first one to find him." Fidel's tone was more matter-of-fact than apologetic. "They've had a bit of time to bond."

"As will we," the woman added, patting Arlo on the flank.

"Well, good luck," Tess said, starting off toward the play areas. "He's a great dog. A real sweetie."

While Arlo was led inside, somehow Riley forced her legs to take her in the opposite direction. She followed Tess up the hillside, wondering how, in the span of just minutes, when everything had been so promising, it suddenly felt as if she'd had a rug pulled straight out from under her.

Chapter 14

By check-in time Friday evening, Riley had racked up over nine thousand steps for the day and anticipated doubling that by the end of the bowling fundraiser. No jogging before work this week. There hadn't been time. It had been an even busier day on top of a busy week, and she'd loved every minute. If only she hadn't missed out on the chance to have been in the running for the permanent job!

For tonight's event, Riley had created signage in the shelter's color palette and font highlighting the dogs who'd been at the shelter longest using photos she'd taken this week. On each poster, she included a few personal snippets about them as well. For Harold, a miniature schnauzer with diabetes who'd been at the shelter for six months, Riley bragged about how he held the shelter record for solving dog puzzles the fastest—Patrick had told her the exact time, but she'd forgotten—and that Harold was a natural snuggler. For Cinder, a seven-year-old rottweiler who'd spent the bulk of her life in a confined yard with little human contact before being surrendered, Riley had taken a close-up of her gripping the corner of her favorite worn baby blanket in her mouth. The sweet dog had one of the larger indoor/outdoor kennels and dragged her blanket with her everywhere, even attempting to take it along on walks, though the staff was attempting to discourage this to encourage her to interact more with her caregivers. While she'd never had the opportunity to warm up to people before, there were signs that she was beginning to do so.

The posters were displayed in placards on break tables at the individual lanes, at the silent auction area, on the information table outside by the entrance, and at the food counters. Next week, she intended to create a series of posts based on them too. Between rounds, images of the dogs would be cycling through on the overhead screens as well. Her personal goal was to get as many of them adopted as she could while she was at High Grove.

Riley had also helped assemble and wrap over a dozen gift baskets for tonight's raffle, a few of which she'd be more than happy to win herself, including the home spa kit and a mouthwatering assortment of fine dark chocolates. There was a "socks for every occasion" gift basket that was a riot too. The whiskey basket, lotto basket, and money tree promised to be crowd favorites.

With a glance at her watch, Riley headed outside to check on Tess and Patrick, who'd be staffing the information table and watching over the dogs they'd brought along as adoptable mascots. While no animals would be going home with anyone tonight, eight dogs of all breeds and sizes were in portable pens outside ready to greet attendees, including Harold the schnauzer. The shelter was stringent about making sure potential new owners were well vetted, but hopefully some forever connections would be made.

"Hey there!" she said, stepping outside.

"Hey," Tess said. "Everything ready inside?" She'd pulled the friendly border collie mix out of the pen and was practicing a few simple commands with her. Patrick was seated behind the eight-foot table, ready to sign people in and hand out food and drink coupons and prepurchased raffle tickets.

"I think so." Riley bent over to give Harold a scratch after he trotted to the edge of the pen for a sniff. The three other dogs he was sharing the pen with were too interested in one another to notice. "I just finished going over my list for the second time. As far as events go, it's orders of magnitude easier than when you're bringing in food and hiring entertainment."

"Makes sense, and I'm betting it's a hit. Who doesn't have fun bowling?" With a glance at Patrick, Tess added, "Unless you don't enjoy all the noise."

How Patrick wasn't fazed by all the barking in the kennels yet got agitated by the sounds of bowling didn't exactly make sense, but Riley figured everybody had their own quirks. As it was, he'd signed up to work outside with Tess until they closed it down in an hour and returned the dogs to High Grove, and he wouldn't have to deal with the noise inside.

"How many lanes did we end up selling?" Tess added.

"Twenty-eight of the thirty lanes," Riley said.

"So, at $200 a team, that makes…"

"Five thousand, six hundred dollars," Patrick answered without looking up from the spreadsheet he was reviewing. "Plus another $465 in donations and $325 in early raffle sales. I predict we top $10,000 tonight."

Riley had yet to see him not remember something related to the dogs who moved through the shelter, previous social media posts, or money, and he was everyone's go-to for such questions.

Tess humphed. "Not bad for an event with such little legwork." Turning to Riley, she added, "Wait till you see how much work goes into our fall fundraiser and our Twelve Days of Christmas celebrations. Those are all-hands on deck." Suddenly Tess frowned. "Sorry, I keep forgetting you aren't staying, as well as you fit in."

Riley wasn't sure if she was happy or sad that Tess wasn't the only one this week who'd mentioned something similar. "Thanks. I wish I was going to be around to see it, but hopefully, I'll be back for Christmas and can catch a few of them."

A car turning into the parking lot caught their

attention. Three more cars on the main road were slowing down and had blinkers on, about to turn in. "Looks like it's go time," she added.

Patrick checked his watch. "It's 6:27. By the time they park and walk up, we can begin checking them in."

Tess gave Riley a knowing smile as she returned the border collie mix to her pen and joined them at the table. What might Patrick have said if someone had pulled in fifteen or twenty minutes early? While the event began at seven o'clock, attendees had been told check-in began at six thirty, and Patrick took that more literally than most.

"I'll head back in and give everyone a heads up that people are trickling in." As Riley turned toward the door, her heart thudded into a sprint. A red Dodge Ram was about to turn into the lot. Levi.

In case he'd spotted her too, Riley waved his direction. Her stomach flipped like a fish when she spied Marcus in the passenger seat and someone else in the back seat. "I'm so not ready for this," she mumbled to herself, stepping inside.

The thing about being so busy today, it kept her from thinking too much about Arlo having been adopted—he left this morning, and Riley had stepped into the bathroom to cry—and from obsessing over who Levi might be bringing in addition to Grant. Lana had confirmed her hubby was getting a boys' night out even though he hadn't bowled since back when he still relied on gutter guards to help the ball down the lane. "And if there was any question as to whether or not that guy of yours is still smitten, there shouldn't be," Lana had insisted.

While Riley wasn't as wholeheartedly optimistic as Lana, Levi had dropped $200 and gathered a team of six for tonight's event on top of all that flirting/not flirting. This morning, he even texted to ask if she needed any help, which she politely refused. She'd wanted to ask who all was joining him but, after practically sliding into a panic about coming face-to-face with people she'd done her best to avoid for twelve years, she figured this was an exercise in trust. Levi wasn't setting her up for failure, and he wasn't holding a grudge, clearly. While his helping to coordinate the friendraiser with her could debatably be for no other purpose than to help out his buddy, his coming here... This was no simple favor for Marcus, no way.

Riley wanted to know what this all meant, but she wasn't ready to ask. Levi wasn't just any guy. Her heart would likely wither and die if she let him in and lost him a second time. And with neither of them having plans to stay in the city, really, what was the point?

In the break room, Riley strapped on an apron loaded with tickets for both the raffle and for additional food and beverage purchases over and above what came with the registration fee, then headed for the food service window. She had just wrapped up a quick conversation with the bowling center staff who'd be working the registers when someone tapped her shoulder. Half expecting it to be Levi, Riley turned to find Grant grinning at her with a look that would have anyone believing they'd been close friends in high school rather than the always-poking-fun-at-one-another frenemies vying for Lana's time after he and Lana joined at the hip junior year.

"Riley Leighton, how the heck have you been?"

Riley did a double take before he pulled her in for what was likely the first hug they'd ever shared. Unlike Levi, Grant hardly seemed to have stepped out of his early twenties yet with his slight build, thick lashes, and smooth-shaven skin. "I'm doing well, Grant. Good to see you."

"Yeah, good to see you too, but not as good as it's been for Lana. She's been glowing all week. Riley this, Riley that. Just like old times."

"Except there weren't little ones in the mix then, huh? But yeah, it's been nice to reconnect with her. Really nice."

Grant pointed a finger her way. "She's crossing her fingers you'll stick around this time."

"She's not the only one," someone said.

Riley looked over to spot the rest of the group walking up. Marcus had made the comment, and

Levi shot him a reproachful look that he waved off. With them were three guys that, despite the twelve years since she'd last seen them, Riley recognized instantly: Chad, Brandon, and Kyle.

While they all smiled, Riley wondered if Kyle remembered the sneering remark he'd made at prom asking how her parents were doing. Perhaps he did, because he was the first to drop her gaze amongst the chorus of greetings. Marcus stepped in and hugged her too, and Riley shot off a prayer of thanks when he didn't mention the flagpole incident in front of his friends. Over the phone, when she'd called to apologize, he'd promised it was undamaged, unlike her dented bumper.

Ignoring the rapid-fire tapping of her pulse, Riley plastered on what she hoped was an everyday smile. "Thanks for coming, guys. I see you got checked in." She motioned to the food and drink tickets in Levi's hand. There was something reassuring in his gaze, more than simple kindness, more like faith.

"Hey, Riley, tell these guys I have dibs on adopting that Weimaraner out there." It was Chad, the middle linebacker on the football team who'd gotten a full-ride scholarship to a college in Texas whose name she couldn't remember.

Riley raised her eyebrows. "If you're looking for a dog, I'll put in a good word for you, but just a heads up. Monti is high energy, even for a Weimaraner. He's been returned a few times, too."

Chad patted the midsection that was fifteen or so pounds heavier than when she'd last seen him. "That's just the kind of dog I'm looking for."

Riley raised an eyebrow. "If you're serious, Tess, one of our head trainers, is the one to talk to. She's outside. With his return history, before he goes home with anyone, he needs a lesson or two with her or one of our other trainers and whoever adopts him."

"Putting the fear of God in them, huh?"

"More like a heavy dose of reality, but he's a great dog. If you're really thinking about adopting a high-energy canine, you should come by. We'll find you something that works." Here she was again, talking like she'd be there forever when her stint at High Grove was anything but.

"Maybe I'll do that. I've been thinking about it for ages."

With a chorus of "Catch you later, Riley," all of them but Levi headed off to get their bowling shoes. Even though the bowling alley was filling with people, and their bustling conversations were raising the energy in the room, time seemed to stand still as Levi closed a hand around her elbow. For a second or two, he held her gaze without saying a thing. "So…better than you were expecting, I hope?"

"Yeah, better than I was expecting. Thanks for coming. For bringing them."

"I wouldn't have missed it."

"Do you bowl often then?"

"Not since I was thirteen or fourteen, but I think we both know I didn't come for the bowling. Not that it won't be fun."

Riley pressed her lips together. Levi and his banter. It would take some getting used to again. "Well, it'll be like riding a bike, I'm sure."

"Bowling, you mean?" The way he said it, it was clear he didn't mean bowling. "Cuz I expect there's some things you never forget."

With a light shake of her head, Riley patted her apron pockets. "I'd better get moving. I have a whole mound of tickets to sell, and you'd better grab your shoes."

"Before you run off, how about I buy some?"

"Sure. For food and drinks or for the raffle baskets?"

Pulling out his wallet, he fished through the bills. "Drinks for sure. One pitcher of beer for my team won't cut it. They haven't changed much that way, it seems. About the baskets, anything good in them?"

"Yeah, you should check them out. Raffle tickets are three for fifteen dollars or six for twenty-five, and food tickets are five dollars apiece."

He took out a hundred-dollar bill. "How about fifty each then?"

"That's generous, but you don't have to, Levi."

"I want to."

Without discouraging him further, Riley fished out blue and orange tickets. He was welcome to spend his money on a good cause if he wanted to. "Blue is for food and drinks, and you turn the whole ticket in at the counter. The orange ones are for the baskets. Tear them down the center and keep this side. Write your name and number on the half you drop in in case you lose the other half. We draw the winners at ten o'clock."

After shoving the blue ones in his pocket, Levi began tearing the orange ones in half. "How about you put 'em in for me? My luck tends to come in spurts, and I don't want to waste it on something I don't need."

"Are you sure you want to leave it up to me? There's a basket of all-occasion socks you could rock, if you ask me."

Grinning, Levi offered over the other half of the tickets. "I trust you."

Their fingertips brushed, and Riley's were like lit fuses, transferring heat along her hands and arms, right down to her belly. After folding the tickets into a manageable size, Riley shoved them in her jeans pocket. "I'll catch up with you later."

"I'd like that."

Riley walked away, wanting to fan her face. The event hadn't even started, but right now, she had the same adrenaline as if it was the most successful one she'd ever orchestrated.

After the last game ended, the yearning to get outside away from the noise was a whole-body one. Levi had known coming here wouldn't be a walk in the park, but the crashing of the balls, the scattering of pins, and the constant buzzing hum all around of laughter, jeers, and shouts had his head pounding like a percussion band, and he craved the quiet of Marcus's place. Still, it was fun. And worth it.

Marcus clapped him on the back. "I didn't think you'd beat Brandon, considering he played in a league in high school."

"How does that explain you beating him then?" Marcus had come in first in their team with a 180 average. Levi ended two points ahead of Brandon's 172. Grant had brought up the rear with 123.

"Why are you even asking, Levi?" Brandon chided. "You know everything with him goes back to the Marines."

Marcus grinned, his white teeth gleaming. "What can I say? Not everyone has the advantage of marksmanship training, do they?"

"Think that would help you caulk my shower in a straight line? If so, what're you doing tomorrow?" Kyle said with a laugh.

The guys were still giving Marcus a hard time as they took off their shoes when Levi spotted Riley headed their direction with a gift basket as big as the upper half of her body.

Grant shook his head. "Death by Dark Chocolate.

Man, I was hoping to win that one. I'd score some major points with Lana."

"Who did win it?" Brandon asked.

Riley walked straight up to Levi. "About that luck of yours... I don't think it's as sporadic as you were claiming."

The guys were pressing in, wanting to tear it open, but Levi held up a hand. "Hold off. You and I can argue semantics later, Riley, but that basket belongs to you, just like the luck that won it."

Riley's eyebrows knitted together. "I may have dropped it in, but you paid for the ticket."

"If neither of you want, I'll throw in twenty-five bucks to take that mountain of goodies home to my beautiful wife," Grant interjected.

"Cheap ass." Chad scoffed. "That's well over a hundred bucks of chocolate, easy."

Levi warded them off. "It's Riley's, guys."

Riley looked down at the basket. "I'd have to up my jogging regimen tenfold if this were all mine, but if you really don't want it, Levi, I'll take it into the shelter with me tomorrow." To Grant, she added, "And I'll bring some to your house tomorrow night. Lana and I are having a movie night."

When she shifted the bulky basket in her arms, Levi offered to carry it to her car.

"Thanks, but we've still got some loading up to do."

Chad looked toward the door. "I know what you

said about it not being so cut and dry and all, but I really wouldn't mind relieving you of that Weimaraner out there. That picture of his has been calling my name whenever it's flashed across the screen."

"The dogs went back to the shelter a few hours ago. They were just here to greet everyone as they came in."

"Yeah," Marcus said with a grin, "and nobody out there would've let your drunk ass make that decision on the fly anyway."

"I'm far from drunk, my friend."

Levi relieved Riley of the basket. "Let us help load. Maybe it'll sober a few of these guys up a bit."

"I'm sober because I'm driving, but I'll help," Grant said.

Riley was passing off the basket when Kyle stepped a foot closer. "How's your family been, Riley?" He'd had three or four beers and was just buzzed enough to ask. The way everyone went stone silent, he held up a hand. "What? I'm just asking a question." Refocusing on Riley, he added, "I see your brother at Ruth's Deli sometimes."

Riley's cheeks darkened just a hint, and she squared her shoulders almost imperceptibly. "I don't mind you asking. My brother's doing great. He's still at the deli. It gives him the sense of community he needs, but financially, he doesn't need to be. He's making a killing at day trading. My parents are good too. My mom's been diagnosed with breast cancer, but most everyone in town knows already, judging by the cards and well-wishes she's getting. My dad's really been there for her too."

Riley's gaze was trained on Kyle like she was poised for him to say more. Grant and Chad were fiddling with their bowling shoes, while Brandon seemed confused, like he was wondering what he'd missed. Marcus was staring Kyle down like he'd flatten him into a pancake if one wrong word was said, but he'd have to get in line behind Levi.

"Good for your brother, and good about your parent's too—except for that cancer bit." Kyle smiled sheepishly. "I don't know if you heard, but my parents divorced. So did Trevor's. And Courtney, her sister's a big fat mess. Got on heroin and is doing some jail time. Which I guess I'm just saying because nobody's perfect." Looking around at his friends, he shrugged. "I don't know what the looks are for, but I've just wanted to say that for a long time. That, and I'm sorry for being an inconsiderate ass back in high school."

Riley blinked a couple times like she was fighting back a tear or two. "Thanks, Kyle. I appreciate it. I bet there are very few of us who don't walk out of high school without at least one big thing they'd change if they could."

Levi didn't think it was his imagination that there was a promise in her gaze as it shifted from Kyle to Levi that was even stronger than the declaration on her lips.

Chapter 15

"So, what do you think of the place? Better than you were expecting, huh?" Gale, Levi's mom, gave an exaggerated blink of her eyes, ones that had his exact same amber-brown hue, and sipped her tea. As far as Levi was concerned, she was pushing the season by switching to hot tea, even if they were sitting in the shade, and there was a refreshing breeze this afternoon. For the third of September, temps could've been worse, but today it was hovering in the mideighties. That was his mom though. She drank hot tea any day she could get away with it. Levi, on other hand, was sipping on a beer.

They were sharing the swing on the covered front porch of the cabin that her boyfriend, Larry, had built out of Missouri pine, relying largely on his own muscle and skill. With his mom next to him with her mug of tea, Levi was resisting the urge to swing a bit more forcefully than this slow, lazy beat. When he'd pulled in a half hour ago and hadn't spotted Larry's Pilot, he'd been a bit relieved to learn Larry had taken off not long before for the grocery store, a trek that was no easy feat this far out.

This bit of unplanned time with his mom was

nice. Sitting here, Levi was reminded of those years when he was little and it was just him and her, back before his sister was born and before there were clients coming in and out for tutoring. "It's great. I can see why you like coming out here so much. Beautiful view. Quiet too."

"Wait till the stars come out. Bet you've never seen this many."

After sleeping in late this morning, thanks to a headache worse than any hangover he'd had, triggered by last night's noise and intensity, Levi had picked his half sister up from band practice before heading out on the two-hour drive here. Before leaving Webster, they'd swung by his mom's for Ivy to pick up her bags. His mom and Larry had driven out last night, and the house had been empty.

Lola the bulldog was sniffing about the bushes at the bottom of the porch, leashless after showing no interest in trotting off to explore the new digs. On a whim, Levi had brought the easygoing dog along with him for the weekend. As far as Levi could tell, she was relatively unfazed about having been carted somewhere new. He still thought Marcus should make it official and adopt her, but his buddy kept insisting that while she was the first dog left behind at his place, she wouldn't be the last, and he wouldn't be able to take them all on.

As dogs went, Lola was as low maintenance as they came. So different from Tank, who'd needed long walks and vigorous runs at the beach or dog park to be zapped of energy enough to resist chewing up Levi's shoes while Levi was at work.

Watching Lola drop and roll on the ground, either scent marking or scratching her back, Levi wondered if she thought about her old owners the way he still thought about Tank. If she did, at what point would she give up wondering if they'd come back for her?

Beside him, Levi's mom shot a glance toward the windows on the other side of the front door. Ivy had retreated to the front-facing bedroom to pout when the cell service had once again proved patchy enough that she could neither text her friends nor use Snapchat. Lowering her voice so as not to be overheard, she added, "Hopefully by then your sister will have made peace with those withdrawal symptoms she gets without her phone. Last time, she had a great time here. At least, she did until the last thirty minutes, then she was a wreck of anticipation, ready to get on the road and reach a patch of good service. You know, in case Webster had imploded over the weekend, taking her friends with it, never to be seen again."

"Yeah, well, that's pretty typical of kids her age." Being twelve years apart and having different fathers, he couldn't say he was as close to Ivy as he'd like to be, but the easy flow of conversation on the drive down had given him hope. Part of it was his fault, no question. In his mind, she was perpetually five and learning how to ride her bike without training wheels, not seventeen going on eighteen, and fine-tuning a list of top-rated colleges to apply to.

"Not you. When you were her age, you'd have come out here, left your phone in the car, and taken off to explore the woods or build a fort or hike to the creek. You never cared about who was moving with what crowd or who'd posted what." Levi was about to interject that social media had ballooned astronomically over the last twelve years when she added, "But you never were like most kids, and believe me, I've tutored enough teens over the years to know."

Levi raised an eyebrow. "I think in some ways the fact that I have a hard time sitting still actually worked in my favor in high school."

Gale smiled before sipping her tea. "You mean by helping you become such a good athlete?"

"In high school, that stuff matters. Not that I did any of it for that, but it did make things easier."

"Like getting the attention of all those girls? So many of them, wanting to be the one who stuck."

Levi had been fiddling with the label on the neck of his Corona but stopped to take a few swigs. *All those girls.* There hadn't been that many back then, had there? He knew there were more, but he could only remember two with any real clarity, one who'd mattered more than anything, who still did, and one other who'd contributed to Riley breaking his heart.

Doing his best to brush away thoughts of those dark days, he stood up and headed down the porch steps over to where Lola had stretched out in the shade. He sank onto his heels to give her a scratch. He'd never admitted to his mom what Riley had meant to him. In truth, he'd kept his feelings for her separate from everyone except Marcus.

Even so, Levi had always wondered if his mom had caught on to the fact that Riley was different. If not for the way he'd come alive that month or so when they were partners in their child development course and getting to know one another, then for the way he'd hit rock bottom after she shut him out of his life.

"How often do you get out here?" he asked, knowing she'd get that he was changing the subject. "Don't you still tutor most weekends?"

Lola's back leg thumped in the air to the rhythm of Levi's scratching. He was glad he brought her. Now that he knew her story, he was on a mission to get her adopted, assuming Marcus didn't change his mind and claim her.

"Yep. Still tutoring weekends and most evenings. It's my third time here, but I'm hoping to start coming out once a month."

The cabin was sitting on twenty wooded acres with close to an acre of cleared land surrounding it.

On the opposite side of the gravel road in front was rolling farmland as far as the eye could see, and a herd of cows far enough in the distance that only an occasional mooing could be heard on the breeze. Off to the side of the cabin was a firepit that Levi had every intention of building an impressively sized fire in tonight.

"You definitely deserve that." Working two jobs, teaching mathematics at two different campuses in the St. Louis Community College system and offering ACT and SAT tutoring on the side, Gale had never had much free time. "Though I can't say I'd have pictured you loving coming out to a cabin in the boonies and just chilling all weekend. Usually, you're busy doing things."

Gale had one foot tucked under her thigh and was using the other to swing her now that Levi wasn't there to do the swinging. "I think it's *because* I've been so busy doing things for so long that I love it here as much as I do."

"I can see that, I guess." He was doing better at Marcus's, but before that, Levi had been going stir crazy with so much time not working.

"Did I ever tell you why I decided to major in math?"

"Ah, because you wanted to be a financial analyst but ended up hating just about everything about it except the money it brought in?"

Gale nodded, sweeping her shoulder-length,

dark-blond hair into her free hand. "I certainly tried my hand at that, yes, but that wasn't why I majored in math. Not even close."

He'd always been proud of her for all she'd accomplished, managing a career and raising two kids spaced as far apart as he and Ivy were, even as untraditionally as she'd done it. He'd been in second grade when she'd bought the house in Webster, a nice one, and in fifth grade when she left her company to teach at the college. "I guess I always assumed it was because you grew up wanting a steady job that paid well."

After giving Lola a final pat, Levi stood. He thought about rejoining his mom on the swing, but he'd spent too much time in a seat this afternoon. After setting his beer on the bottom step, he gripped the smooth, circular pine railings at each side of the steps, and hoisted himself into the air, locking his arms, attempting to ascend the stairs that way.

"You can never be still, can you?" If Gale had said that once over the years, then she'd said it ten thousand times, though her tone was more amused than annoyed as it had often been when he was younger and fidgeting about in a checkout line or whatnot.

Since they both knew she was right, he didn't bother to reply.

"But I can see why you'd think that about me," she said, continuing their conversation, "especially with me having watched your grandparents always working so hard." Levi's grandparents had run their own screen-printing shop until they'd retired. They'd worked hard and scarcely managed to get by. "But the reason I went into math in the first place was because of a summer camp over on the Illinois side where I worked as a counselor my junior year."

"Oh yeah?" He was a bit breathless, having scaled his way to the top step. He hopped down to the porch floor, the muscles in his arms burning in a good way after the recent weeks of neglect.

"Yeah. One week, one of the themes was finding math in nature. Part of every day, we trekked campers into the woods to find evidence of mathematical patterns."

"Like the Fibonacci sequence?" Levi had a vivid memory of a coffee-table book on mathematical beauty that he'd flipped through countless times as a kid. Images of fern leaves, interiors of conch shells, spider webs, and more, many of which formed the famous pattern. He'd not thought about that book in years.

"Yes, that and tessellations." Levi must've given her a look because she added, "You remember, tightly fitted shapes that form repeated patterns without overlapping. Like in a honeycomb."

He grinned and started making his way down the stairs the same way he'd come up. This way was easier but required a stronger grip not to slide.

"Yeah, that's right. I remember you pointing them out all the time when I was a kid."

"I did, didn't I? I've always loved patterns and predictability, especially in nature. There's something that feels inherently safe and secure about them, a 'this is how it is and how it always will come to be' sort of thing."

"I can see that."

"The thing is, it wasn't until I started dating Larry and coming out here that I remembered how much of that part of myself—the explorer who lived in wonder—I've left behind in the busyness of raising kids and earning a viable income. Not that those weren't good choices. They were, and I have no regrets. They just didn't represent all of me."

Levi swung his legs in a wide arc and landed several feet out in the grass. Lola lifted her head and barked once, as if attempting to keep him in line. His mom's words had him thinking back to the life he'd been living, the way being in the water had given him the grounding he needed. But the last couple days at Marcus's, watching the stars at night and thinking about how what he wanted more than anything right now was to make things right with Riley, he'd experienced a different sort of contentment that had largely been eluding him these last several years.

"Does that make any sense?"

"Yeah, absolutely."

"Good, because I'm hoping you'll understand when I tell you I'm thinking about making some big decisions in the next year or so."

He turned to look up at her. "You mean with Larry?"

"With Larry, yes."

"I thought things might be getting serious."

"I've been more worried about telling Ivy than you, given her age, so I'm thankful for the opportunity to bounce it off you first." She shot a glance toward the window again, keeping her voice low. "It never would've worked out for me with either of your fathers had I wanted to raise my children differently than I did."

"You mean like had my father not already been married?" Maybe it was a low blow, but her words triggered him. As much as Levi thought he'd made peace with coming into the world as he had—the result of a passionate evening spent with an investor who came in from Cleveland looking to invest in the company Gale worked for back then—he obviously hadn't.

"I mean your father being who he is in *every* way," she replied, her tone anything but on the defensive. Some days she was better at not taking the bait than others. "Adventurous. Polygynous. Wildly driven. And Ivy's father being the polar opposite. Not an ounce of adventure in his veins, that one."

Twelve years after Gale had given birth to Levi,

Ivy had come into the world as the result of a planned decision with a perpetually single man she worked with at one of the college campuses, a socially awkward history professor. He'd wanted a child; she'd wanted a second one.

Levi hadn't understood his mom's decision to have Ivy then, to intentionally bring a child into the world like that. No surprise, he was twelve at the time. Almost all his friends had lived with both their parents, though a few had parents who were divorced. He'd been angry about the thought of having to explain this to them and couldn't see the decision from her perspective, that she was a woman going through life without a partner who still wanted children, two of them.

It had been hard enough talking to his friends about his own father, hard enough watching people do the math whenever he talked about his other half siblings in Cleveland as they figured out that his father must've already been married when he and Gale had gotten together.

Thankfully, Ivy didn't seem any worse for the wear, growing up in a world where she was split between two intentionally and habitually single parents.

"Larry's different, a good mix of both of them," she continued. "But it's not just that. I'm in a different space now too. I'll be the first to admit it was a bit untraditional, the way you both were raised, but I don't regret a minute of it, and I hope you don't either."

"A *bit* untraditional?" He tried to have some levity in his words, but it didn't seem to carry through. "I don't," he added. "At least not any of the time I spent with you." Those years he'd attempted to spend half of his summer vacation at his father's, that was another story. There, he was always something between a fifth wheel and a black sheep.

"Good, because sometimes I think you have a tendency to forget what I told you about the night I spent with your father."

Levi sank onto his heels and started petting Lola again, comforted by the feel of his hand moving over her padded but wrinkly skin. Enjoying it as well, she stretched out onto her side and let out a contented grunt.

"Yeah, I know. You weren't drunk. You knew what you were doing."

"It's more than that, Levi." She looked at him pointedly. "You were *wanted*. I'd already started researching and filling out questionaries to find a donor, the right one. It wasn't easy, all those profiles to choose from. I had no intention of shacking up with a man I met at a bar, and I didn't. You have your beef with him, I know, but I followed my heart that night, and it gave me you. As I've shared, I wasn't on any form of birth control—obviously— and what we used didn't work. But however you go about it, a part of what makes you *you* is a smart, compassionate, talented man who'd made a mutual decision to stay in a marriage that wasn't working for him—or for his wife—until their children were raised."

He'd heard this story enough times before to know it by heart, so why it took until now to wonder if this might be part of the reason he and Riley had clicked so deeply when they'd finally started breaking down barriers, he couldn't say. Not because of any words they'd exchanged, or any confessions Levi had made. Riley hadn't realized what was truly going on with her parents until the moment things fell apart so completely. But because of a similar, shared energy, the unspoken stuff people labeled intuition but seemed not to understand half as well as the animals and insects that didn't get bogged down in the language of labels and definitions.

Levi didn't understand it, this energy humming under the surface, and he wasn't claiming to, but he'd be the first to admit paying attention to it had kept him safe in the water until it didn't. The fact was, in their senior year, Riley had been living in a home like the one he'd spent a handful of summers and winter vacations in Cleveland, a home with parents who were only going through the motions for the sake of their kids.

He was still processing this when his mom

continued. "What I'm saying is there was a time when I wasn't ready to let any of those men in, not in a way that would really be a game changer, but things are different now. I'm on the cusp of being an empty nester, and I'm ready for something I wasn't ready for before. When Ivy heads off to college, I'm thinking about selling the house and moving in with Larry. Pulling back a bit, from tutoring, at least. Finding myself in a different way."

"Then why'd you sleep with Riley's dad?" It was a strange question to tumble out on the heels of his mom telling him she was going to sell the only house he had any real memories of living in, seeing as he'd spent the last twelve years bouncing between apartments and hotels, but it was the question at the top of his mind.

She stopped swinging and shifted her cup in her hands. It took her a few seconds to respond. "Of all the questions I'd have thought you might follow that up with, that certainly wasn't at the top."

"Why did you?"

"I didn't, if you remember. He followed your friend out of the house. I never saw him again. That's not true; I saw him once in the grocery store; he was with his wife, and we pretended not to know each other."

Lola had started letting out slow grunts in rhythm to Levi's petting. When he stopped and stood up, she lifted her head and gave him a pleading look, but Levi turned and began pacing the grass in front of the porch. "But you were going to."

"Yes, I won't pretend I wasn't. I'd talked to him a few times over the years at the varsity football games. He was usually alone, like me. He'd always ask how number 27 was doing."

"Why'd he go to those? It wasn't like he had a kid in football."

"Because he likes football, I suppose. You asked why we got together, and I'm telling you."

Tension had knotted his shoulders into rocks. Levi took a long breath and nodded. "Thank you."

"We always said hi when we passed in the halls at parent-teacher conferences or at PTO meetings." She paused and shook her head. "Then we showed up at the same bookstore in the kids' section, looking for copies of *Oh, The Places You'll Go* as graduation gifts." She pressed her lips together long enough that Levi wondered if that was all she was going to say before she continued. "We started talking. He wasn't in the best space. He and his wife were on the brink of divorce. They were keeping it from their kids until they decided." She shrugged again. "What can I say? Your sister was at a sleepover. I didn't think you'd be home before midnight at the earliest. Your car wasn't in the driveway. I certainly had no idea you were already home and in the basement."

Levi took a minute to respond, taking this in.

He'd thought about that a lot over the years, how he'd parked along the street, closer to a neighbor's, rather than in his spot in the driveway because he'd really wanted to kiss her before going inside and wasn't sure who was looking out the window. "If I hadn't been there, would that have been it, or would you have seen him again?"

"I don't know. If it had been up to me, maybe." Gale turned her mug in a slow circle as if in contemplation. "But maybe not, maybe that was just loneliness talking back then. You may have noticed, this thing with Larry, it's the first time I've had feelings for someone who's one hundred percent available and able to reciprocate them." She looked up, meeting his gaze. "Why these questions? Why now?"

Levi shook his head. It was as if poison ivy covered his body on the inside. He doubted the coldest of showers could quell it.

"This Riley, was she different? Is that why you're asking?"

That was one thing he could answer. "Yes."

She closed a hand over her mouth. "I'm so sorry, Levi. I wondered if that was the case, but you'd shut me out so completely back then, it was hard to tell."

Her words stabbed at him. "I'm sorry for that." If he'd wondered that once, he'd wondered it a thousand times, how different things might've been if he'd talked about Riley to his mom. Would she have put two and two together and known who her father was? The truth of it was, even when he'd talked to Gale about his and Riley's joint project, he'd been careful not to so much as say her name, as if shining light on a flower could make it wilt faster.

"It's okay. Roots and wings. I figured you were getting your wings."

He huffed at hearing such a simple truth.

"What happened to her?"

He kicked a rock in the grass. "She ran. Not right off, but kids found out, and it was a big thing, and too much for her, obviously. She was gone for a long time."

"But now she's back? I've been wondering why you showed up out of the blue."

He nodded. "For now, at least. She isn't planning on staying."

Gale took a drink of tea that by now had clearly gone cold. "I've been thinking about your predicament a lot lately, about you not being able to do what you love any longer."

"Oh, yeah?"

"Yeah, and even before we had this conversation, what I've been wanting to tell you is that sometimes the world breaks us open in ways that seem ugly and harsh."

"*Yeah, it does.*"

"It might not seem like it today, Levi, but in doing so, it makes way for something very different that might not have come otherwise."

Levi turned to look out at the field on the other side of the gravel road. Far off on its opposite side, the herd of cows was making their way from the shade of a copse of trees to a gate.

He'd made an assumption years ago that his mom didn't fit in with most people because she was so different. It wasn't until now that it occurred to him that maybe it was because she was so different that she'd never cared to fit in in the first place. In either case, even if he wouldn't admit it aloud, he suspected she knew just what she was talking about.

Chapter 16

LEVI WAS PROVING TO BE HARDLY ANY BETTER than Ivy when it came to disconnecting. As the day wore on, he itched to check his phone for new texts, no matter that there was only one person he cared to be in contact with, and he had a date with her on Monday evening.

Around sunset, when it was nearing the time to head outside and start the fire, he broke down and admitted why, as his mom put it, he had ants in his pants. "Hey, Larry, there's a text I need to send. When I get to the main road, which way might I head to reach a spot of service faster?"

Ivy was curled up on the couch reading *Jane Eyre* and snapped the book shut. "I'm going with you!"

Gale stopped wiping down the counters and frowned. "What about intentionally recharging our personal batteries with a technology break? You're on a four-hour streak of being unplugged, Ivy. You don't want to break that, do you?"

"Yeah, I do." Ivy sat up and pushed her glasses up higher on her nose. "I *so* want to break that streak."

"Sorry," Levi murmured, catching the look his mom shot in his direction.

Larry shrugged at Gale sheepishly before turning to Levi. "When you get to the end of the gravel drive, head west, opposite the way you came in. About a mile up the road, you'll climb a big hill that winds to the right. At the top, there's a gravel bar wide enough that you can pull over safely. I can usually get a decent spot of service there. If not, you can head into Annapolis."

Ivy headed for Levi's car barefoot, phone in hand. She'd been pulling it out every fifteen minutes to see if things had improved.

"Yeah, yeah, Gale, last time this weekend, I promise," Levi assured his mom before heading to his room for his keys, wallet, and phone. "Just need to let someone know I don't have service here." When he got to the car, Ivy was already buckled and had her feet pulled up, her knees tucked against her chest.

"Nice here, isn't it?" Levi said, a grin playing on his lips. Whenever his sister wasn't making it known how much she disapproved of her forced weekend detoxing, she did seem to be enjoying herself.

"You mean in a 'look what a happy family we are' kind of way?" Ivy rolled her eyes as Levi started down the gravel drive. "I mean, seriously, I'll sit by the fire, but I'm *not* playing board games afterward."

"Why not? Board games are fun."

Ivy gave an adamant shake of her head, sending her curly black hair tumbling over her shoulders. "And just a heads up, those cabin windows are really thin, and there's nothing here but silence for distraction."

Levi pressed his lips together a second. "I'm guessing that's your way of telling me you heard our conversation earlier?"

"Some of it. Most of it, honestly. I can't believe she's thinking about selling the house. Thank God I'll still have my dad's place to go to. I mean, it's a safe bet *he's* never going to make it work with anyone. He's got an entire room full of Civil War paraphernalia. A few of which have their own insurance policies, even. Who'd want to deal with that?"

"You ever think maybe your dad's choosing to be alone?"

"My dad? Not likely. Not anymore, at least." She gave an adamant shake of her head, sending her curls in all directions. "I'm pretty sure he's gone through all the dating apps at one point or another. Honestly, I used to think you were choosing to be alone 'til I heard you talking about that girl. What's her name? Riley? I'm guessing this text you need to send is to her?"

"It is."

Ivy pursed her lips. "So, Mom almost slept with her dad? That's, like, horrible."

Levi couldn't disagree, so he kept silent.

"None of my friends' families are as weird as ours."

"That you know of, anyway. And the way I've learned to look at it is this: I'm glad to be here, however I came to be. My dad's kind of a douche, yours is kind of a recluse, but we're here, and Gale's been a good mom, as far as moms go."

"Yeah, whatever, I guess. The fact that I grew up hearing you call her Gale instead of Mom is a little weird though, isn't it? And she's up in my business like *all* the time." After falling quiet for a bit, she added, "Other than that, I guess she's not so bad."

Levi turned onto the main road and, in less than a mile, spotted the winding hill up ahead. They were heading in the direction of the sunset, and the western sky was aglow with a brilliant red orange.

"You know how they met, her and Larry?" Ivy asked.

"At an art class, wasn't it?"

"Yeah, watercolor. The thing is, before Larry, and before I heard that disgusting bit earlier about her and that guy, Riley's dad, I always figured Mom was kind of like my dad that way."

"Like in what way? Reclusive?"

"Like being the kind of person to use a turkey baster to have a kid. That kind of way."

Levi was sorry he'd asked for clarification. He was saved from having to reply by her phone suddenly dinging like mad as a series of texts and chats came in.

"Thank you, God." Shifting in her seat, she unlocked her phone, and her fingers began to fly.

It was such a short drive, he hoped he hadn't

created something with Ivy by doing this. "So, uh, not to be all big brother on you, but for our mother's sake, we need to make this our only trip up here this weekend."

If she heard, she didn't acknowledge him. After pulling over onto the gravel embankment, Levi slipped his truck into park and unlocked his phone to find a handful of texts from work buddies—old work buddies, that was—one from Marcus, and two from Riley, which he opened first. There was a picture of the Great Dane they'd walked standing somewhat awkwardly by a woman in a medical attire and tennis shoes who was smiling ear to ear and holding one of the shelter's preprinted signs that read "It's a match. We're going home together."

Levi was about to text congratulations when he glanced down at what Riley had sent next.

> **Didn't get to share this with you yesterday, but I thought you'd like to know since you walked him. :)**

Three minutes later, a second text had followed.

> **The thing is I'm trying to be happy about it, but I really, really wanted to keep him. I know I'll fall in love with a lot of the dogs here but finding him is what got me back**

**here in the first place. Seems he's going to
a good home though. There's that, right?
Sorry to be a downer.**

She'd sent it three hours ago and hadn't texted
since.

"Be back in sec, Ivy. Gotta make a call." After
checking the sideview mirror, he stepped outside.
It was the kind of text that warranted a phone call
in return, not a text, and sooner than three hours
after it was sent.

He dialed her number, and the phone rang several times before going to voicemail. "Hey, Riley,
it's me," he said. "Hope you can hear me. There's
close to zero reception out here, but I'm sorry about
that Dane. There was definitely something special
about him, and I'm sure you're feeling it. I only saw
him once, and it was obvious he'd bonded with you.
I didn't realize you found him." He paused, hoping
the reception was good enough that she'd be able
to make sense of this.

Everything he'd just said, that was it, the easy
stuff that didn't suck the air from his lungs to say.
Didn't require him to fall back into a joke rather
than saying nothing at all. He cleared his throat
and switched his phone to his other ear. "Look, I'm
stuck out here in the middle of nowhere through
Monday afternoon. Once I head back to the cabin,
I won't be able to call or text, so just know…"

There were so many things needing to come out, and the vulnerability in her text stirred them to the surface. Apologies and vows for doing better than he'd done lined up like toy soldiers, waiting for a chance, waiting for him to say something truly significant, but either he was a chicken, or he was just good at convincing himself that now wasn't the right time, not with questionable reception on top of the day she'd had.

"Just know I can't wait for Monday night. I'll pick you up at the shelter at five. Hang in there tonight. You'll feel better tomorrow, I bet."

In the grand scheme of love declarations, maybe it wasn't much, but it was the most vulnerable he'd been with the girl in twelve years. No sense in ripping that Band-Aid off all at once, was there?

He hung up and stared at the sunset, wishing he'd done better. He pulled up his texts, debating what he might add. Finally, he held up his phone and took a picture of the sunset right as the sun was beginning to dip below the horizon, and red-orange flames were shooting out in all directions over a green and gold field in a way that had him feeling small again and full of wonder. He sent it off to her, hoping it would go through, hoping that for now it would suffice for the thousand words he'd somehow find a way to say.

It wasn't until John Bender did his infamous fist pump, Brian Johnson's voiceover essay was finished, and the credits began rolling on *The Breakfast Club* that Riley realized her phone had disappeared between the voluminous cushions of Lana's basement couch. Tonight's triple movie feature had been Lana's suggestion in hopes of keeping Riley from feeling too blue about Arlo being adopted. With the first movie under their belt, Riley could attest to it helping. For just over an hour and a half, it had kept her mind off the fact that Levi hadn't replied to her text either.

"I always wanted a sequel to this," Lana confessed, stretching out on the opposite side of the sectional and stifling what must've been her thirtieth yawn of the evening. "I want to know that Claire and John beat the odds and find a way to be together. I want Andrew to stand up to his father, and Allison and Brian to find their way."

"I'm glad they didn't make a sequel," Riley said as she fished between the deep cushions. "Sometimes the happily-ever-after ones are forgettable."

"I'm guessing that's why you wanted *La La Land* next?"

Riley snorted. "Hey, I voted for *The Princess Bride* too, didn't I? What's happier than that? And as much as you're yawning, I highly doubt we're making it through three classics tonight, so you can pick whichever one you want most. Except *The Notebook*. Too sad."

Lana gave her a sour look and reached for one of the dark chocolate–covered almonds on the coffee table. "But it's a beautiful kind of sad."

"Yeah it is, but who ends up with their forever person at that age? Weren't they like midteens in the book?"

"I did." Munching the almond, Lana pointed toward the two baby monitors on the coffee table. "Thank God, or I wouldn't have those two angels—I call them that when they're sleeping well, by the way. The nights they're waking up every twenty minutes, they're my holy terrors."

"They're sweeties, for sure, and you and Grant aren't exactly your average couple."

"You and Levi weren't either."

"Levi and I weren't even a couple, not really." Finally, her fingers brushed against the cool metal of her phone. "There it is." Pulling it out, she spotted a couple missed texts from various friends and a call and voicemail from Levi. Sitting up, she opened the text from Levi first. It was a picture of a gorgeous sunset and a rolling hillside out in the country but was unaccompanied by any text.

Her heart sank a bit to find that he hadn't replied to her text, but he'd left a voicemail as well. "Levi called." She pressed play on his voicemail and turned on the speaker. When a heavily broken up message began playing, she turned her phone to full volume.

Lana leaned in. "I didn't get any of that," she said when it was done playing.

Riley hit play a second time. With the volume up fully, she was able to make out a few broken and isolated words as his message went in and out of reception. "...hear me...sorry...zero re... definitely...feeling it..." Then there was nothing intelligible for a short stretch before she was able to make out a few more words. "...Monday...cabin... just know..." Then it clicked off and that was it.

"Just know what?" Lana folded her hands over the top of her knees expectantly.

"He's out with his mom and sister at a cabin this weekend. Do you think that last bit is canceling dinner Monday or confirming it?"

"Play it again."

"He sent a picture too. A sunset." Riley held out her phone for Lana to see.

"That's positive." Lana leaned in even more, peering closer. "Gorgeous. And romantic. He was confirming dinner. For sure."

Riley played it again but couldn't make out any more words than before. "That 'zero re' has to be zero reception, don't you think? Ugh, why didn't he text something if he knew the reception was so bad?"

Lana shook her head. "Because he's Levi, and he sucks at communicating."

"If he's canceling, I'm going to trust it's not

because he's had a change of heart." Riley was mostly assuring herself with this declaration. "He was great Friday. Perfect, really, even if we didn't have much time to talk."

"Grant said you two are still perfect together."

"We aren't together."

"Yet."

Saving the rest of her texts for later, Riley peered at the image of the sunset once more before dropping the phone on the coffee table. It had been entirely too long since she'd stood out in the middle of nowhere and watched the sun set. She closed her eyes a second, wistful, imagining being there with him, doing nothing but holding hands and watching the sun drop below the horizon.

"He showed up at your work on your first day and brought you a coffee," Lana added. "Heck, he drove through three states after he found out you were here, didn't he? My guess is that he knows what he wants."

Riley nodded slowly. "Thanks, I'll hold on to that whenever I get inundated by the waves of doubt that this'll never work."

"That's my girl."

"Do you care if your girl picks next then?"

Lana lifted an eyebrow. "What're you picking?"

"*The Princess Bride*. Definitely."

Lana's skeptical smile spread into a giant one. "Happy is as happy does." Suddenly, she cocked her head, squinting at Riley. "You know, I've never thought about it before, but put some crimp in your hair and a thin little 'stache on that boy, and you two kind of even look like Buttercup and Westley."

Riley shook her head, the last of her unease waning even before she pictured Levi dressed in a medieval outfit, hair in a ponytail, and donning a thin moustache. "I needed that laugh, and you're kind of right, about him anyway, even though he's better looking than Westley."

"Yeah, but we should give Westley credit. He was a victim of '80s fashion, after all."

Riley held up a finger. "Good point."

As they settled in for movie number two, Riley couldn't help but be reminded that most people weren't Lana and Grant and didn't end up marrying their high school sweethearts. People changed. Love changed. Not everyone was meant to be. But Riley wasn't about to count her and Levi out of the running for a happily ever after yet.

Chapter 17

EVEN THOUGH RILEY'S TO-DO LIST HAD BEEN growing steadily her first week on the job, she figured she might as well embrace today's chaotic flow. Better too busy than to have time to obsess about tonight's date-but-not-a-date with Levi.

One of Riley's favorite things about working at High Grove so far was the unpredictability. On her way here this morning, she'd never have guessed she'd be taking a crash course on how to care for juvenile mini pigs, thanks to the three young ones found first thing this morning curled up in a dog bed against the back of the building. There'd been no note and nothing keeping them from wandering off.

A replay of the video feed from the cameras out back had shown the piglets being unloaded from a Kia Sportage about 4:30 a.m. The dumper was a woman wearing baggy sweats, a hoodie, and sunglasses—in the dark. Even though her vehicle was in plain sight, she'd covered her front and back license plates with paper, making it obvious she knew she'd be on camera. The footage had shown her treating the little pigs with care, placing each one in the soft-sided dog bed she'd left them, and scratching their heads until they settled down and stayed in the bed rather than rushing for the cover of her legs. Once she was gone, the frightened piglets hadn't so much as wandered further than a foot or two until Patrick pulled up this morning.

Clearly, the woman who'd left them had wanted to make sure the little pigs wound up here as much as she hadn't wanted to get caught. The problem was that the shelter wasn't licensed to care for mini pigs. No matter how good of pets they could make, they were still categorized as farm animals. Adorable as the little creatures were, they needed to be placed with an individual or organization qualified to give them adequate care—and pronto. Megan figured they had twenty-four hours to relocate them before any real violation occurred, seeing as the pigs were dumped and not taken in. Until then, the staff and volunteers were soaking up as much time with their unexpected guests as they could get.

"I've never thought of myself as a pig person," Kelsey said, "but I could seriously see having a mini pig as a pet." She'd gotten up from her desk, beckoned by their grunts and squeals now that they were awake again, and was sitting crossed legged on the floor in front of the temporary pen they'd set up behind the staff's work stations.

"They're sweet, aren't they?" Earlier, Riley had turned into a puddle by their whole-body bliss when being scratched, from those little piggy smiles to them rolling over and grunting in pleasure. "But I'm not letting myself get any ideas," she added. "I suspect wherever I end up next will be just as strict about pets as all the apartments I've had so far."

Riley was attempting to work through the unread marketing emails, but Trina, High Grove's resident senior cat, was camped out next to her, watching the pigs with enough heightened interest that she was emitting a series of erratic, half-silent meows while flicking her tail back and forth with a whiplike flair. Although Riley was happy to share her desk with Trina, the normally agreeable kitty had no interest in cuddling today.

"Yeah, pets and apartments can be tricky. Ever think about renting a house? I had a friend who did that, and her landlord let her foster a whole litter of puppies—after upping her pet deposit a bit."

"That's cool. I wanted to do that in Atlanta, but I couldn't find anything I could swing cost-wise close enough to my work. Maybe I'll give it another try, depending on where I end up. Though I'd feel super guilty if I did."

Kelsey stopped scratching the black-and-white pig's belly and looked up. "Why's that?"

Riley was hesitant to admit here how much Arlo had meant to her. It'd be all too easy to assume she was going to want to adopt a slew of animals. There was something about Kelsey though; she didn't have the look of someone who'd place judgement, so Riley went for it. "Because I really loved Arlo. There was something about him that really clicked with me."

Kelsey's answering expression was without judgement. "That's rough. I've had that happen to me too, so I know the feeling. I heard Patrick say that Arlo had really bonded with you too, and that's saying a lot, because Patrick's not one to offer up compliments, as you've probably guessed."

"Well, thanks. I keep reminding myself he went to a good home, and it's helping. A bit," she added with a smile.

"Hopefully, it'll keep getting easier. Most of us go through that at one point or another." When Kelsey started to get up, the littlest pig she'd been petting the most squealed in distress. "I can't hang out all day, little one." She attempted to herd her toward the stuffed animal "comfort" pig that had been placed inside the pen with them that she'd been cuddling against earlier. "They're quite used to human touch. I'll give whoever had them credit for that."

Earlier this morning, Margie, one of the longtime supporters of the shelter, stopped by with a fresh supply of gently used stuffed animals. Margie frequented garage sales most weekends and was always on the lookout for good ones to drop off here. A skilled seamstress, she'd first make them pet-safe by replacing any plastic eyes and noses with ones she sewed on with her sewing machine. Thanks to a string of Labor Day weekend garage sales, this morning's delivery was Santa Clause–sized. When it had included a large stuffed pig, pink and super soft, there'd been zero question as to who got dibs.

Whether the piglets realized the similarities they shared with their cozy stuffed kennel mate was another question, but they'd cuddled up around it after an improvised breakfast of rabbit and dog chow with some fruit and veggies mixed in.

The cuteness of all the cuddling gave Riley the perfect opportunity for an impromptu video post— one that took off shortly after she posted it and was generating more leads than the cold calls the staff made in hopes of securing a place to take them. By lunchtime, the perfect place came forward, a farm-animal rescue organization about an hour west of the city. The only catch was that they couldn't spare the staff to pick them up, so someone from the shelter would need to run them out.

After mulling it over, she texted Levi the photo she'd posted of the piglets cuddling with the stuffed pig and asked how he'd feel about putting their dinner off an hour or two in order for her to do a good deed. She sent it off, crossing her fingers that the garbled message he'd left Saturday had, in fact, been him saying he was looking forward to tonight and not canceling. Otherwise, she was about to look like someone who couldn't take no for an answer.

It took him close to an hour to respond, and when he did, he did it with his typical Levi flair.

> **How 'bout that? I was gonna to take you to Club Bacon tonight, but now I think I'd better not. And what's this good deed about?**

She knew without searching online that there was no such thing as Club Bacon. As she was deciding how to respond, another text came in.

> **What time are you thinking?**
> Well, these little ones were dumped here this morning, but we can't keep them. I found a place to take them, but it's out past Washington. I skipped lunch and can leave early to run them out. Still, I doubt I'll be back before six thirty. Work for you?
> **Nope.**

Riley bit her lip and waited for another text, which came a few seconds later.

> **I'll ride with you. What time are you heading out?**

Riley shook her head, her smile spreading wide.

You can be such a Levi. :) I was thinking 4 or
4:15.

**Good. Gives me time to shower. I was in
a creek with my sister earlier. You don't
want to be in a confined space with me
until I shower.**

THEN TAKE YOUR TIME

Levi responded with a nose and a green-faced
emoji. Riley snorted lightly as she dropped her
phone back on her desk. Well, he wasn't canceling
with that garbled message of his, that's for sure.

Reaching for her water bottle, she realized her
breathing had gone shallow. It seemed the one
thing that had seemed impossible for so long was
happening. She was getting another chance at the
one thing she'd been wishing forever she could
undo, and she didn't think it was just her imagination that he wanted the same thing.

Whatever this led to, she was darn certain she
wasn't going to let herself fall into another I've-
lost-Levi-and-it's-killing-me funk. No, this time
they were both adults, and Riley was committed
to acting like one. This meant big conversations. It
meant being real and taking it slow and acknowledging all that might be at stake.

And terrifying as this was, it had the potential
to be the best thing that had happened to her in a
long time.

Chapter 18

LEVI SPOTTED RILEY THROUGH THE LARGE front windows of the shelter. She was standing in full view while in conservation with two other people, smiling at something that was being said. Energy mounted inside him at the sight of her. "Don't you get it?" his body seemed to be saying. "This is what I wanted all along."

After parking in one of the spots at the side, he dragged his palms along the top of his steering wheel, taking a second to collect himself.

He didn't think it was his imagination that she wanted to explore what they might be able to step into as much as he did. Like there was a bridge to the twelve years since she'd last been in his arms they could cross and get back to what they'd lost. The skin of his leg tingled, as if anticipating an experience of her calf pressed against his like when they'd been sitting on opposite sides of the booth, bantering back and forth rather than studying, their fingers brushing as they reached for their shared plate of fries.

As he crossed the parking lot, his attention was drawn to the towering thunderheads building in the patchy clouded sky and blocking out the sun, promising late-afternoon storms the same as the smell of rain on the wind did.

Riley must've spotted him pulling in because she met him at the door, smiling deep enough to bring out her dimple. He caught something in her expression, something welcoming and standoffish at the same time, and it reminded him that crossing that bridge to get back to where they'd left off might not be as easy as he'd like to think.

If that was the case, he was willing to work on it.

As Levi was stepping inside, Riley knelt to stop Chance from trotting out. The stocky, senior dog raised his head and sniffed the air, his tail beating contentedly. Levi bet he was smelling the rain too.

"Thanks for coming early."

"Yeah, no problem. I'd have come earlier, had you asked." The larger truth in this simple statement didn't occur to him until she dropped his gaze, a blush lighting her cheeks. To make it easier for her, he added, "Looks like he wants to go out. Want me to take him while you're wrapping up?"

"I'm ready aside from logging out." After giving Chance a pat now that the door was closed, she stood up. "And Chance was outside a little bit ago. A lot of the dogs in back are getting riled up by whatever's happening with the barometric pressure and wind right now, though he seems more excited than nervous."

"Maybe he appreciates a good thunderstorm every so often."

Riley smiled. "As far as dogs go, he's one of the wisest. And just so you know, I have a change of clothes in my car, but I figured we're heading to a farm, so what you see is what you get." She was in jeans and a heather-gray V-neck T-shirt that was just fitted enough to remind him how nice it had been to finally savor the incredible body underneath. To stop the blood from rushing to his groin, he refocused on the cartoon outline of a dog on the front alongside a quote from Rudyard Kipling that read "...our friend always and always and always."

"Works for me. Nice shirt."

With the door closed, Chance lingered long enough to sniff Levi's shoes, then shuffled behind the counter. For being a half hour from closing, the place was anything but empty, with a handful of people milling about the gift shop, others in front of the cat kennels and at the varying adoption stations.

"So, these pigs. Want me to load them in the truck while you're finishing up?"

"I was thinking we'd take my car. I've got a travel crate loaded in the back seat already."

Figuring it was best to keep it to himself how much less fun, at over six feet tall, a few hours in a Mini Cooper would no doubt be compared to his truck, he nodded. "Sure thing."

Proving she could still read him, she tilted her head. "You know, there's more leg space than you might think."

"Oh yeah? Well, I'm willing to let you make a believer out of me. So, where are they now?" he asked, following her over to her desk.

"They were up here all day, but we moved them to a playpen out back a half hour ago in hopes of them going to the bathroom and getting some energy out before we head out. Wait till you see them. They're really cute."

"They looked cute enough in that picture you posted that I considered bringing one back for Marcus, though I doubt he'd appreciate it, full as his hands are right now."

"I bet. And the way I see it, he needs to claim that adorable bulldog as his own before any more animals come his way."

"Amen to that." Levi checked out the cat kennels as she was entering her time and logging out for the day. He stopped in front of a kennel where two scrawny and long-legged kittens were tousling about in play. He waggled his fingers and, after they skittered away long enough to determine he wasn't a threat, they began pouncing and batting their paws at the side of the kennel, bodies fluffed and tails erect in that playful but serious way kittens had.

After a minute or two, Riley joined him, a sling bag over her shoulder. "Ready if you are."

It took a few minutes to get the piglets loaded into the soft-sided travel crate that was more like a tent than a crate, but soon enough they headed out with the piglets squealing in the back seat, and Levi sandwiched in the front passenger seat. After winding through the still-familiar streets of Levi's youth and finally hitting the interstate, Riley shot him a hopeful look. "So, more space than you were expecting?"

Levi cocked an eyebrow. "When we're back, you can hop into my truck and let me know what you think about the difference in room. Not that I'm complaining."

"No, not that you're complaining," she said, a smile playing on her lips. "But sure, so long as after that, we figure out how much gas we saved by taking the Mini instead of a Dodge Ram."

"I wondered why you wanted to drive. I thought maybe you didn't like the idea of my absconding with you to who knew where once we drop these pigs off."

"I guess there's that too."

"Well, you're safe there. Pretty soon, I'll have too big a kink in my calves to carry you off anywhere far."

She laughed. "You certainly haven't stopped being Levi, have you? And you know you can still push your seat back aways."

"Guess that depends who you ask. Marcus

would probably tell you I haven't acted this much like Levi in a while."

Her smile faltered just enough to know he'd hit home. For close to a minute, there was nothing but the grunts and soft squeals of the pigs to break through the tension.

"So, how was your weekend with your family?" she said, adjusting her hands on the steering wheel.

"Better than expected. The cabin was nice. The stars were really nice. So was the quiet. Ivy survived without her phone. That was a plus. It was touch and go those first couple of hours."

"That's good. It's nice you got some real time with her. How old is she now?"

"Seventeen, closing in on eighteen."

Riley's eyes widened. "I guess I should've figured, but I still think of her with those uneven pigtails, chapped lips, and the Dora backpack that was almost as big as she was."

"So do I, most of the time, but she's going away to college next year."

"Wow."

"Yeah, and my mom's talking about selling the house when she does." It was a touchy subject, knowing where it could lead to, but he took it anyway. "Seems like she and this guy she's seeing—the one who owns the cabin—are getting pretty serious."

Riley shifted her hands on the steering wheel so they were at ten and two and nodded. "Oh yeah?"

"Yeah." He gave her a bit of space to process, to let her step into this slowly. But the truth was, no matter what they talked about from their past, sooner or later, they were going to have to go there. As far as Levi was concerned, he was ready now. "That in itself is a bit weird," he added. "Seeing how she's never been in a committed relationship before."

She adjusted her grip again, locking her hands in like she was driving through hurricane-force winds even though the highway traffic was light. "I wondered if that had ever changed."

"Not until now."

She pressed her lips together long enough that he was starting to think she wouldn't respond. "My parents—like I said Friday, they're still together. Not just living in the same house either. They're really together again, like going to bed at the same time and going out to movies and stuff." She merged onto the middle lane, flipping on her blinker, and checking her blind spot with the same calculated Rileyness he remembered from the few times he'd been a passenger in her car, back when she'd driven a Jetta.

"How do you feel about that?"

Her lips parted, and she shook her head slightly, tousling her blond waves over her shoulders. "No one has ever asked me that quite so point blank.

Then again, I haven't had this conversation with that many people before either."

The sky in the horizon was dark and heavily clouded, promising storms, heading west as they were. With her Maps app showing they had another 48 minutes to reach their destination, Levi doubted they'd arrive before encountering them. "Seems to me that it's as good a time as it'll ever be to have it then."

She sat straighter in her seat, and Levi got the sense that this was the real reason she'd wanted to drive, to keep some semblance of control in a conversation that was inevitable.

"I know my answer should be that I'm happy," she said when she continued. "I should be happy that they're together. Not just together but happy together, if you know what I mean." She shook her head harder, sending her hair in all directions this time. "Any decent person would want their parents to be happy together, wouldn't they?"

Levi shifted in his seat, frustrated for a second by its confinement. He wanted to face her, but compared to his truck, he might as well be buckled in next to her for a ride on the Screaming Eagle. "If you want the truth, maybe the question you need to be asking yourself is what do you need to do to get in the space that you can honestly say you're happy for them, and for whatever it is they've found in each other now."

No doubt it was a coincidence, but even the pigs fell quite for a few seconds as she was taking this in. Levi dragged a hand over his mouth, noticing the tension lining her frame, in her shoulders and thighs, tension that hadn't been there minutes ago.

"I don't think…" Riley's shoulders sank, and her eyes pressed closed a second. "Damn it anyway, Levi. I hate that you do that so well."

"Do what so well?"

"Act like you don't know a thing, when in fact, you're the most intuitive person I know."

"Intuitive, huh? I don't know if I'd go that far, but I do know three things well enough that I trust my intuition with them wholeheartedly."

"Let me guess. Water being one of them, right?" she said, shooting him a look and a soft smile. Some of the tension locking up her thighs and arms seemed to be fading.

"Yeah, water being one. The career I'm leaving behind being the second." Go big or go home. "You being the third."

She blinked, and her left hand abandoned the wheel to sweep her hair over her shoulder, leaving him with an unobstructed view of the delicate skin of her neck and earlobe. "I'm not ready for this."

"Nobody said you had to be."

"Twelve years is a long time, Levi." She sounded like she was trying to convince herself as much as she was him.

"I won't argue that."

"We were eighteen," she added, still arguing with herself as much as him. "Now I'm less than a month from hitting thirty, and you already hit it. We're basically strangers."

"Is that what you really think, or what you feel you need to say?"

She blinked several times in a row. "You know, we haven't even been in the car fifteen minutes. Can we just talk about the weather or something for a bit? Actually, there's the whole friendraiser we need to be planning, though I imagined doing that at the restaurant where I can take notes."

"Sure thing." He chuckled. "As far as the event goes, it's simple. Tell me what you'd like me to do, and I'll do it. Whether it's distributing flyers, knocking on doors to solicit donations, talking to my buddy at the radio station, I'm in." With a nod toward the rapidly darkening sky ahead of them, he added, "And while normally I'm not big on talking about the weather, it does look like things are about to get pretty interesting."

Chapter 19

THEY'D LEFT THE HIGHWAY BEHIND AND WERE winding through a hilly and picturesque country-side on two-lane roads with thirteen minutes left to their destination when both their phones went off simultaneously with tornado warnings. "A warning, not a watch?" Riley gripped the steering wheel more firmly. The wind had picked up a good ten minutes ago, the sky overhead was dark gray, and the grass and trees were glowing bright green in the eerie light.

Not that the first half had been what she'd call a relaxing drive through the country. First, there'd been getting used to sitting so close to him, even before that declaration of his. Who'd have thought he'd just put it out there like that? Not her, certainly. After the adrenaline rush that created had faded, there'd been getting used to his hand on her knee. Of course, she could've asked him to move it, but the most unsettling part about the whole thing had been how much she *hadn't wanted* him to move it. Her knee was a thirsty sponge, soaking in all the Levi it could get. All that happened before the strong winds hit, whipping at the car, threatening to blow them into the other lane or off the shoulder.

"A warning," Levi confirmed. "We've been under a watch the last few hours." A quick glance away from the road in front of her confirmed that he'd pulled up the emergency weather alerts. "Damn," he added. "Looks like a funnel cloud was spotted straight west of us."

Riley glanced at the minutes to arrival on the Maps app displayed on her dashboard screen, willing its countdown to tick away considerably faster than it was. Hadn't it been thirteen minutes to their destination for a while now? Perhaps it was stuck. "Think we'll be able to wait out the storm there?"

Levi leaned forward in his seat, glancing up at the sky directly above them and then out his passenger window. "That'd be nice, but I have a feeling we're going to hit it any second."

"By 'it,' please don't say you mean the *tornado*?"

"I hope not. I meant the front edge of the storm."

Seconds later, a burst of wind hit so strong it was all Riley could do to keep from swerving off the shoulder. Still-green leaves whipped through the air and in no time, hail pummeled down, hitting the pavement and the top of her car and bouncing off like Ping-Pong balls.

After coming out of a steep curve, they reached the top of a winding hill. Levi pointed toward the bottom in the distance. "I can't tell if it's a driveway or a side road ahead, but I think we should pull over to let this front pass." He was practically yelling to be heard over the hail hitting the roof and the squeals of the piglets, who clearly didn't care for the sound of the hail.

Riley wasn't about to argue. Large splats of rain joined with the hail, and she needed to turn her wipers on. Just as they neared the bottom of the hill, and Riley was slowing down to turn left onto what turned out to be a narrow county road, the rain and hail stopped as suddenly as they began, and the wind stopped whipping the trees like they were inflatable tube men. If the sky wasn't so dark and there wasn't such a lingering eerie glow, she'd have breathed a sigh of relief.

A massive bolt of lightning burst across the sky, temporarily lighting the countryside like a giant halogen bulb. Thunder cracked loud enough to rattle the vents in her car as she pulled onto the narrow lane with fields on either side and sporadic trees and shrubs along both fence lines.

"Keep going a bit," Levi directed after surveying the sky. "It's darker behind us, and whatever you do, don't stop under any trees."

Riley nodded. Her hands were shaking, but she had a stern grip on the wheel. Her GPS warned her that she'd made a wrong turn before Levi silenced it. They'd gone less than half a mile when the wind started up again, strong enough to shake the Mini and make steering difficult.

"You hear that?" Levi cracked his window an inch.

"Is it a siren?" Riley wanted it to be a siren, even if it was unlike any siren she'd ever heard, but this was lower, more of a rumbling roar.

"No, not a siren."

Her skin went cold. "Levi, what do we do?"

His hand closed over the back of her neck. "You've got this. Keep going. It's behind us. We're heading south. It's heading east."

Every hair on Riley's body stood on end as the roaring intensified. She resisted the urge to tell Levi to close his window, knowing it wouldn't make a bit of difference, but was glad when he did seconds later anyway. "It sounds like a freight train."

"*Yeah, it does.*"

They'd made it another mile down the road, and Riley was no longer wondering if it was her imagination that the roar was lessening when the sky opened up, and torrential rain began falling down in sheets too intense to navigate even at slow speeds. Another wickedly intense bolt of lightning lit the sky.

Levi's hand was still on the back of her neck, and he squeezed reassuringly. "Why don't you go ahead and pull over? No sense trying to find a place to pull into right now."

"What if someone rams into us?"

He reached out and pressed on the hazard lights. "No one's driving fast in this, if anyone around here is driving at all."

Riley slowed to a stop and numbly slipped the Mini into Park after getting as close to the fence line flanking the side of the road as she dared given such poor visibility. She left the engine running in case they needed to get moving quickly. It wasn't until a handful of seconds passed of her not driving that she realized how wildly she was shaking. "Could you see it?"

Levi shook his head. "Not the funnel. It seemed like it was north of us on the other side of the hill back there. But I could see a mass of clouds blacker than the rest that seemed to be turning in a circle."

"I kind of feel like I'm going to be sick." Riley pressed her eyes closed, willing her stomach to still. Rain was pummeling the car hard enough that the visibility was close to zero even while sitting still.

"If you need to step out, I'm game." His words carried a touch of jest, but his hand moved from her neck to lock over her hands which were resting numbly on her lap. He squeezed gently, and Riley remembered back to the first time he'd closed his hand over hers and how, in that moment, it had seemed like she'd never worry about anything ever again. Where might they be now if things hadn't played out as they did? If she'd not shut him out like that? An image of Jackson and Rosie from their day at the farm tugged at her heartstrings. Would they have gotten married like Lana and Grant? Were there little ones who'd never exist because she'd made a decision to start running and never stop?

Fighting back tears, she blinked her eyes open again, attempting to stare through the sheet of rain sliding down her windshield rather than look in Levi's direction. "I bet the rain's cold," she said, forcing herself to say something. "With hail that size." The hail had stopped completely, at least for the moment, though the tree limbs—what little she could make of them—were whipping about again in the wind. Her car rocked gently like it was on a raft and going down Thunder River at Six Flags. Resisting a shiver, she flipped off the AC.

"I bet you're right."

Suddenly, she realized the pigs had gone completely quiet for the first time since they'd pulled out of the shelter parking lot. She twisted in her seat and looked through the dark mesh sides of the travel crate to spot them curled up together in the corner next to the stuffed animal pig, their eyes wide open and ears perked, listening with a keen observance she'd not have expected of such young things. "It seems they know when not to make a fuss."

"Who'd a thunk it'd only take a tornado to get them to settle down?" Levi grinned, his teeth gleaming in the dim light.

"I hope… I hope everyone's okay. Everyone in its path. Something that loud…" She shivered and pushed the thought away.

"Yeah, me too."

The car seemed to be rocking less, and the rain was coming down in straighter sheets, so Riley's best guess was that the front was past them now. "I've been through a hundred thunderstorms, but I've never been that close to a tornado before."

"Me neither."

"You were in a hurricane though, weren't you? When you were working down in the Gulf."

The way he looked at her threatened to suck the breath from her lungs the same as the roaring of the tornado had. A hint of a smile played on his lips too. "Were you keeping tabs on me, Riley Leighton?"

She wanted to look away, but the rain was still coming down too hard to see much beyond the glass. Even if she wanted to, his gaze was holding her too strong. "Kind of." Was there really any sense in denying it? Her gaze dropped to his lips for a second or two before locking on his eyes again.

"That's alright. I was keeping tabs on you too."

She knew he was going to kiss her even before he leaned in. His lips brushed against hers, slowly at first, and his thumb and fingertips traced her jawline before moving down the side of her neck as she opened her mouth to his. His tongue met hers, and soon the kiss was intense enough that their front teeth brushed against one another. Even then, his hand was locking behind her head, and he was drawing her closer still. Riley didn't mind. She wanted to drink him in like he was the rain and she was the desert.

She heard the click of their seat belts releasing—Levi's doing—before his hand locked around her hip, pulling her closer. Her blood heated faster than if she was hooked up to an electric tea kettle, and she had to fight off the urge to crawl onto his lap and savor his neck the same way she was savoring his lips and mouth. Had it really been her idea to take her car when they could have had the spacious interior of his cab? What had she been thinking?

This. This is what you were thinking. You aren't supposed to be letting him in again. Certainly not this fast.

Her body was at war with her mind, and all odds seemed to be on it winning. Suddenly, the argument that this wasn't the way to let Levi back into her life didn't have as much strength to it as it had this morning when she'd promised herself no hanky-panky. Who cared that she wasn't one to jump in the deep end without first dipping her toe in to test the water, or that she blew on her fries before biting into them? That she'd been the last one of her friends to let her dad take off her training wheels.

Levi was the one to move in leaps and bounds, not her. She needed her wits about her to keep the pace for the both of them. The problem was the storm had shaken her up, dropped her right into her body and out of her head, so much so, all she could do was let out a throaty murmur of appreciation when he his hand slipped underneath her shirt. Where the rain had been a torrent, it suddenly sounded like a lullaby. She entwined her fingers in his hair and drew him closer, soaking in his scent and the taste of his skin—both of which her senses remembered intimately. The ache between her legs might as well have been a furnace being fanned by a pair of bellows.

Levi had been her first, and every single one of her parts remembered it. Their bodies seemed to be moving on auto play, as if it had only been a day rather than a countless string of them since he'd been inside her. Riley slipped one hand underneath his arm and was soaking up the strength in his deltoids and torso when one of the pigs grunted softly from where they were cuddled in the corner of their crate, and just like that, the world flooded back in. Not enough to entirely quell the fire in her veins, but enough to dull it. Enough to hear the warning in her head not to do this. Not right off the bat like this, at least.

Sucking in a deep and intentional breath, she pulled out of his embrace and tugged down her shirt. "Levi, no, not like this."

He must've caught her expression because alarm flooded his face even before she spoke. "What're you saying?"

"That we've been apart for twelve years. Picking things up right where we left them—that sounds like crazy talk. Like we're still eighteen and raging with hormones." A smile broke out on her face after catching his look at that last part. "Okay, so maybe we're still raging with hormones, but we aren't eighteen anymore, and we've been apart a long time. I don't even really know who you are now."

He twisted in his seat so that he was facing her more directly. "You know everything that's important. None of that's changed."

Something raw and penetrable flashed over his face, something that had far older roots than this moment. How badly she must've hurt him, shutting him out the way she did.

She leaned over the console and brushed her lips against his, silently wishing away his pain. "Probably so," she answered after pulling away enough to look him in the eye again. "But if you care about getting this right half as much as I do, then you'll support me in taking this down a notch."

It was a leap of vulnerability she almost never permitted herself, admitting this aloud. This thing between them had never been given parameters. The word "love" had never been spoken. She'd been close to saying it that night in his arms before they'd been interrupted, but that didn't help her now. "Because, the thing is, I don't want to spend another twelve years regretting all the things I might've done differently this time."

His whole body seemed to exhale in relief. He

kissed her again, but this time there was no sense of urgency to it, and his hands kept to less volatile ground. Even if neither of them was ready to admit it aloud yet, she was pretty darn sure it wasn't only her who could go her whole life and not feel as deeply for anyone else as she did for him.

While no longer torrential, the rain was still coming down hard enough that it seemed as if they were tucked away in a private cave. Undoubtedly, the world would start pressing in, but she wanted to hold it off as long as possible. They had enough to overcome when it was just the two of them.

"I don't either, Riley, so name your pace, and I'll match it, turtle slow or rabbit fast, because I'm not going anywhere, and I'm praying hard to a god I'm not entirely sure I believe in that you don't either."

Riley locked her arms around him, burying her face in his neck and closing her eyes. A dozen worries stirred to the surface, including how neither of them had plans to stay in St. Louis, and how her career could very well take her anywhere, but she did her best to let them fall away like the rain on the windowsill. Right now, it wasn't about the could've beens or the might bes.

"Then how about we aim for the middle and see where it takes us?"

Chapter 20

"Looks like you're in seventh heaven." Levi's tone carried a hint of easy laughter.

Eyes closed, Riley continued to burrow her forehead against the silky-smooth neck of the friendly equine who'd come over to greet them, sticking his head over the fence, sniffing their hands and pockets in hopes of a treat. It had stopped raining, and the evening sun was shining brightly in the clear western sky, while the eastern sky on the other side of the rolling hills and trees was still dark and forbidding. The horse's hooves and lower legs were wet and muddy, but the rest of him was dry, so either he and his buddies had hung out under the lean-to shelter on the other side of the paddock during the storm, or they'd recently been let out from a stall.

While he didn't seem to mind being doted upon, the gelding was clearly more interested in food than companionship. There were two other horses in the paddock with him, but they hadn't been interested in their visitors enough to stop grazing and come over. "I'd forgotten how much I miss horses."

"I wondered if you'd ever started taking riding lessons again."

Riley pulled her head up from the horse to look at Levi, who was standing next to her, leaning his arms over the top of the fence. It shouldn't surprise her that he remembered her love of horses even though she'd not been riding when they'd known each other. She remembered a hundred little things about him too, right down to the way he alternately tapped his middle and forefinger on the table when he was deep in thought. "I haven't done half the things I meant to do," she admitted. "Things are always just so busy, I guess." In her tweens and early teen years, Riley had gotten weekly riding lessons and spent a week each summer at an equine camp.

As she ran a hand along the gelding's smooth neck, he inadvertently tickled her by sniffing at her hair, his strong breath blowing against her neck. "If I'd have known I was coming here when I left this morning, I'd have packed some carrots in my lunchbox, you sweet thing."

She'd given riding lessons up in high school to help ease her parents' mounting expenses and focused on track, but looking back, maybe going a few years without a car in exchange for more time with these magnificent creatures would've been the better decision.

"There's time yet." Levi scratched the dapple-gray gelding on his forehead underneath his fore-lock as the horse began to nuzzle Levi's T-shirt.

His words stirred up all the indecision floating

inside her, from where she'd land next to how Levi might fit into that picture. "Yeah," she said, opting not to give voice to any of the insecurities floating around her head. "For sure."

As anticipated, they'd arrived at the rescue farm after public hours, but there were still a few employees bustling about between barns, busy with whatever task was at hand. Mrs. Reyes, the adoption coordinator and Riley's contact here, had disappeared back into the smaller of the two barns to get the piglets' stall ready after telling Riley and Levi they were free to have a look about the place.

Levi took a step back to prevent his shirt from being munched on. "Someone thinks it's dinner time." Shaking his head, he looked around at their surroundings again. The rescue sat on over fifty acres. There were multiple paddocks along the sides of the two aluminum-sided barns, most of which had a handful of horses in each, though a few of the paddocks had cows, and one had three very large pigs. "It sure is beautiful here. Great land— which is something I'm not sure I appreciated enough until recently."

"Land?"

He nodded. "Yeah, how peaceful it is to be on a nice piece of land. Like at Marcus's or that cabin I was at. Here, even. I'm sure I appreciate it more because of how much time I spent in hotels and condos the last decade or so."

"I bet, and it is beautiful here. Peaceful too." All that rain had soaked the ground but left the grass and surrounding trees with a vibrant-green look that didn't match the late-summer season. "I can't believe I didn't know about this place growing up. It's not that far from the city."

"Yeah, me neither." Levi raised an eyebrow. "We should invite them to set up a booth at Marcus's open house."

"Oh yeah, good idea. If you don't think he'll mind."

"You know Marcus. The more, the merrier. Besides, it's like you said, the goal is to raise friends, not funds."

Riley's mind was buzzing with all the angles she could spin this in a marketing campaign when Mrs. Reyes came their way in a golf cart from the smaller of the two barns. The gelding knickered at her approach, tossing his head up and down ecstatically. "Someone's ready for dinner," she said with a laugh.

Riley's best guess was that Mrs. Reyes was around her mom's age, maybe a bit younger. She had sun-aged skin with a splattering of freckles across her nose and the top of her cheeks that were as welcoming as her smile.

"Sorry about making you wait," she said after letting go of the pedal and the electric whir of the cart silenced. "That storm put us back a bit."

Levi huffed. "It was some storm."

"You can say that again. Turns out a tornado touched down less than ten miles from here," Mrs. Reyes said. "A family who has adopted horses from here a few times before lost the roof of their barn and a whole section of fence along with it, so we've got a handful of horses coming in tonight now too. We've been playing musical chairs with some of our stock to clear out a paddock for a few days for them."

"Wow. I bet we weren't that far from there. It was bad enough we had to pull over." Riley was as quick to look away from Levi as she'd been to glance in his direction. If she let herself recall the intimacy of the experience in her car, she'd lose her train of thought. "We couldn't see it, but we heard it."

"With any luck, it wasn't on the ground long. Out here, we tend to get besieged with strays and surrenders in tornado season every bit as much as we do when it floods."

Riley humphed. "I don't have any experience on the livestock side of rescue, but now that you say it, that makes sense."

Mrs. Reyes smiled. "You'd be surprised how many people around here have never even heard of us, but as most people east of Franklin County don't exactly have a spot for livestock, I guess that makes sense."

"Well, that doesn't mean you couldn't get a bunch of new supporters if more people knew about you."

Mrs. Reyes let out a huff. "We try, believe me. I guess like a lot of nonprofits, we're understaffed, so getting the word out can be a struggle."

"I'm sure." After warding off the gelding who'd begun to chomp her hair with his lips again, Riley motioned toward her car where the pigs were still crated inside, having settled into a doze again after the storm passed. "Speaking of getting the word out, as long as you're good with it, I'll do a post tomorrow in follow-up about how you all stepped up to take the pigs. I'll highlight your organization while I'm at it."

"That'd be great. I've been following High Grove's posts for years. You guys are an inspiration for us here, as much community awareness as you do."

Riley felt a rush of warmth at being connected with the shelter in such a way, not just as a returning volunteer but as a staff member—even if a temporary one. "I'm new there, so I'm not taking credit for any of it, but they really do a great job, don't they?"

"A friend of ours who runs Coleman Boarding and Training is having an open house later this month, just outside St. Louis County," Levi offered. "It's not equipped for these guys," he added with a nod toward the gelding. "But you could bring some pigs and chickens and pass out flyers." He motioned toward the townhouse-sized, multistory chicken coop at the edge of the gravel parking lot where a handful of colorful hens and roosters were pecking about their enclosure.

"Oh yeah? Well, I wouldn't put that stress on the chickens, but if we have the staffing, we could bring a mini pony or two and the piglets, if they're still around, or Morti. He's one of our resident potbellied pigs."

Levi grinned. "Marcus'll love it."

Mrs. Reyes nodded. "Well, it sounds like it could do us some good. Once we get your piglets settled, I'll check our calendar."

Riley and Levi headed for Riley's car, and Levi eased the kennel out of the back as Riley grabbed her phone from the center console to snap some pictures. "They have an observant air about them, don't they?" he noted.

"Pigs are smarter than most people give them credit for," Mrs. Reyes said from where she was still seated on the golf cart. "Smarter than dogs, smarter than three-year-olds, if you believe it. Smarter than horses, that's for sure," she added, "and I'm a horse lover. Before you go, you'll have to meet Morti. He's our therapy pig. A few of our volunteers take him into schools, even."

"A therapy pig? I definitely want his picture. I knew they were smart, but I had no idea pigs were being used in therapy."

"The kids love him, and they always ask to have him back. He's a gentleman, I'll give him that."

"That's cool. Well, after just one day with these little ones, I get it. I'm so glad to know they'll be going to a good home." Riley slipped her phone into her pocket after spying a missed call from Kelsey. She'd call her back when they got on the road.

Riley and Levi piled into the golf cart at Mrs. Reyes's invitation, Levi taking the rear-facing back seat and settling the crate next to him.

Unlike the larger barn which Levi and Riley had taken a quick walk through upon arrival, the smaller barn at the opposite end of the gravel parking lot was full of a menagerie of animals, including miniature horses and ponies, a few donkeys, several pigs, turtles, goats, geese, and a handful of rabbits in wire cages in the center aisle.

"Depending on how long they're here, we'll move them to one of the larger stalls with access to an outdoor run, but for now, they'll have an indoor stall with fresh bedding every morning."

"Do you tend to have problems placing them?"

"Ones this age? No, not typically. They practically fly out of here. It's when they're older like Morti that people pass them by. But I bet you get that at High Grove too."

"We do, but thankfully we get a lot of people committed to adopting senior animals too."

The piglets' new home, even if a temporary one, was warm and inviting with plenty of bedding, fresh hay, food and water bowls, even a few balls of various sizes and colors, but they had no interest in checking out their new digs. To get them out of the cage, Riley needed to kneel by the door and coax them.

After Mrs. Reyes stepped away to get ready for the arrival of the horses, the pigs tentatively made their way out of the crate, though they clung next to Riley for the first few minutes. When they finally began exploring their new surroundings, Levi started to close the travel-crate door. "Want to leave them the stuffed pig?"

"Good thinking. If anything, it's something safe and familiar."

Once the pigs were settled in, and Riley had gotten a handful of photos of them in their new digs, she walked around the barn taking photos of their barn mates, including Morti, who seemed to be every bit the character Mrs. Reyes promised he was. Rather than being confined to a stall, he had free rein of the barn and surrounding area and was currently camped out in the front of the geese, slipping in and out of a doze with what looked like a lazy grin on his face.

Riley had just snapped a picture of a somewhat cantankerous looking donkey with the long, furry ears when her phone rang. "I'd better get this," she told Levi, spying Kelsey's number. "It's a coworker from the shelter. Bet she wants to make sure we made it here after that storm."

"Yeah, sure." Levi had paused near a pair of miniature horses and was tickling the friendliest one's upper lip, making it quiver.

"Hey, Kels," Riley said, answering on the third ring. "Sorry I didn't have a chance to call you back yet. We were late getting here."

"Yeah, no problem. I wouldn't have called again, but I wanted you to know he was found. It's all a big mess, but—"

"Wait, I didn't listen to your message yet. *Who* was found?"

"Arlo. I figured you'd want to know he was missing."

"Oh my gosh. I had no idea, and absolutely. Thanks for calling and thank goodness he was found. What happened?"

"From what she shared, his owner was out walking him, and he just bolted. I guess it was the second time he got away from her since she took him home Saturday, only this time, with the storms, he kept running and didn't stop."

"Thank God he's okay!" Catching Levi's concerned expression, she lifted the phone away long enough to whisper what had happened.

"Well, that's the thing," Kelsey continued, hesitation lining her tone. "They say he's being a trooper, but he ran right in front of a car. The driver hit the brakes but still hit him—not badly—but he's a little banged up, it seems."

Riley clamped a hand over her mouth. *Not Arlo!* "Oh no!"

"The driver dialed 911, and animal control was brought in. They called us since his chip hasn't been processed over to his new owner's name yet."

Tears stung Riley's eyes. "Where is he?"

"That's the second reason I called you. Aren't you out near Washington?"

"Yeah, we're still here."

"They took him to a twenty-four-hour veterinary center that's maybe ten or fifteen minutes from you. If you're interested in stopping by, I'll text you the address."

"Yeah, absolutely, but what's he doing way out here? I thought his new owner lived in the city."

"She does. I think she was at a sister's or something. The thing is, when I got a hold of her and told her he'd been hit, she broke down. She says he's just too much dog for her, and she wants to surrender him back into our care."

Riley felt like a mountain of dominoes was both falling and lining up at the same time. Arlo was being let down by those whose care he was in a second time. But also for the last time. "Text the address, will you? We'll be on our way in ten minutes."

Levi was watching her and nodded his agreement even though he couldn't fully know what he was agreeing to. That was the thing about Levi. He'd always been the adventurous sort. If she was about to ask him to drive with her to Kansas City, it was unlikely he'd have a single complaint.

Before hanging up, she thanked Kelsey again for calling her and promised to keep her posted. Slipping her phone back into her pocket, she turned to Levi, whose normally playful expression was void of everything but empathy at the moment. "He was hit by a car, but he's okay. At least, they told Kelsey he's okay. I'd like to go to the veterinary center where they've got him and see for myself. It turns out it isn't far from here."

"Wherever it is, we'll go." He pulled her into a hug. "I'm sorry, Riley. I know what he means to you."

His kind words picked at a splinter of guilt. "I should've adopted him." She lingered in his arms, soaking in his strength in hopes it would ease her frayed nerves. She'd be falling asleep for a week with images of a terrified Arlo running out in front of a moving car. "I know I'll love a hundred dogs who pass through the shelter doors before it's over, but he's different. The last two days I've done little else but regret not finding a way to keep him. I know it sounds crazy, but it just feels like he's supposed to be in my life. It has since the morning I found him."

Levi wrapped both arms tighter around her and pressed his lips against her forehead. "If it helps, I don't think that sounds a bit crazy. How could I when I know that feeling so well?" His words took her off guard enough that she pulled back to meet his gaze, a different sort of adrenaline warming her veins. This Levi showing up now, the one he worked so hard to hide from the world behind a mask of playfulness, this was the one she'd fallen for. She was still choosing the right words to respond when he added, "The thing is, some second chances take a bit longer to come around than others, so I'm for going all out when they do."

Riley blinked away the tears stinging her eyes. "Even if this one comes with a 110-pound Great Dane who doesn't much seem to like being walked on a leash?"

"I've always wanted to date a girl who owns a Great Dane," he said, that easy grin returning.

"Have you really?"

"I do now. Maybe a bit more than dating too."

Heart pounding in her chest, Riley brushed her thumb along Levi's lower lip. "You sound… confident."

"It's easy to be confident when you know what you want."

"Since we're being honest here, I know what I want too. What my heart wants. I want to adopt a dog even though I don't have a place to keep him. And I want to give this thing between us my best shot." When she pressed her lips against his, she was serenaded by a string of happy grunts from Morti, who'd woken up from his doze and was sauntering over to check out the new arrivals.

Chapter 21

Riley gave Levi credit for not going stir crazy in the sterile waiting room with its stark lighting, hard plastic chairs, and the handful of brightly colored cat and dog pictures punctuating its sterility rather than softening it. She remembered sitting across the room from him in precalculus and noticing the way some part of him was always moving, whether it was an ankle bouncing or fingers twirling a pencil. She suspected he still resisted confinement every bit as much as before, but for the last twenty-five minutes, he'd been planted in the seat next to her, his hand on her leg, his thumb gently caressing the top of her thigh.

Riley had no intention of budging, at least not until she had an opportunity to speak to the vet treating Arlo, and it seemed Levi was committed to waiting it out with her. She doubted he was even aware of the hard looks he kept giving the two receptionists behind the counter, the ones doing anything but acknowledging Riley as she waited for an answer to her plea to see Arlo. Or at least be made privy to his condition.

She and Levi weren't alone in the waiting room

this late in the day on a Monday, and a holiday Monday at that. Given that it was well after 5:00 p.m. and typical business hours were over, the only people showing up now were doing so for urgent matters and picking up animals who were going home this evening. Currently, an older man with his very unhappy kitty, who was making her plight known from the confines of her soft-sided crate, was seated on the opposite wall. Not long ago, a twenty-something and her pet Chihuahua who'd gotten in a scrape with a neighboring cat had been called into a room, and two people had come in to pick up dogs who'd been neutered today.

"You hungry?" Riley asked, nudging Levi gently with her elbow.

He shrugged. "Not too bad, though that vending machine by the bathrooms is starting to call my name. You?"

"I'm okay, but looking on the bright side, wherever we end up shouldn't have a wait list any longer."

He cocked an eyebrow. "You mean closing in on eight o'clock on a Monday isn't prime dining?"

"You've got a point, but it's a Monday that's more like a Sunday, so there could've been dinner crowds."

"I hadn't thought about that. You're off tomorrow, right?" When Riley nodded, he added, "Good. I'll take you out to breakfast. My mom told me about a place you'll like."

Riley nodded, letting this settle in, both that he was talking to his mom about her and that she was unclear if this meant he was assuming they'd still be together come morning or if he figured he'd be picking her up from her parents'. After a quick debate as to which way she'd prefer the next twelve hours to play out, she decided it was more complicated than any split-second decision she could come up with on the fly. "Sounds good."

Actually, she knew exactly which way she wanted them to play out, but the part of her that always stayed in control noted the difference between what was wanted and what was right. "If you're really hungry, we could order take out and eat in the parking lot or something."

"We're kind of in BFE," he said, "but we can look." He pulled out his phone and typed in "restaurants near me."

Riley leaned her head against his shoulder as he scrolled through the search results.

"Looks like anything decent is a good ten to fifteen minutes in either direction," he said.

Lifting her head, she blinked at him teasingly. "Then how about I treat you to something in the vending machine to tide us over?"

Levi had just agreed when a woman in scrubs and an overcoat pushed through the swinging door behind the receptionists' counter and leaned in to confirm something with one of the two young people working the desk. After a second, she nodded and looked at Riley. "You're with High Grove?"

Riley popped up from her seat like she'd just sat on a stove, figuring she was one of the vets on duty even before confirming so on her name tag. "I am. We were in the area and wanted to know how Arlo's doing."

Dr. Patel gave a single nod. "He was brought to us by county animal control, but I understand the Dane recently moved through your facility?"

"Yeah, he was adopted out Saturday after being with us just over a week, but I don't think the transition has been easy." Riley was normally a glass half-full sort, but the downturned look on the woman's face was less than promising. "The woman who adopted him wants to surrender him back into our care. Like I said to your receptionist, we can take him tonight if he's okay to leave. If not, I'd really like to see him."

The vet stared unblinkingly. She had a look about her that was every bit as severe and sterile as this waiting room. "I understand, but there's both the matter of current ownership, and of who's footing his bill. I'm not able to disclose anything about his condition until I can determine the former, and the latter will need to be worked out before he's cleared to leave, as his bill will need to be paid in full."

Riley pulled out her phone, hoping for a new

text or email from Kelsey but not finding it. "We're working on the ownership part. The woman gave a verbal surrender, and she's been emailed a surrender form to sign."

"And until she signs and returns it, there's nothing I can share with you. As Monica told you when you came in."

A childlike urge to scream and stamp her feet rushed over her. *Is this woman for real? She doesn't even blink.*

Beside her, Levi shook his head and let out a "Sheesh." He flattened a hand on the counter hard enough that it came across as a smack. "Seriously? Can't you cut the crap and tell us if he's okay?"

Riley put a hand on his arm. "Hold on a sec. I have an idea." Straightening her shoulders, she turned to the vet. "Look, we get it. That's the world we live in. So don't tell us a thing. *Blink* it."

Riley didn't think it was her imagination that this was the first time since the conversation started that Dr. Patel blinked. "Pardon?"

"One blink for yes, two for no, three for you don't know."

Dr. Patel shook her head. "I don't play blinking games."

"This isn't a game. I love that dog back there more than I ever thought I could, and I should've been the one to adopt him. Whether it's me paying for your services or the shelter doing so and me reimbursing them, I intend to adopt him the second I'm able. So, what I need to know more than anything right now is if he's okay."

Dr. Patel had opened her mouth in what looked as if it would come out in an objection. A second later, she closed it and blinked rapidly.

"I'm sorry. Can we start over?" Riley asked. "That was a lot of blinks, more than three, I think."

"I wasn't ready." After a glance at the only other patient currently in the waiting room, the old man waiting for his unhappy kitty to be seen, she blinked again several times and held up a finger. "I still wasn't ready. Ask again."

Riley's hands knotted into fists in anticipation. "Alright. Is Arlo okay?"

Dr. Patel leaned forward an inch and blinked deeply a single time. There was something undeniably comical in the moment, and Riley spotted Levi clamping a hand over his mouth, but given the circumstances, she was too relieved by the single blink to be swayed by humor. "Thank God." After collecting herself, she added, "Can I see him?"

Blink blink.

Riley's shoulders sank. "Was anything broken?"

Dr. Patel pursed her lips before blinking three times.

Riley took a breath, processing this. "He's okay, and maybe something's broken," she said to which Dr. Patel gave something like a nod.

"Did you take X-rays?" Levi asked.

Dr. Patel's pointed glance Levi's direction communicated quite clearly that she hadn't agreed to play the blinking game with him too; however, she blinked once before turning her attention back to Riley.

"No internal bleeding though?" Riley confirmed. "Or you wouldn't have nodded that he's okay?"

Blink.

"Shoot, was that blink for the last part of the question? That he's not bleeding internally or anything terrible like that?"

Blink.

Relief flooded her as Riley's largest worry was alleviated. "Thank you. This helps a lot." She swept her hair over her shoulder. "Look, you're open twenty-four hours, and we'll be here until he can either go home, or we can see him, but thank you for this. If you think of anything else you want to blink, you know where to find us."

Dr. Patel looked over at the man who was waiting and then at her two receptionists who both seemed to be trying hard to look busy while clearly hanging on every word playing out before them. After shooting a deliberate glance Riley's direction, Dr. Patel held up a finger before disappearing through the door.

Riley grabbed Levi's hand in anticipation, hoping she'd pop back through with Arlo. Levi squeezed it reassuringly. "This was a great idea, Riley," he murmured. "Here's to thinking on your feet."

"Thanks. You know what they say about the mother of necessity."

Riley's swelling hopes burst when Dr. Patel walked through the door alone less than two minutes later, but they lifted again when she held up a phone their direction with a picture of Arlo inside a large stainless-steel cage. He was awake, eyes wide, and he was curled into as much of a ball as he could get himself into.

Riley leaned forward. "May I?"

Dr. Patel blinked, and Riley lifted the phone from her hand, expanding the picture to get a closer look at the two large patches of missing hair and scrapes on his shoulder and hip and what looked like a boot brace on his back left leg. A wash of tears flooded out as she held the image out for Levi to have a better look as well.

"Thank you," she said, offering the phone back to Dr. Patel. "Thank you *so* much."

Dr. Patel nodded and whispered something to one of the receptionists before disappearing through the door again. The receptionist stood up and nodded toward the old man with the cat. "We're ready for you now, Mr. Timms."

As the man shuffled off with his cat, he gave them a nod as he passed by. "You know, sometimes I get to thinking how everything's going to hell in a handbasket, but when I see things like this, it gives me hope. You youngins have got a resourcefulness about you that's inspiring."

After thanking him, Riley offered well-wishes about his unhappy kitty. After he'd passed through the side door, she collapsed against Levi. "Arlo's okay. He's *going to be* okay. He hardly looked that much worse for the wear, don't you think?"

Levi's arms locked around her. "Yeah, he looked really alert, and that's a good sign. A lot of times, it's the shock they fall into after trauma that proves to be the worst thing that hits them."

"I was most worried about internal bleeding, but now that you say it, I remember hearing that about shock."

"But he's doing okay, that's what you need to hold on to. And that boot he was in, I had a dog who needed to wear one once. I'm guessing the potential break is in one of his foot bones or an ankle bone. Not a terrible injury to have."

"Oh yeah? How long did it take your dog to heal?"

The fact that he was quick to look away told her as much as his answer. "His case was a little different, so a bit longer than expected."

Levi had never been big on posting pictures on social media, but in his random and infrequent posts over the years, a chocolate Lab had been the star of most of them. Yet, in the few times she'd seen Levi recently, not a single thing had come up about the dog. Riley suddenly felt ashamed for not having asked about the dog sooner, but at the same time, something guarded in his expression gave her the sense that it was likely by design that the dog hadn't been brought up.

"So, vending machine time?" Levi asked, running a hand over his stomach. "My tank is officially empty."

Now that the adrenaline was beginning to fade, she was experiencing equal waves of exhaustion and hunger. "Mine too. I don't think I've eaten anything out of a vending machine since college, but a Snickers and a bag of Cheez-Its are equally calling my name. A root beer too."

"Oh yeah? I think I'm going for a Slim Jim, some Doritos, and a Twix."

"And let me guess, you'll wash them down with a Mountain Dew?"

He winked as they headed down the hall. "You got me."

"I'm glad some things about you are still exactly the same."

"Why's that?"

A rush of vulnerability threatened to lock up her throat, but she pushed through it. "Because that way I don't feel as bad about the twelve years that've slipped away."

He locked a hand over her shoulder. "At the risk of sounding like an overeducated millennial working in a coffee shop, the only thing that matters in all this is right now."

Riley raised an eyebrow as they reached the vending machines. "Barista philosophy or not, I think that's exactly what I needed to hear."

Chapter 22

AS HE SANK INTO THE PASSENGER SEAT OF RILEY'S Mini, Levi figured this wasn't the time to point out the merits of driving a truck. Arlo took up every inch of space across the back seat, his booted back leg was lifted awkwardly to the side, but he fit, and Riley had been through enough today not to be messed with.

The interior already smelled like nervous dog, and Arlo's anxious panting promised it wasn't going to get any better anytime soon. Riley hadn't yet turned on the ignition, so Levi left his door open in the mostly empty parking lot. It was just after 8:30 p.m., and the sun had set, though full darkness hadn't yet set in.

"Well, he isn't officially mine, but he isn't someone else's any longer either." Riley gave a little nod as she said it. "And most importantly, he's okay."

"That he is, and he's clearly happy to be with his human." Arlo's gaze was glued on Riley like she'd vanish if he glanced away. It had been something the way the giant of a dog had whined like a baby upon seeing her a few minutes ago. There was a connection there, no question. A dog and his person.

A sliver of pain stabbed at Levi, recalling the way Tank had come to cue off him in his adult years, after some of that wild puppy energy had faded. It was the first time Levi had become privy to the way two different species could so easily communicate. Like the way Tank would start to stare him down, thumping his tail, hoping for a late-evening walk or a run on the beach when Levi lazed around too long after a tiring day in the water, or the way, even when off leash, Tank would flank Levi's side at the sound of Levi's hand clapping twice against his thigh, beckoning him without words.

Riley deserved that too. Whatever this turned out to be between her and him again— and he had specific hopes—he'd never begrudge her decision to go to the ends of the earth to keep this charismatic canine. She hadn't so much as flinched at paying a four-figure vet bill even though she had nowhere to keep him officially, and the adoption paperwork hadn't yet been completed.

"This so isn't me," she said, as if reading his thoughts, "to leap before looking. I mean, I don't have a place of my own, and my mom's anything but a dog person." Levi was about to throw out a suggestion she may or may not be ready for when she continued. "And my employment's temporary. Like really temporary." She raised her eyebrows. "And I have no idea where I'll end up."

"Why not stay here?"

Riley looked down at her hands. "A week ago, I could've given you a laundry list of reasons why staying in St. Louis would never work, most of them having to do with things that happened a long time ago that were out of my control."

"And now?"

"I don't know. Maybe it should be an option. I know my family would love that. She's doing good, but my mom's breast cancer diagnosis got me realizing my parents aren't going to be around forever. And I've made friends everywhere I've gone, but I've never had a friend like Lana, and her kids are flipping adorable. I'd love to spend more time with them."

"I know what you mean. I've missed a lot of time with my sister, and who knows where she's headed next year."

"Whenever I think about staying though, I feel the need to strap on linebacker-sized emotional padding. But ever since Friday night... That whole gang of guys you brought to the bowling event, not a one of them could've cared less what kind of gossip there was about our parents back in high school. I don't know if that was your plan all along, but it's got me thinking that maybe instead of trying so hard to distance myself from it, I could...I don't know..." She shrugged. "Just let it go."

After letting her words hang in the air for several seconds, Levi leaned over and brushed his lips across her brow. He sensed she wasn't looking for an affirmation, not with something this big. She was thinking about it, processing it, and he was here if she needed him.

Behind them, Arlo's nervous panting had slowed somewhat, and he was looking back and forth between them like he was attempting to discern the underlying mood of what was playing out before him. When he whined softly, Riley turned to give him a scratch under the chin.

"I just hope my mom is in bed when I get home, so I can sneak him upstairs tonight and explain all this tomorrow. Assuming her cats don't call me out first, which is the more likely scenario if I'm being honest."

Levi grinned at that last part. "You're doing the right thing, Riley."

"Thanks, I'll remind myself of that in the middle of night when I'm explaining Arlo to my parents. In all honesty, it's kind of like moving a pony in without asking. At least he's potty trained, right?"

"How about making sure you don't have to tell her tonight?"

Her mouth fell open half an inch as she searched his gaze. "How would I do that?"

"Well, for one thing, there's Marcus's place. You could stay there tonight. That spare bed I've been sleeping on will fit you better than it fits me. We could swing by somewhere and pick up the biggest dog bed they make—or two, if needed."

"What about you?"

He shrugged. "The couch will be fine."

"I wouldn't want to put you out like that."

"Considering how much I've been looking forward all weekend to tonight, extending our date into tomorrow isn't putting me out one bit, regardless of where I catch some shut-eye." Riley was still processing this when he took a leap. "Option two is to mix things up a bit and get a pet-friendly hotel. I'm betting all three of us could use a night off from our new norms."

Riley switched her gaze from Levi to Arlo. Considering what had just happened in this car earlier tonight, clearly, she knew where a decision like this might lead so long as she wanted it to. "I didn't exactly plan for that sort of thing when I headed out today, if you know what I mean."

"If it helps, we can always swing by your parents' and grab your things." When she didn't seem too excited by that prospect, he added, "Of course, you could aways sleep in your clothes, if that's less complicated. Or *not* in your clothes. I'd be good with that."

She bit her lip to lock down a smile. "Speaking of leaping before looking…"

"If you ask me, twelve years ago, that might've been leaping without looking. Not this."

"What is this then?"

She shifted her gaze from his eyes to his mouth,

so it was all too easy to start kissing her again. He locked a hand in the back of her hair and brushed his lips over hers. "This? This is getting things back on track, that's all."

If she had a difference of opinion, she was too busy returning his kiss to reply, and Arlo was shoving his big head into the mix, sniffing their hair and tickling them by sticking his wet nose in their ears, and Levi figured if he wanted any privacy with the woman he loved, he'd be needing to secure a room with two queen beds, because their back-seat companion was going to take up one of them.

───────────

As she pulled into the circular drop-off for the hotel, Riley forced down the butterflies fluttering up her throat. This was really happening. She reminded herself that her choice of "option two" had as much to do with Arlo needing a good night's sleep after his ordeal as it did her dreaming for the last twelve years about having another chance to lounge in a bed next to Levi—a chance to unweave the tapestry of life and create an entirely new pattern.

"Pretty place you found," she offered. The hotel Levi had snagged using an app was a newer one in the outskirts of St. Louis County in Wildwood and looked like it would fit right in to the mountainous hillsides of Europe as much as it did here, with its peaked roofline and spires sticking up into the night. "A bit too pretty to haul in my stash of toiletries in my reusable bags, don't you think?" A laugh escaped at the thought of her looking like a character in a Jeff Foxworthy joke.

She'd opted not to waste time heading home to her parents' house to pack a bag and instead popped into Target after the pet store to snag an assortment of travel-sized toiletries and a short-sleeve nightshirt that read "Dog Mom." Considering she'd spotted it just minutes after Kelsey sent a text confirming that she could wait to fill out the paperwork until she worked Wednesday but that Megan had said to consider Arlo hers, it seemed fated for her. Since Levi had been hanging outside with Arlo, and the question of birth control had yet to be discussed, she'd also erred on the side of caution and grabbed a box of condoms.

Levi shrugged in response to her comment about the bags. "What're they going to do? Turn down their noses at us? If it makes you feel better, let's get him settled, and I'll run back out for your stuff before I head out for food."

Riley flipped off the ignition and fished her keys from her purse to pass them Levi's direction. The vending-machine visit hadn't quite done the trick for either of them, and he'd been talking food options as Riley drove. They'd settled on pizza in the room, though Riley suspected this bout of nerves would chase her hunger pangs away for some time. Reminding herself that Levi had already seen her without her clothes on wasn't entirely helpful. Last time, she'd been eighteen, an age that was considerably more synonymous with tight and perky than a few weeks until thirty.

Once his door was opened, Arlo took a bit of coaxing to clamber out of the back seat, his booted back leg mostly going along for the ride. "Poor baby. I bet you're sore as all get out."

Up close, the hairless patches of skin looked more like rugburn than cuts, and the vet had promised that his dislike of using his booted leg had more to do with the apparatus than it did injury. "He limped less before we put it on him," she'd insisted, "but he'll heal faster this way. From what I was told, the driver really slammed his brakes when Arlo dashed into the street. So much so, she was nearly hit from behind. The impact could've been much worse."

Free from the car, Arlo shook himself off hard enough that he sent a trail of slobber flying that missed Riley by less than a foot. She gave Levi a wide-eyed look as he laughed heartily. "You got lucky there. That wouldn't have been pretty."

Riley held the leash tight as they headed through the sliding glass doors to the ornate lobby with cherrywood paneling, granite counters, and a towering vase of flowers. Arlo was hesitant to enter but allowed himself to be coaxed inside while staying glued to Riley's side.

The receptionist, an older woman who looked to have enough hair spray to keep her hair in place in a high wind, had been typing but stopped to gawk at Arlo. "What a monster of a dog! And with a boo-boo too. I'm honestly not quite sure what to make of him."

"He's a Great Dane," Riley offered, "and he's a sweetie."

As they crossed the otherwise empty lobby, the woman dug around for something behind the counter and held up a bone-shaped dog treat. "Would he like one?"

"Thanks, I bet he would." Riley took it as Levi fished out a card from his wallet, but Arlo was too busy eyeing the towering vase of flowers like there might be a goblin hiding inside them to do more than give the treat a quick sniff. "I'm sure he'll love it later. He's a bit slow to warm up to new things."

"What do you make of that? A big dog like that nothing more than a scaredy-cat. Who'd a thought it? Not me. Even so, I have no complaints at staying on this side of the counter," the woman said before taking Levi's card and typing his name into her reservation system. A few seconds later she gave a nod. "Levi Duncan, I've found you." She looked up over the top of her glasses. "And where do you all hail from?"

Levi shot Riley a quick glance before answering,

"Webster Groves, actually." It was the simplest answer to a complicated story.

Her eyebrows lifted slightly. "Not far at all, then."

Levi had the look of someone about to say it was none of her business where they hailed from when Riley placed a hand on the back of his shoulder and answered for both of them. "Not far. We're just looking forward to a relaxing night away."

Lips pursing slightly, the woman turned back to her screen. "Two queen beds?" When Levi nodded, she spouted off a reminder that the rooms were all nonsmoking and that there was a two-hundred-dollar incidental deposit being charged to his card. "Nine times out of ten, it's human activities and not animal ones that cause our guests not to be refunded their deposit," she added.

Riley suspected it was Levi's way of meeting attitude with attitude when he winked in Riley's direction. "I won't argue that."

Before Arlo had decided whether goblins were in fact hiding in the flower vase, Levi was handed the card to the room. As they headed down the long, quiet hall, Riley poked him playfully in the back. "All I can say is good thing we weren't hauling a bunch of grocery bags in with us. She'd have turned us down flat."

Levi shook his head. "Well, I for one am about to take great pleasure hauling in every shopping bag in your car right in front of her."

Riley laughed. "If it makes you happy, but not the dog bed, at least, seeing as to how he won't need it tonight."

Their room was at the far end of the hall, and Levi held the door open with a wink. "After you."

Riley headed in with Arlo sticking close enough that he kept stepping on her toes. His tentative whine petered off when she flipped on all the lights and unhooked his leash. He sniffed deeply, looking around without stepping further in.

The room was well decorated, and the two queen beds looked clean and cozy with their down comforters and mounds of pillows. Levi's hand landed on Riley's hip the exact second the heavy door swung shut, making her jump. "Nice room, don't you think?" he said. "Even if that receptionist was competing for world's most nosey."

Riley's arms locked in front of her before she was aware she'd done so. It was entirely too easy to imagine a wild escapade in the nicely tiled shower or underneath—or even on top of—those fluffy comforters. "Pretty. And clean."

Levi fished out his wallet and handed over his credit card. "How about you call in the pizza while I grab the bags? Then you can get busy doing whatever it is you want to do with all that stuff you bought while I run and pick it up."

Suppressing a laugh, Riley placed a finger-tip against the tip of his chin. "For the record, no one's going to be voting for you as world's most romantic."

"Never say never."

"So, I've heard." Riley slipped the card into her pocket. "Normally, I'd buy the pizza since you paid for this," she said with a nod toward the beds, "but considering I've charged more on my card for this dog tonight than I typically do in a month, I'll let you be the gentleman and pay for this whole… whatever you call it because 'date' isn't flying off the tongue for any of this tonight."

After Levi stepped out and the door closed behind him, Arlo looked at Riley questioningly, those expressive brows knitting into peaks. Riley walked over to the nearest bed and patted it in case he was waiting for a cue to join her. "You being here cost an extra forty dollars, so I'm guessing they don't mind a little bit of hair on the comforter."

Arlo tottered over without losing a beat and clambered up onto the bed.

"Guess what, you sweet thing? It may take a week or two to sink in for both of us, but I'm adopting you. Considering how cautious they are with adoptions and how I have no idea where I'm keeping you after tonight, clearly I'm getting an insider perk. But all things in time, right?"

After circling the bed a few times, Arlo laid down with an exaggerated grunt, leaning his shoulder heavily enough against Riley that she needed to brace her feet on the floor not to slide right off the bed.

"You seem even bigger this way than you do standing, if you'd like to know." She was practically looking him straight in those expressive eyes. After a minute or two, Arlo stretched out with a whine and laid his sizeable head on her lap, his eyes open and watchful. "What an adventure you've had the last few weeks. I wonder if you're still wondering when you'll go home?"

Knowing there was no use putting it off, Riley placed a call to her mom after she'd finished the pizza order. There was little chance of her mom answering her cell since she hardly ever had it with her when she was home, but Riley tried it first anyway. Her parents still had an ancient landline that her dad was a quick to answer as her mom, and this wasn't a conversation Riley wanted to have with him.

Brenda answered her cell on the third ring. "Hey babe, what's up?"

There was noise in the background, other adults talking. "Do you have people over? Is this a bad time?"

"No, it's fine. We're still over at the Reynolds."

Surprise rolled over her before she remembered that her parents had been invited to a Labor Day barbeque with a few other families from the neighborhood, something they'd done dozens and dozens of times over the years. Nothing risqué about it, even if, God forbid, they were still living a night life Riley wanted to know nothing about. *They aren't. There's no way.*

"Oh, yeah, well, I won't keep you, but I wanted you to know I'm staying out tonight. With a friend." Levi was a friend, wasn't he? "I didn't want you to worry."

As much as she didn't want to admit it, if she wanted to let go of this thing her parents had done once and for all, she was going to have to have a private and undoubtedly awkward conversation about it with her mom. Under no circumstances would she be including her dad in the mix. He'd never been one to talk about anything of any sensitivity with her—the birds and the bees, her period, teen abstinence, birth control, all those fun things parents like to drill into their children's heads. In Riley's family, those talks had always happened while her dad was at work or away on a business trip.

There was a second or two of silence on her mom's end that had Riley wondering if her mom had heard over the din of voices in the room when she said, "At Lana's?"

"Ah, no, not with Lana." Riley heard the door's electronic lock beeping unlocked the same time Arlo did, and he let out a baritone woof that hurt her ears.

"Did that come from an actual dog or a speaker? I don't think I've ever heard a dog bark that loud."

Levi began piling in with not only the shopping bags from earlier, but also with every reusable tote in her trunk, and the satisfied grin on his face showed he'd made the impression he'd wanted to make.

Shaking her head, she held up a finger and mouthed, "One minute." To her mom, she said, "A dog. A Great Dane, actually. The one I told you about."

"I thought he'd been adopted."

"Long story, but he was returned."

"Oh, that's a shame. Well, I won't keep you, but I'd love to hear more about it tomorrow, but where did you say you were staying?"

"I didn't, actually. This is me not wanting you to worry about my not coming home tonight while being an almost thirty-year-old and maintaining a bit of privacy in my life."

"Oh. Okay." There was another slight pause. "Well, call if you need anything. And be safe."

"I will. See you tomorrow." After a split second of deliberation, she added, "Have fun tonight."

"Thanks. We're heading home soon. This radiation has bumped up my bedtime up an hour, no question. Talk to you tomorrow."

Riley hung up and patted Arlo on the chest, a hollow thump filling the room as she smiled at the still-smirking Levi. "I see you made your point. You look like a cross between a homeless person and a hoarder."

He grinned, plopping the bags on the credenza. "And you called your mom."

"That I did, and thankfully she stopped herself before it turned into twenty questions. I ordered the pizza too. It'll be ready in about forty minutes."

"Nice on both counts."

Riley slid out from underneath Arlo's cuddle puddle and joined Levi at the credenza. "I bet he's starving." She fished out Arlo's new stainless-steel food and water bowls. As she did, it hit her that Levi had undoubtedly spotted the condoms near the top of the tote.

"You know, I came with a few of my own," he said as if reading her thoughts, "but I was glad to see we wouldn't run out."

Pretending to misunderstand him, Riley held up the two bowls. "Oh yeah? These should do just fine." Doing her best to hide a smile, she headed for the bathroom sink to wash them out.

Arlo's ears perked forward so much that they were nearly touching as he followed the bowls with his gaze. When she disappeared behind the door, he clambered down from the bed, letting out a whine in the process.

Perhaps sensing the nerves suddenly hitting her, Levi let the joke slide. "Poor guy has to be sore, but man is he lucky. Running in front of a car could've had much worse consequences."

"That's what keeps resonating with me." Riley

dried one bowl, leaving the second one filled with water. Carrying them in, she placed both next to the wall beside the credenza, then worked free the thick string to open the kibble as Arlo lapped up water. Figuring she'd work on manners after he had a night or two of rest between him and the accident, she allowed him to dive in as she was filling the food bowl.

"Wow," she said, seeing the vigor in which he ate. "Makes you wonder about the stress he'd been under."

"Yeah, it does."

With that done, Riley was struck with her second wave of "holy crap, this is happening" since pulling into the hotel. After closing the kibble the best she was able without a clip, Riley excused herself for the bathroom to wash her hands, no doubt putting entirely too much thought along the way as to whether to leave the door open and ending up doing so.

She closed her eyes as the warm water flowed over her hands, attempting to slow her rapidly beating heart as doubt rushed in. When she looked up, Levi was standing in the doorway, one hand resting on the top frame, watching her.

"I just wanted to say if you're second-guessing things, we can always stick to separate beds tonight."

Pressing her lips together, Riley nodded. "Thanks for saying that."

"Fair warning, I'm not an HGTV guy, as much

as I know most chicks dig it. I've been known to binge *The Food Network* though, and I'm always up for some old episodes of *Gunsmoke* or *Bonanza*. I'll even lose an hour or two in reruns of *The Brady Bunch*, here and there."

As Riley laughed, a bit of her nerves receded. Turning around, she rested against the counter while drying her hands. "Spoken like someone who's spent considerably more time watching hotel TV than me."

"True that."

After biting her lip a second, she went for the biggest truth she could muster. "Levi, I want this, I'm just a bit terrified. For more reasons than one."

"Tell me the biggest one then. If we can knock it out, maybe things won't seem so daunting."

The way he was leaning in the doorframe like that, Riley suspected nothing about him was daunted right now, but she summoned the courage to answer him truthfully. "How big this is, this thing between us. I think that's what scares me most."

"Yeah, well, I don't think anything I can say will take the energy off of that except for admitting I feel it too, and I'm pretty sure that's nothing more than an invitation to lean in." He stepped inside, his eyes dropping from her mouth to her body as he closed the distance between them. "What's the second thing? Maybe I can do a little better with that one."

Riley closed her eyes as his lips brushed her

forehead. "You did pretty darn good with the first one just now." His fingertips traced her cheekbone and her chin, and Riley locked her hands over his arms, relaxing into it.

"What else?" he murmured, his lips brushing her brow, then dipping to her nose, cheek, and lips. "I've got a solid twenty-five minutes to knock away at this bout of nerves before I need to head out for the pizza."

After what must've been a full minute of kissing, this second fear slipped out so easily, it hardly carried the weight it had been taking up inside her. "I guess there's the bit about getting naked in front of you twelve years later, and you figuring out I don't have the body of an eighteen-year-old anymore."

Levi slipped his hands under her T-shirt, letting them close around her waist as his kiss intensified. "I was hoping you'd give me an easy one. Yours is the only body I'm interested in seeing, and I can tell you right now I'm only going to be thinking good things."

Riley's head fell back as he kissed her neck before lifting off her shirt.

Finished with his dinner, Arlo came over and paused in the doorway, front legs splayed, cleaning off his jowls on the carpet after his meal. Then he stepped inside the bathroom, looking past the toilet into the tub as if to confirm there were no exits to worry about Riley slipping away from him.

Seemingly satisfied, he backed up and limped off to the bed, grunting again as he clambered on top.

When he was gone, Levi slid one bra strap off her shoulder, then the other. The overhead light was still on, a fluorescent one that didn't do a single good thing for her complexion, and she hadn't yet taken that shower she was hoping for, but Riley found herself not caring one bit any longer. Reaching back to unhook the straps, she let it fall off, the last of her worries slipping away with it. "It's been a while, but if memory serves, you really know how to make the most of twenty-five minutes, Mr. Duncan. I say we go for it."

"I can't think of a single thing I've wanted to do more for the better part of a decade," he murmured as his hands closed over her, "so you won't be hearing any complaints from me."

Chapter 23

THE MUTED TV CAST A SOFT GLOW OVER THE night-darkened room, and, from the other bed, Arlo's soft snores were an easy lullaby as Riley drifted closer to sleep. She was still getting used to being curled against Levi, whose even breathing almost perfectly matched Arlo's. An empty pizza box was on the counter, and the leftover slices of the pizza Levi had been nearly a half hour late picking up were in the mini fridge.

The world wasn't going to start pressing in here, she reminded herself. Not tonight, at least. The door was bolted, and no one knew they were here. Their silenced phones were on the desk, screen-side down. She was free to lie awake, soaking this in, this thing she'd all but dared never to hope for again.

The truth of it was, around Levi, Riley felt like a bubble getting bigger and bigger but never bursting. Her skin still tingled from all the places his hands and mouth had been, and her muscles were spent. No surprise, the physical stuff had been every bit as good as before. Come to think of it, it had been better, with none of the initial fear and discomfort hanging over her. Add to that, she knew her body better, and there was a confidence about him that suggested he'd had a good deal more practice figuring out how to please a woman too.

The bubble feeling threatened to deflate a touch, thinking of him with other women and of how, had she not run, perhaps there wouldn't have been any. But Levi was right about one thing. Wishing away the past wasn't the answer.

Letting any troubling thoughts fall away in the face of all that was right, Riley focused on the sensation of their bodies breathing in unison. Eventually, she must've dozed again because she woke up with a start when Arlo clambered onto their bed around two in the morning. He was turning in a circle, making it rock like a ship under his weight. After a bit, he lowered himself with the grunt that spoke of stiff, sore muscles. He sprawled across their legs and rested his twenty-pound head atop Riley's stomach.

Beside her, Levi had woken up and was dragging a hand over his face. "I've never woken up getting steamrolled by a Great Dane before."

"No kidding. My feet will be asleep in minutes if he doesn't move."

Stifling a yawn, Levi glanced at the clock on the side table between the beds. "Two o'clock? Man, was I out. Ever since the accident, when I crash, I crash hard. Sorry about that, seeing as I had plans to empty that whole box of condoms tonight."

Riley pressed her lips against his shoulder in a

kiss. "I think it's always important to know when good enough will do, don't you think?"

"Good enough, huh?" Levi twisted underneath Arlo's splayed body to face her. "Sounds like we've got room for improvement."

Ignoring this last bit, Riley planted a second kiss on his shoulder. A glance at the muted TV showed that *ET* was airing on the classic movie station, and Arlo had his head turned toward it, watching the wobbly but endearing alien meander around the house drunk on a beer, making her wonder if he thought ET was a dog with those pug-like eyes.

"How's your head now? Did that sleep ease your headache any?"

"Yeah, quite a bit." Levi draped an arm over her hip atop the comforter. "I'm good to go. If you'd like proof, I'm happy to offer it to you."

"Ha ha." Riley brushed her lips against his. "Maybe in a bit. If you're up for it, right now what I'd like is to talk about one of the things I have a feeling you don't much care to talk about."

"Oh yeah, what's that?"

"Your injury."

He was running his hand along the length of her hip and thigh and paused. "What about it? I told you about all I know last week."

"I know, but I'd like to know more about the terms of your recovery. You aren't going to be able to dive again. You're sure?"

"Can't and shouldn't aren't the same thing, are they?"

"That's what I'm worried about most, that you'll dive anyway."

"If it eases your worries any, I won't be able to find work as a commercial diver again, in the union or otherwise. I'm uninsurable now. Beyond eight to ten meters, I'm a seizure risk."

"I'm sorry, Levi."

In the dim light, she saw him raise an eyebrow. "It's a tough industry. I knew that going in."

"And you've never been one to let daunting odds hold you back."

"You could say that."

"So, I guess you've been thinking a lot about what it is that you want to do next?"

"I have, but if you want the truth, I haven't been good at getting past *you*."

Riley snorted softly. "Pun intended, huh?"

"Aren't the hardest truths best told in a joke?" Something in his look stabbed at her heart. "In answer to your question, I don't know what I want to do next. Teach high school kids about the skilled-trade industry, maybe. It'd feel good to reach teens who don't quite fit into the college mold but think they should so they can follow the norm. And there's a lot of opportunity in machining right now, solid careers that pay better than a lot of degrees do."

"I could see you doing really well at that. Connecting with teens."

"Thanks."

"But I guess what I want to know most is would you stay here if it weren't for me? I know how you love the water, and murky rivers don't cut it, do they?"

"I love the water. You're right about that. But I've had my time by water. What I haven't had is time with you."

Riley pressed her lips together. As tricky as this subject was to talk about, it was even trickier now that they'd spent a few hours tonight exploring one another. "There's something I didn't mention earlier. When we were talking about the merits of staying in St. Louis."

"What's that?" Levi shifted slightly, the muscles of his torso tensing.

"On Friday morning, I had an impromptu first-round phone interview for a job in Kansas City I applied for a while back. I'd be doing PR for an organization dedicated to building hiking and biking trails along old rail lines. It seems like it could be a pretty cool job, not on par with the shelter, but staying there's not an option."

"You know that for sure?"

"Someone's already been hired. He's just finishing out an internship in Seattle." In Levi's ensuing silence, she added, "But if I'm being completely honest, there's a good possibility that I've been running away from life more than I've been running toward it, which is why I never saw the posting."

He raised up on his elbow. "How about you stop running then?" He abandoned her hip to play with the ends of her hair. "Find something else around here you love as much as the shelter. Move in with me."

"I bet Marcus would love that." There was so much else she could've said in reply, but that was what slipped out, no doubt thanks to her defenses being up.

If Levi was bothered, he didn't let on. "I don't mean at Marcus's. I've got some money. Even before the accident, I was putting it away pretty steadily. You have to in this career. It's boom or bust. The point is I could buy a place." When she didn't interject, he went on. "Maybe something in Webster. Then again, that drive this afternoon on the heels of this weekend with my family has got me thinking a place on the outskirts of the city could be nice. Something with a bit of space to it. Maybe a lake or a creek running through it. Something drivable so you could still get to work, and I could get to wherever it is I end up."

Riley flattened a palm against her chest. Her heart was beating a mile a minute. Not only was he open to staying here, but he also wanted her to move in with him. This was most certainly rabbit fast, but then again, he was never going to stop being Levi. It would be her job to set a pace she was comfortable with.

"What's going through your head right now, if you don't mind my asking?"

Her mouth curled into a small smile. "I'm thinking about what a baby I am, to be so afraid of something I want so much."

"A place in the country?" His tone was playful.

"*You*, you goof." She leaned close to brush her lips over his nose. "You."

"A couple hours ago, you didn't seem that afraid." Before Riley could protest about a failing in his short-term memory, he added, "After the clothes came off, I mean."

"A couple hours ago, we weren't talking about something this big. As a matter of fact, we weren't talking at all."

He cocked an eyebrow and trailed his fingertips along her neck, down her sternum, and underneath the sheets, and all her parts revved into overdrive again. "Maybe if we pick up where we left off, it'll calm those nerves a bit."

Her eyes closed and her lips parted as she savored his exploration, though it was hindered by the fact that her legs were still pinned tight underneath Arlo, whose steady breathing had her suspecting he was close to dozing again. "We're going to have to do something because my legs are falling asleep, but I'm not sure this oversized baby is going to be that easy to move back to his bed."

Levi shook his head. "This bed's closer to the TV, and he's pretty transfixed with that bug-eyed alien. I think we'll have more luck switching beds and leaving him here."

"Makes sense, though I can't believe you just called ET a bug-eyed alien." Riley started to pull her legs free from underneath Arlo, but he stretched out, sprawling further across her. "Something tells me he and I aren't starting off with me as the clear alpha in this relationship."

Levi grinned as he pulled out from underneath Arlo's sprawled form as well. "*Ya think?*" Stepping out from under the sheets, he stood up. Of course, he didn't even flinch at standing there without a thing on, and the sight of that physique turned Riley to goo considerably faster than a wax warmer on high. She shimmied her legs free inch by inch even though Arlo wasn't having it and stretched out even more on top of the comforter. "Feels like I'm under a pile of rubble."

"Want to bet as to whether or not he had free rein of the bed at his last place?"

"Nope." Legs and feet finally free, Riley attempted to minimize her time spent moving between beds, though Levi stopped her in the middle for a few long kisses before following her underneath the sheets of the second bed. "It's considerably colder over here," she complained, cuddling up against him.

"We'll fix that."

Realizing he'd been abandoned, Arlo's expressive brows peaked and his whiplike tail flicked, but he didn't follow them. With what sounded like a sigh, he turned back to *ET* with the fixed gaze of someone paying attention to the plot, leaving Levi and Riley to do what they'd switched beds to do.

This time around, after a pause to locate the strip of condoms that had fallen off the nightstand at one point or another, it didn't take long before Levi was inside her, and their bodies began a dance more ancient than words.

"I love you." It was throaty and deep and took Riley a full second to realize those three immensely powerful words had been spoken for the first time by her, right against Levi's ear in a moment of mounting pleasure for both of them.

It wasn't until that pleasure was receding some minutes that he answered her. "I know you do." He brushed his lips against her temple. "I knew it back when we were kids, before we'd even gotten together, and I knew it when you showed up at Marcus's." He paused, letting the tips of his fingers trail over her collarbone. "If I didn't, I wouldn't have had the courage to pop in at the shelter like I did. I guess I'm a bigger baby than that dog over there when it comes to matters of the heart. So, you'll forgive me, I hope, for not saying it back."

Riley popped up onto her elbow with a start, causing Arlo to glance her way, thumping his tail.

Levi held up a finger. "It isn't that I don't. I trust you already know that. The thing is, I know me. Losing what I lost this year—my career, the ability to dive—adding you to it a second time, there'd be no coming back from it."

"What are you saying?"

"Not saying, asking. Asking to not go there until you decide if you're staying."

Riley waited for the punch line a second or two even though she knew it wasn't coming. "You want me to tell you that I'll stay here, find a job, and move in with you, but you don't want to talk about love?"

He frowned, brows furrowing tightly together in the dim light. "When you put it like that, I sound like quite the ass."

"*You think?*" she said, mimicking his earlier comment, half surprised to be able to find a bit of humor in the moment. "The thing is, Levi, if I move in with you in a month or two, and it doesn't work out, then what?"

"It'll work out."

She could spy the unwavering confidence in his expression, but it didn't mean she was buying into it. "It doesn't work out for everybody. Our parents, for instance. Mine especially, even if they are still together."

"We're not everybody, Riley, and we're certainly not our parents."

Riley settled back onto her pillow, tucking it closer to her shoulders and eyeing him in the dim light. "No, we're not."

Levi ran a hand under the sheets and along her hip and thigh, causing her blood to heat all over again.

Sliding his hand further down her thigh, he rolled onto his back and pulled her on top of him. "In dive school, one of the first things you learn is how to recognize when fear is getting the best of you, making you panic when staying calm might save your life. But *this* kind of fear, it's different. It won't lead to a stupid decision that'll burst your lungs or get you washed away in a down current."

"Well, if I didn't have nightmares about what you did for a living before, I'm going to now. Neither of those are something I ever wanted to envision you having risked."

"My point is that this kind of fear might not be life or death, but it could hold you back all the same."

"You think fear's holding me back?" She raised up for a better look at him, and he brushed her hair back from her face.

"What I think is that I don't want to lose you a second time, Riley Leighton. Tonight, that's the most honest thing I can tell you."

She nodded slowly. "Okay. But this is my life we're talking about, Levi. My career, my home. I can't just decide on the fly."

"Then don't. Take the time you need."

"And this?" She ran her fingertips down the length of his torso, appreciating the definition along the muscles of his chest and ribs. "What about this?"

He locked his hands on either side of her hips and pulled her closer. "Consider me a real estate agent, showing you all the city has to offer while you're thinking it over."

She giggled. "Not fair." She dipped low, exploring his neck and earlobe with her lips and tongue. "Not fair at all."

"Probably not."

After their lips met and the kiss heated again, Riley pulled away enough to ask, "What about taking you with me somewhere new?"

"That's on the table someday, absolutely. Right now, even. Assuming you can convince me that being here isn't the best thing for you. For me too. For now."

Before he'd answered, Riley had a line of arguments like toy soldiers ready to stand up in her defense, but the truth in his words laid siege to them. "I think," she said when she'd gotten her senses about her once more, "that you'd have crushed the debate team in one fell swoop had you ever gone against them."

Chapter 24

RILEY FLIPPED ON HER BLINKER TO TURN INTO the shelter parking lot. "It feels like we left here a lot longer than, what is it, seventeen or eighteen hours ago now." It was 10:30 a.m., and Riley was having a hard time shaking the feeling she was late for work even though Tuesdays were one of her two scheduled days off.

Levi's red Ram was in the far corner of the parking lot where he'd left it last night, making this the obvious spot to bring their date to a close. On the way here, they'd stopped for coffee and breakfast sandwiches, and Levi had loaded up with a couple dozen doughnuts, a box for the shelter staff and volunteers, the other for Marcus's.

"Yeah, it does," Levi agreed. "And I'd never have guessed when we started out that we'd be trading mini pigs for a Great Dane as a back-seat traveling companion either. The hotel though, that was inevitable, if you ask me."

"Ha ha." Riley rolled her eyes. "I'm trying not to spiral into a panic about walking inside and having Megan tell me she's had a change of heart, and I'm not a good fit for Arlo." After parking next to Levi's truck, Riley slipped the Mini into park and leaned her forehead against the steering wheel a second to collect herself.

Levi ran a hand over her back. "Want me to come in with you for moral support? I've got time."

Riley shook her head and sat upright as her dashboard screen lit up with an unknown call from an 816 area code. "Thanks, but no thanks."

"816. That's Kansas City, isn't it?"

She nodded, suspecting they were both wondering if the call had to do with the phone interview she'd had last week with the Kansas City nonprofit.

"I'll step out and let you take it," Levi offered when Riley didn't make an immediate attempt to answer it.

"It's okay. Whoever it is, I'll call them back."

After unbuckling, Levi pressed his lips against her temple before Arlo shoved his head between the seats and wiped his big tongue along the sides of both their faces. Pulling back, Levi dragged the back of a hand over his temple. "Call me and let me know how it goes, will you?"

"Yeah, of course, about this, and about my mom's." Riley rolled her eyes at the last part.

He grinned. "You've got a place to stay if you need it, you know."

"Trust me, you're the ace up my sleeve here. I'll check in with you for sure, wherever this big lug and I end up later." Riley ran a tongue over her lips, wanting to say something more but not sure where to begin. There were so many monumental things hanging between them still. After sleeping in late this morning, they'd showered together and taken Arlo for a walk on trails near the hotel, hoping that a bit of movement might work out the stiffness in his hips, and it had certainly seemed to. Compared to yesterday, he was more accepting of the boot and was hardly favoring his back foot any longer. He'd also been so perfectly behaved on the leash that Riley was hopeful whatever had happened yesterday was a fluke.

All morning, both Riley and Levi had steered the conversation away from things that might put a heavy spin on the day, including all the decisions awaiting her. Now, Riley was second guessing this. Maybe parting ways would be easier if they'd talked about them.

As he reached for the door handle, she closed a hand over his arm. "Levi…"

"Yeah?"

"Thanks for giving me time to think this through. It's a lot to process."

"Take all the time you need." His lips brushed hers. "I'll be here." Leaving her with one box of the doughnuts, he took the other and his coffee and stepped out, then leaned in again before closing the door. "For the record, this dog of yours is growing on me."

As if he knew he'd become the subject of the conversation, Arlo stuck his head between the seats again, whining after Levi.

"I don't see how he couldn't." Riley scratched Arlo on his jowls. "I'll bring him by later, assuming you don't have plans. I bet he'd enjoy being at Marcus's."

"I bet he would. Bring him by. He can meet Lola. We'll barbeque."

Riley's phone beeped with a new voicemail as Levi shut her passenger door and opened his own. "I'm not sure what to hope for here," she mumbled to Arlo, whose head was still shoved between the seats watching Levi get in his truck and wave before backing out.

Opening the voicemail that had already been converted to a text message, Riley skimmed as the message played aloud over her speakers. It was indeed the man who'd interviewed her, asking if there was a time later this week or weekend that she could come to Kansas City for an in-person, second-round interview. The message ended with him saying it seemed like she could be a good fit and that his team was looking forward to meeting her.

Riley's shoulders sank when she would've expected to be delighted. She'd been down this road enough times to be confident a comment like that meant she had a strong chance of landing the job. Rather than being excited by the prospect, it was as if a lead ball had been dropped in her lap. A month ago, it was a job that would've had her doing back-flips. Now, it would mean leaving the shelter poten-tially earlier than she had to, and at the very least complicating things with Levi. On top of that, the idea of being a road trip away once more from her imperfect family and from Lana was disheartening.

Numbly, she dropped her phone into her purse and picked up the box of doughnuts, then freed Arlo from the back seat as Levi drove away. "The worst she can say is no."

Halfway across the parking lot, Arlo planted his feet and wouldn't budge an inch more toward the shelter. Riley shifted the box of doughnuts to the other hand and squatted in front of him, smoothing a hand over the side of his chest. "I know, I know, but we aren't going in to stay, bud. However, I *do* need to get you through that door. For a little bit, at least."

Reminding herself how he'd bolted free from his handler just yesterday, she tightened her grip on the leash.

Staring at the shelter, his tail stuck straight out behind him, Arlo woofed a single time, a bark loud enough to hurt Riley's ears.

"I won't leave your side. Promise."

Riley had hoped this stubborn streak he was displaying was lessening up when the shelter door jangled open, but Arlo began backing up rapid fire, his booted foot slipping a bit and likely giving him a touch less traction. Even so, for Riley, it was trail along or be dragged. Abandoning her purse and the box of doughnuts on the pavement, she locked both hands over the leash and leaned in the opposite direction with every ounce of strength she could muster while Arlo backed across the lot with the power of a backhoe, pulling her along with him like a hunk of grass caught in one of the blades.

"Come on, boy...it's all fine." Words of encouragement spat out in a grimace didn't help matters one bit. Arlo seemed stuck in permanent reverse as he pulled her closer to the back row of cars. "I see obedience training in our future, just so you know."

Arlo stopped and sidestepped so fast that Riley fell smack on her butt with a thud. "Oof!" Out of the corner of her eye, she caught Patrick circling the big dog at a jog with the intent of cutting him off.

Spotting him, Arlo bolted forward and away from Patrick, prancing behind Riley like a thoroughbred at the starting gate before panicking further and yanking her in the opposite direction. Already on her butt, Riley was yanked hard enough that she was instantly stretched out, belly up and stomach exposed, arms stretched overhead. In the middle of the shelter parking lot. *Please don't let the cameras be catching this.*

A minivan paused not far inside the entrance, the driver and passengers witnessing the performance.

Riley heard other voices joining in the commotion, though she was too discombobulated to make out who they belonged to. As Arlo was encircled, a series of "easy boy" and "easy now" reached Riley's ears.

Arlo must've realized he was surrounded because he stopped pulling immediately and flanked Riley's side, his baritone bark sounding both territorial and terrified. Sidestepping, he landed on her boob hard enough that she let out an "Oof!" and rolled onto her side.

So much for confident first impressions.

Fidel was the first to step in and lock a hand around Arlo's leash. "Easy now, big guy. Nobody's going to hurt you."

Megan stepped in as well and offered out a hand to help Riley up. "Nice grip. For a minute there, I thought he might pull you into the road. You okay?" In addition to her, Fidel, and Patrick, two of the volunteers had also run out to help.

Riley got to her feet, wiping her hands on the back of her pants. "Yeah, I'm fine. I was just terrified he'd get away again. He's got some pull, it seems." Whether it was from rug burn or a blister, there was a hot spot on her right palm, and her back was stinging from being dragged on asphalt.

"And a wild streak," Fidel said. "That recommended additional training I put in his notes before he left, I'll upgrade it to mandatory training. We'll start working on what we can while he's here this time too."

Riley looked at Megan in confirmation. Did Fidel not know Riley's plans, or were they not going to give her a chance any longer?

As if sensing her fears, Megan gave her a sympathetic smile. "Fidel, I don't think you were in the room earlier. Riley's made the decision to adopt Arlo."

Fidel did a double take, and Riley had no doubt that he was refraining from commenting on how well that was likely to turn out given what they'd just witnessed, but at least Megan hadn't had a change of heart. That was the most important thing.

Riley rubbed the elbow that had taken the brunt of her fall. She'd have an ugly bruise to show for it, no question. "And you can consider me sold when it comes to the additional training. As much as is needed. I'm getting the sense he's a gentle giant until something scares him or sets him off, then he's out of here."

"Yeah, me too. And be sure to make use of Tess and Fidel while you're in St. Louis," Megan said. "They're excellent trainers."

"Arlo would benefit from a training harness too" Patrick said. "The other Dane who moved through here last June with a nervous streak like Arlo's was fitted with one upon adoption. In those early first few weeks, it proved essential in keeping her from taking off while she was getting acclimated to her new surroundings."

"I'd forgotten about her," Megan said. "Hopefully, since we've not heard about her in a while, she settled in well."

"Well, I'm all for trying one out," Riley added. "Whatever it takes to keep this baby safe while exposing him to potential triggers."

Megan had walked over for Riley's abandoned purse and the box of doughnuts. "Not only did you not lose your grip during all that, but you also had the sense to save the doughnuts. Well done," she teased.

Riley smiled. "Priorities. What can I say?"

Even despite the crowd bringing up the rear, getting Arlo through the door was a challenge, and he pulled and jerked for Fidel just as strongly as he had for Riley. Once he was inside, Megan had the idea of heading straight for the break room in back rather than attempting to keep him put alongside one of the adoption desks.

A few minutes later, Riley found herself on the break-room couch, nursing a sore elbow and raw back as she filled out the paperwork. The oversized canine towered above her, camped out next to her on the couch like he was, and Riley needed to tilt her head up to meet his gaze. For the most part, he was looking back and forth between the closed door and Trina, the shelter's resident three-legged cat, who was curled in her kitty bed atop the fridge, her eyes blinking closed every so often and her tail flicking as she watched the newcomer from the comfort of her favorite napping space. Riley wasn't entirely sure Arlo could be trusted with cats, so she'd kept his leash attached to his collar just in case, but she suspected he wasn't in the mood to chase down a cat, even if given the opportunity.

Smashed as close against her as he could get, Arlo hadn't even seemed interested in snagging a bite of her doughnut, which now lay half-eaten on a napkin on the table next to her as she filled out the rest of the adoption form.

When the break-room door opened, and Megan popped in to check on them, Arlo showed no inclination to flee. Unlike ten minutes ago, he seemed to want nothing more than to stick by Riley's side. The occasional ripples of fear that shook him broke her heart. "You know," she said to Megan, "it's taken this experience to really hit home how traumatic it probably is for most of these guys who wind up here."

Megan gave a light shake of her head. "No kidding. Patrick could tell you the exact percentage, but we figure about half of our intakes come here from cozy homes where they've been loved. The rest who move through here are mostly the strays and confiscations. But for sweeties like Arlo, all that chaos in the kennels, I imagine it's a bit like a war zone, no matter how sedate we attempt to make it back there."

"I bet you're right." Riley flipped her form back to a few of the questions she'd left blank. "Hey, so I know you said it was fine to use my mom's address for the top portion here, but I wanted to clarify the question about access to a fenced yard or a dog park. My parents do have a fenced yard, and wherever this big guy and I end up, I intend to make a fenced yard a priority, but I'll happily commit to joining a dog park too."

Megan's face lit up. "Yeah, that's perfect, but that reminds me. In all the chaos of getting him inside, I forgot to tell you that I had a call this morning from that nonprofit in Kansas City you mentioned might be calling."

"Really? That's moving fast."

"Well, I can't say I'm surprised. They'll be lucky to get you, but the conversation left me with no doubt they're interested. They even asked me to confirm that a handful of our recent posts are yours. They're impressed with your work. As they should be."

"Wow, thanks." Why did what should be good news make her want to cry? She could hear Levi's voice in her head telling her this meant something.

"It's fine if it doesn't work out but, depending on your start date at your new place, I'm hoping you'll be able to work jointly with the new hire here for a week or so, to show them the ropes and all."

Riley swept a lock of hair behind her ear, and Arlo leaned down for a fresh sniff of her face, no doubt having gotten a whiff of the unshed tears stinging her lids. "Yeah, sure. I bet that could work."

Megan headed back to her office while Riley finished up, stumbling through the rest of the paperwork. Patrick came in, wanting a doughnut and choosing a chocolate glazed with sprinkles but scraping off exactly fifty percent of the sprinkles into the sink before heading out, something Riley refrained from commenting on.

When they were alone again, Riley scratched Arlo's shoulder. "How come everything has to be so complicated, buddy?" Arlo looked from Riley to Trina, those expressive eyebrows of his knitted into peaks. "That kitty's not going to get you, bud, but if you're worried about her, you're really not going to like where we're headed next, and I'm not even kidding."

Setting the completed application aside, Riley folded forward and rested her head in her hands to collect herself. These last few weeks, everything had been about Arlo, Levi, and the shelter. Maybe it was the fact that she was utterly spent from staying awake half the night and bruised and battered from the fiasco in the parking lot, but suddenly it was if she was in the middle of a juggling act, and the odds were dismissal that she'd be able to continue juggling all three.

Yet, there wasn't a single one she was willing to part with.

A bit surprisingly, Riley realized the one person she suddenly almost desperately wanted to talk things through with was someone she hadn't turned to for advice in a very long time.

Digging out her phone from her purse, she pulled up her mom's number in her contacts and shot off a text, asking if she had any plans for lunch.

Also, a touch surprisingly, her mom must've had her phone nearby because she was quick to reply.

I'm free. Why don't you come on by? I'll place a take-out order.

"Well, there you go, Arlo," she said, leaning her head against his shoulder. "You're going to get to the meet the Leightons. Fair warning, they're cat people to the core. But don't worry, they'll come around. I'm sure of it."

Chapter 25

RILEY POKED AT THE SOFT-BOILED EGG FLOATING in her ramen bowl but ended up pinching a bit of noodles with the ends of her chop sticks to eat instead, saving the egg for later. "I'm glad you were in the mood for this," she told her mom between bites. "I haven't had ramen in forever."

They were seated in the backyard on the patio under the shade of the big white oak that had begun dropping what promised to be a bumper crop of fat, healthy acorns this year. A couple had dropped since they'd sat down five minutes ago, and each time, Arlo lifted his head and perked his ears from where he was resting in a patch of sun a few feet from the table.

The acorns got Riley thinking of the dozens of art projects she'd done over the years, both with her Girl Scout troop and with her mom. The most memorable had been pinecone mice, with acorn heads and tails of twine that she'd given out as Christmas presents when she was in third grade. Something about the memories stirred up a sense of both transience and permanence, reminding her how far and, at the same time, not so far, childhood was from her.

"Well, I for one am glad you went along with my request," her mom replied. "Your brother has yet to give ramen an honest shot, not even the instant kind, and your dad could easily do without it, so it's not something I get as often as I'd like."

Riley nibbled a wrinkly noodle hanging from the tip of her chopsticks. "Yeah, I can never see Tommy eating this."

"Given his inability to consider any foods that aren't thoroughly solid, you mean?" Brenda said with a smile. She meant it too. Despite his sweet tooth, Tommy turned his nose down on pudding, Jell-O, whip cream, and even cereal with milk, though he was a fan a several brands of cereal when eaten dry, most especially Reese's Puffs, his longtime favorite.

"No kidding."

"And whether it's the result of the radiation or not, I can't say, but this last week, I haven't been able to get enough of anything brothy."

"How are the treatments going now that you're more than a week in?"

Brenda shrugged, winding her noodles with a fork. While her pallet was diverse for a member of the Leighton household, she'd never been one to attempt eating with chop sticks. "No real complaints yet. My skin's a bit sore where I've been getting zapped, but it's not bad. Not yet, at least."

"That's good. From what I read, not everyone's skin burns badly. Hopefully yours won't."

Arlo lifted his head to sniff the breeze, catching Brenda's attention from the opposite side of the wrought-iron table. Earlier, when Riley had first let him off leash, he'd trotted around the big, quiet yard sniffing the furniture and Brenda's well-cared-for plants. Her mom had frozen in place while Arlo sniffed her, not daring so much as to pet him.

"You were going to tell me what happened, why he was returned, but looking at him, while he seems friendly enough, I have to say, I'm not surprised. Who on earth would want a dog that big in their home?"

Riley took a drink of water. *I'm guessing not you.* So far, all she'd shared was that she had Arlo with her today, and they'd have to eat outside. "A lot of people, actually."

"Well, I'm sorry he has to go through the system all over again. Is that why they let him tag along with you for the day?"

"Uh, not exactly."

Brenda wiped her mouth with one of the linen napkins she'd carried out. "Something tells me I'm not going to like this."

"Probably not, but I figure I'd better tell you anyway."

Brenda dropped her head into her open palm and closed her eyes. "Please don't tell me you want to adopt him."

Here goes nothing. "That's exactly what I need to tell you. Actually, I already did."

"Riley, you didn't." Brenda gave an exasperated shake of her head. "I know you've always wanted a dog, but your life is so unsettled right now. Wouldn't waiting to see where you end up make so much more sense?"

"Yes, of course it would've. But while I've always wanted a dog, I never wanted a dog the way I want Arlo."

Brenda took a controlled breath. "Where do you keep a dog that size? A barn? For goodness sakes, you might as well have bought a horse."

"Someday I hope to do that too, but right now, it's just him and me."

"And you plan to live *where* exactly? Because in case you've forgotten…" Brenda pointed her fork toward the sliding glass doors where all her cats were staring at their backyard visitor. All three had looks of obvious displeasure, ears flat, heads ducked, and fur ruffled. True to form, Hercules was most visibly frustrated of the bunch, hissing Arlo's direction and occasionally pouncing on the glass with enough might that Riley wasn't sure who'd she'd put money on winning in a fight, him or Arlo.

"I haven't forgotten. How could I when Hercules wakes me up by attacking me every morning or rattling my door if I dare to close it?"

"He just wants a bit of your attention, that's all."

"Like he wants Arlo's attention?" Riley quipped, though her mom didn't seem to see the humor in it. "To answer your question about where I'm going to live, that's what I'm trying to figure out. I've been here two weeks already. While I hadn't planned on staying long, a lot has come up since I got here. A *lot* lot." She let this sink in. "So, once you process the fact that I have a dog now, and I'm keeping him, that's really what I want to talk to you about."

Brenda had paused with a forkful of noodles halfway to her mouth. "Does it have to do with where you were last night?"

Riley nodded. "Yeah."

"You're a grown woman, Riley, and you probably don't think I have room to talk, but there are a thousand good reasons not to jump into things too quickly with someone you've just met."

Her mom's not-so-subtle reference to the infidelity didn't go unnoticed. Maybe she was ready to talk about it too. "I won't argue that, and the same probably goes for jumping in too quickly with someone you've known a very long time."

Her mom looked up in surprise. "Who do you mean?"

"Levi."

Her mom flushed beet red before stabbing at a mushroom. "You two... Wow. I didn't even know he was in town again."

"He hasn't been here long."

Her mom sat back in chair, processing this. "I don't know what to say. I guess I always thought there might be more between you two than what you shared. Before you stopped talking to me about him, I mean."

Riley gave up attempting to catch a mushroom sliver floating in the broth with her chopsticks to focus on what needed to be said—on what she'd held back for entirely too long. "I was just hurting too bad to tell you, and I was angry."

Brenda fiddled with her napkin. "Your dad and I can't take back what happened, Riley. I wish we could, but we can't."

"I know that."

Brenda met Riley's gaze. "Levi, huh? They say opposites attract and all that, but wow. I didn't know him well, but I wouldn't have guessed that. For the most part, I thought he was one of those jocks you couldn't stand."

"That was the judgement of a teenager who didn't fit in well with that crowd. I'm starting to realize most of those guys weren't nearly as bad as I made them out to be. As for Levi, I think that's what pulled me in at first, how different from me he was. But it wasn't until I realized all the ways we're similar that I really fell for him."

Her mom shook her head. "I guess I thought you were just testing the waters with him. I tried talking about it with you, but you wouldn't have it. You shut me out so completely back then."

"I was hurting—finding out what was going on with you and Dad the way I did." Riley's heart thudded into a sprint to finally be having a conversation she'd avoided so long. "And I was eighteen. No eighteen-year-old wants to talk to their mom about their love life."

Brenda smiled sympathetically. "That's probably true."

"But the truth is, it was so painful that I just wanted to escape and not deal with it. Then the disaster that was prom happened, and I just wanted to disappear."

"What happened at prom?" Brenda's expression was a mix of equal surprise and concern.

"You really don't know?" Suddenly parts of that weekend Riley hadn't thought about in forever came rushing back. After walking up from Levi's room in the basement and finding her dad in an intimate make-out session with Levi's mom, Riley spent a string of nights at Lana's, including prom night. When Riley went home to get her dress, shoes, and extra clothes the next day, Brenda pulled Riley into her room to talk while Lana waited in Riley's room. Riley had been hurting so bad, she'd stood there, arms crossed, staring at one of the then-cats on her mom's bed, full of teen venom. *"I can't believe you knew what he was doing. And how can you defend him? You and Dad make me sick. I never want to see either of you again."*

Yes, she'd said that to her mom. "That's been one of my bigger regrets, not knowing a thing about how prom turned out when I'd spent so much time helping to plan it. I was supposed to chaperone, remember?" Brenda fiddled with her napkin again. "I begged out of helping at the last minute because I assumed you'd have a much better experience without me."

Riley sat back in her chair. All these years, she'd only ever considered Courtney and her minions finding out about what happened from Lana or Marcus. With all the school-related hats Brenda Leighton had worn over the years—PTO president, room mom, and Girl Scout troop leader—she'd developed as many friends through the school system as Riley had. When her daughter cut her out so completely, wasn't it logical she'd have confided in someone? "Mom, was Courtney's mom on the prom committee with you?"

Brenda blinked. "Yes, why? What happened at prom, Riley?"

"Did you tell her what happened at Levi's house?"

"God no, Riley. I never would've told her anything, gossipmonger that she was. Why?"

"Because they knew. They *all* knew. Everyone on homecoming court, dozens of others. It was the big laugh of the night. They'd even..." Riley blinked and looked away. Hadn't it been long enough that this shouldn't hurt anymore? "They'd even had buttons made up, and a ton of kids were wearing them."

Brenda closed a hand over her mouth. "Buttons?"

"Keeping it in the family buttons. They were supposed to fly under the radar of the chaperones but still make a point. I didn't even get what was happening until I was dancing with Levi during one of the slow dances, and all of a sudden some of the kids started singing 'Riley and Levi kissing in the family tree.'"

When tears flooded Brenda's eyes, Riley dragged her hands along her thighs and blinked back several of her own.

"I'm so very sorry, Riley. Your father and I had no idea."

"Rather than talking about it, I just shut down, and not only with you two. I ended it with Levi even though doing so crushed him as much as me. I hardly talked to anyone the rest of senior year. I put my head down and studied and skipped out at lunch and made it through to finals."

Brenda shook her head. "And then went away to the furthest college you could find."

"And the thing is, I worked so hard not to look back that nothing ever went away. It was just sitting there, waiting to bring me down anytime I thought about it."

"I'm so sorry."

"You don't have to keep apologizing. But I

would like to know if you told anyone on that prom committee."

When Brenda was quick to look down at her lap, Riley knew the answer even before her mom said it. "One person. I thought she was a dear friend."

Riley closed a hand over her wrist. "I don't need to know who. All that matters is that rumors spread. The person you told, most likely told someone else. Maybe it doesn't make sense, but it helps that it was more than just Lana and Marcus who knew. Maybe Dad and Levi's mom told people too. Whatever the case, the truth is, I suspect it didn't start maliciously."

"But it grew that way." Brenda sat back in her chair. "Oh, Riley. I would never in a million years have wanted that for you. Looking back, there's so much I could've done differently to help get your father and I out of the rut we were in. I blame it on a stupid TV series we watched, if you want the truth. The idea of spicing up our marriage seemed... exciting, I guess."

"Eww, Mom." Riley held up a finger and shook her head. "There are some details I'll never need."

Brenda let out a small laugh that relieved some of the lingering tension in the air. "I guess that's neither here nor there. But as for Levi, I thought he was working down south on an oil rig or something."

"He was working as underwater welder, but he hasn't been down south for a while. When he found out I was here, he came back too."

Brenda lifted an eyebrow. "It's quite serious then?"

"He'd like it to be."

"And you? What do you want?"

Riley hadn't touched a bite of her ramen since the real talking had started. Her appetite had fled. "I want that too. The problem is that when we talk about it, I find myself thinking more about what I *don't want* than what I do want."

"And what's that?"

"To not be afraid of what happened between you and Dad happening to me and Levi someday."

Brenda blinked back a few sudden tears. "Happily ever after is a nice way to end a book, Riley, but life isn't only the fun parts. Hardly so for anyone. Those early years with your brother..." She shrugged. "I was spent. Every ounce of my energy went to raising him. At the end of the day, I had nothing left for your father. For a very long time. He didn't have much left for me either. It's no surprise we grew apart."

"A lot of people grow apart. The divorce rate's fifty-fifty or something."

"Isn't it dropping for you millennials? I admire the way you all seem to know yourselves so well now. When your dad and I were growing up, people married young, and we were no exception. But even so, love changes for most people, maybe not as drastically as it did for us, but it changes. For years, your father and I stopped thinking of one another as lovers, but we were still partners, bringing up a family, maintaining this home. In the end, we stayed together because we realized we were still good together."

"But he's not... You don't still—"

"Have an open marriage? No, not since you found out. Not since then. Seeing yourself through the eyes of your children can be a life changer."

"Are you happy you stayed together?"

"Of course, I am. Your father's my best friend. There's no one I'd rather fall into bed with at the end of a long day. There's no one's hand I'd rather hold on to during a cancer treatment plan appointment either."

Riley pinched an edamame bean between her chop sticks and nibbled on it, processing this.

"Your dad and I had a lot of growing up to do," Brenda added, "and we didn't always go about it the best way. We didn't talk about things like your generation does. We each just expected the other one to be our everything, and that hardly ever works."

"I bet when you really love someone, that's an easy trap to fall into, regardless of your emotional IQ."

"Do you love him? Levi?"

Riley nodded. "Very much so. He's not perfect. He's a bit impulsive and never sits still. He chose a career that nearly killed him, and now he can't risk practicing it any longer. Who knows what he'll do next. But he's also fun and playful and steers clear of being vulnerable in this charming way, and when I'm around him, I feel…expansive. Like my feet don't touch the floor."

Her mom murmured appreciatively. "That's love, alright."

"The whole thing's a bit terrifying, if you want the truth."

"You know what they say about the difference between fear and excitement being only what you make of it?"

Riley sat back in her chair, mulling this over. "I can see that."

Fifteen feet away, Hercules pounced at the glass door especially hard, and Arlo lifted his head and woofed in the cats' direction.

Brenda jumped upon hearing Arlo's baritone bark. "Somehow, we've sidestepped around talking about this dog you've adopted. You do realize how chaotic it'll be with a canine his size in a home with those three felines?"

"Forget the other two; it's Hercules I'm worried about. Arlo's a bit of a baby, if you haven't noticed, but it'll work out one way or another. I'm not staying long."

"Because one of those job's you applied to is coming through or because of this thing with Levi?"

Riley dipped her head sideways a touch. "One

of the jobs does seem to be coming through, but I think I'm going to call and turn it down. I want to give this thing with Levi the best shot I can give it, and that doesn't include trekking across the state to see each other on our days off, nor does it include asking him to leave St. Louis when he's ready to call it home again."

Her mom processed this for a second or two. "While doing my best to keep my personal wishes out of play, I'm compelled to ask, are *you* ready to call it home again?"

Riley nibbled on a bite of noodles, considering her answer. "That's what I've been thinking about all morning. I'm finished running. All those other cities—Atlanta, Chicago, Memphis—they had their merits, and it was fun to get a taste of different American cultures. But someday I want kids, and the thought of having them here makes my stomach flip with what I'm confident is more excitement than fear, now that you put it so aptly. The idea of scheduling playdates with my best friend and her kids or arranging a date night with Levi and dropping our kids off here where I have a million good memories of childhood feels like the most *right* thing I could ever do."

Her mom had set down her fork and was brushing tears from her cheeks. "I never stopped hoping you'd come home, but sometimes it's felt like a pipe dream."

Perhaps sensing a change in energy in the conversation, Arlo got to his feet with an exaggerated grunt and walked over, his stiffness having set in again. Practically eye to eye with Riley, he pressed in close and nuzzled her ear, and Riley wrapped an arm around him.

"Well, you can breathe easy. Now that I've said it, there's no going back. I want this. All of it."

Brenda laughed as Arlo swept his big tongue across Riley's nose like he was in perfect agreement. "At the risk of sounding overly sentimental, you've just made my year, my decade even, even if it means my cats will be shedding like they're in a hurricane-force wind with this big guy in the house."

Considering how wild her mom's cats were, Riley wasn't going to disagree with her there.

Chapter 26

IT TOOK RILEY THE BETTER PART OF A WEEK before she began telling people at the shelter that she'd had a change of heart and would be staying on in St. Louis indefinitely. It was a big decision, focusing only on available jobs in St. Louis and turning down a great opportunity in Kansas City, but she had no regrets. Thankfully, with her temp work at the shelter, she could afford to be a little picky when it came to sending out new résumés. With some luck, she'd find something she liked almost as much.

The next Sunday, when Megan invited Riley to join her at her house for a late-afternoon doggie playdate, Riley walked the three blocks from her parents' thinking how much she wanted to keep growing these newfound connections, even when her internship ended. Even Arlo was making out from the experience.

"You may not be big on playing with other dogs yet, Arlo, but Megan knows you well enough to know what you can handle. If today is nothing more than exchanging a few sniffs with some curious canines and sticking close by me, that's fine."

Megan's house turned out to be just a couple addresses down from a house Riley had played in as a kid with a girl who'd moved away with her family some years ago. It was ironic the way life was circling around again, bringing her back to a world she'd thought she'd left behind forever but now wanted very much to be part of.

Compared to his unease when she'd first started taking him on neighborhood walks, Arlo had an easiness to his gate, like he was enjoying the stroll down the tree-lined sidewalks that had been pushed up every here and there by roots as much as Riley was. He sniffed at occasional mailboxes and under bushes, but for the most part, he hung next to her like a gentleman. Even so, Riley kept a secure hold on his leash just in case something made him want to bolt again, though she suspected the more comfortable he grew, the less chance there was of him bolting.

Megan's house was lovely…and large, though Riley had suspected as much from the address and from Megan's comment earlier this week that her husband was a successful entrepreneur and self-proclaimed recovering workaholic.

When Arlo seemed undecided about approaching the house after hearing a few barks from within, Riley hung back and pulled out her phone to text that she was here. Even before she sent it, Megan was opening the door and welcoming her.

Perhaps it shouldn't have been a surprise, but

Megan's two dogs were well trained enough that they sat on command, waiting with rapt attention rather than attempting to bound through the open door. The German shepherd was as still as a statue while the beagle wiggled in place like a worm.

"How's he doing?" Megan asked. "I can bring them out for a sidewalk greeting so he doesn't feel like he's stepping into the lion's den, if you think he's good."

Riley shrugged, picking up on a slight, hopeful wag of Arlo's tail. "Sure."

Megan disappeared behind the door and reappeared seconds later with leashes in hand. Before she was finished hooking her dogs up, a toddler waddled into view, fingers shoved in her mouth, her striking blue eyes wet from recent tears.

"Aw, what a cutie."

"Thanks. This is Evie. Her molars are coming in something fierce, so she's pretty clingy this afternoon."

"Poor girl."

After hoisting her toddler onto her hip, Megan headed down the brick steps with both dogs. Arlo pushed forward as well, giving both dogs a thorough sniff when they met up.

The German shepherd, Sledge as Megan called him, was the first to step away to the end of his leash, scent marking on one of the hostas lining the walkway. On the other hand, Tyson, the beagle, didn't dial back an inch with his whole-body wiggle even despite the towering size of his visitor.

"Look at that," Megan said. "I thought they'd be easy friends. Tyson has yet to meet a dog he doesn't like, and Sledge is pretty laid back as well, especially given his breed." Megan's baby pulled her hand out of her mouth to point at Arlo and ruff like a dog. "Yes, Evie, ruff ruff. It's another doggie. I bet you didn't know they came in such big packages, did you?" To Riley, she added, "She loves dogs more than toys, I swear. Between her and Tyson, I can't say who's happier to follow whom around the house."

"Oh yeah? Cute."

Megan glanced between the dogs. "So, no one else is home, but I'm still thinking it might be best to start them off leash out back. It'll likely be less stress on Arlo than inside the house. There's a gate at the side of the yard if that works for you."

Riley shrugged. "Sure thing, though fair warning, I'm not sure how much running around Arlo will do with these two."

"That's okay. Tyson will do all the running for all three of them, I bet, and honestly, it may keep him from knocking things over in the house in excitement. He's small in stature, but he's taken out chairs, side tables, stools, you name it. My husband's always saying we should've named him Dozer, short for bulldozer, obviously."

Riley laughed. "Beagles and their energy. How old is he?"

"Not quite two. He was supposed to float between houses and be here only half time since he belongs to my stepdaughter. He still does sometimes, but mostly my husband's ex prefers the kids don't bring him when they're with her."

As soon as they were in the backyard, and Tyson was off leash, he tore around the yard, bounding in circles as fast as he could go, while Sledge trotted off calmly to sniff along the fence line. After he was unhooked, Arlo glanced tentatively at Riley before eyeing the energetic beagle. He wagged his tail hopefully but didn't so much as move a muscle to join him, making Riley wonder if he expected *her* to join in the play first.

"We call that the zoomies. Once Tyson gets them out of his system, I bet he'll try to get Arlo to play with him. At least, he always does Sledge."

"He looks a bit like the Tasmanian devil tearing around like that," Riley offered, laughing.

As Megan promised, after a few minutes, Tyson stopped running and bounded over, panting hard but wagging his tail. He yipped at Arlo, dropping into a play bow, while Arlo backed up a foot or two, not quite sure he wanted to play.

When Arlo didn't take the bait, Tyson trotted off to the wide stone patio and grabbed a half-mauled Frisbee that was lying under one of the chairs. Finished with sentry duty, Sledge trotted over to where they were standing and sank onto his haunches as if watching for his next cue.

The baby yawned in Megan's arms and burrowed her head against her. "Someone's going to need a nap soon, so I'll get to this before any meltdowns ensue. I have some news that I'm hoping you'll find to be good news, but I also don't want you to feel pressured either."

Riley could feel her eyes widening. "What kind of news?"

"The marketing coordinator position, turns out our guy in Seattle doesn't want it after all. He called yesterday and turned it down. The nonprofit where he's interning offered him something permanent, and he'd like to stay in Seattle."

Riley's jaw fell open. "Wow. I guess…wow. Does this mean you'll be posting the job again? Because if you are, I'd love to throw my name into the hat."

Megan ducked her head sideways as Evie poked at her cheek to get her attention, letting out a series of "Mama, Mama."

"Hold on, baby. Mommy's talking to Riley." She switched Evie to her opposite hip as if trying to buy some time. "Sorry, but no. I'm afraid you can't throw your name into the hat." Just as alarm rocked through Riley, Megan broke into a wide smile. "Because if you want it, the job's yours."

Riley stood there a second or two, waiting for an

entirely different punch line. "Are you kidding? You don't even want to interview anyone else?"

"I'm perfectly serious." Megan shrugged. "You've already interviewed—even if it was a bit informal, and you sent me your résumé and portfolio. Had you been applying for the permanent position then, you'd have gotten it, and you've more than proved yourself these last few weeks. You're a great fit, Riley. You're talented, and you're dedicated to the shelter. I can't think of anything else we could be looking for."

Riley folded over in disbelief, gripping her knees as Arlo dipped his head under her hair to sniff her face, perhaps having caught a whiff of her rush of tears.

"There are some formalities, of course," Megan added when Riley had gotten her composure again. "Paperwork to sign, etc., and we can take a second look at what you're earning. There's a salary range we can't go above, but I think you could end up with a couple dollars an hour more than what you're making now, plus you'll get insurance, and you'll start accruing vacation and personal time too."

"Megan, I don't know what to say. I'm still trying to wrap my head around all this. And you're sure you don't need me to interview again? Do you think any of the staff will mind the way this is playing out?"

"Of course not. When I shared the news ear-lier, rather than being disappointed, everyone was hopeful this meant you'd be staying on. Even Patrick, and that's saying a lot. But if it makes you feel any better, I'm happy to schedule a mock interview before formally announcing that you've got the position."

Riley laughed, her body still abuzz with happy shock. "That's okay. I just…wow. When I made the decision to stay in St. Louis, I never imagined anything this good."

Megan smiled, lifting her daughter in the air to keep her from grabbing at her hair. "If the last few years have taught me anything, it's the way that, when we have good intentions and the time is right, the things that're truly right for us just sort of fall into place. Like when you find that missing piece in a puzzle that didn't seem to be anywhere, and all of a sudden everything comes together."

Riley's gaze traveled to Arlo, who'd tentatively meandered deeper into the grass this last minute. He was watching Tyson trot around the yard with his tail erect and the Frisbee in his mouth. Spying his company, Tyson abandoned his toy and dropped into a play bow again. This time, Arlo did the same, dipping low on his front feet and wagging his tail, only with his massive size, he looked a bit comical doing so.

"Well, after finding so many wrong pieces for a long time, it feels really good to be finding some perfectly right ones."

Chapter 27

As upturned as his life had gotten two months ago when he'd geared up for what he was expecting to be an average day in the water, Levi would have to give some merit to what he'd heard about things needing to fall apart in order to fall back together again. He didn't regret leaving St. Louis at nineteen, and he didn't regret his years spent as a commercial diver. He was, however, finished living out of apartments and hotels. It was time to create a life that didn't have him escaping to bars at the end of the day to fill the emptiness that seeped in when things weren't entirely wrong enough to force a change but not quite right enough to experience the easy satisfaction he'd recently stepped into.

Being home, being with Riley, Levi's compass was finally pointing due north again. Even his headaches receded considerably this week, another good sign he was healing. While he was committed to giving Riley as much time as she needed to figure out how right this whole thing was for her too, Levi had no doubt the next right step was moving in together.

After spending most of the week helping Marcus knock chores off his list for the upcoming open house, Levi passed the downtime he didn't spend with Riley lounging around in the shade with Lola stretched out by his side, mouth gaping open in that perpetual bulldog grin of hers, as he searched for houses and land for sale, both closer to the city and farther out past Marcus's.

There were a handful of contenders in Webster, cute homes with decently sized yards, and just as many outside of the city with acres and acres of land. If it were up to Levi alone, he'd chose the latter, somewhere quiet with room to the stretch their legs—his and Riley's and that long-legged canine of hers.

A couple of the listings were intriguing enough that Levi made appointments to see them later in the week. He debated whether to text pictures of them to Riley but decided to hold off. While he didn't want to keep her out of the loop, he didn't want to pressure her either.

Around 4:00 p.m., he stepped in to help with the day's pickup, playing dog caddy for owners who'd dropped their four-legged companions off for a day of training or simply to expend some energy while their people were at work.

Lola had the goings on here down pat. At pickup time, she headed for the circle driveway where she hung out on the sidewalk, watching the dogs get loaded into cars and occasionally getting called over to a vehicle for a treat.

"Think she's still waiting to get picked up too?" Levi asked Marcus, having noticed the way she studied the cars.

Marcus watched Lola a few seconds before shaking his head. "Nah, man, I don't think so, though maybe that's only because it would bring me to my knees if I did."

"You need to make her yours already and quit forcing her to camp out every night with the boarded dogs. She's already a mascot of sorts for you."

Marcus shook his head. "It's like I told you before. I promised myself I wouldn't be adopting any abandoned dogs. If I break down and start with her, I guarantee you another one'll get left behind as soon as I do, and before I know it, I'll have more dogs than I can handle vet bills for. Besides, do you have any idea what kind of tab her owners have rung up by now? I'll connect with 'em eventually, one way or another, and I'll get paid too."

Levi clicked his tongue. "Someday, someone's gonna come around and break that steel trap of a heart of yours wide open, and when they do, it's not gonna be pretty, all that goo and blubber you've been holding back forever."

Marcus chuckled. "Keep betting that all you want, bro. Ain't no skin off my back if you're delusional."

When the pickup rush was over, Levi headed inside to shower. Halfway across the lawn, he stopped and turned back, whistling for Lola. She lumbered to her feet and trotted over, looking up at him expectantly. He bent down and scratched the top of her head to which she happily thumped a back foot in the air. "No sense watching for a car that's not coming. How about following me inside, and we'll beg forgiveness later?"

Either reading his body language or picking up on the invitation in his tone, Lola trotted after him like she was in on the plan, hardly hesitating when Levi beckoned her through the open sliding glass door at the back of the house. "I'd get you set up smack in the middle of Marcus's bed while I'm showering, but that might be taking it a bit too far, even for me."

With the exception of the cabin trip, it had been a few months since the dog had been in a house that hadn't been converted into a boarding facility, but Lola didn't seem fazed by the change of pace. She trotted over the threshold like she belonged, heading for the kitchen, and sniffing along the bottom of the cabinets in the kitchen before trotting into the living room where she lost no time snatching a few fallen crumbs from under the side of Marcus's recliner.

Levi headed into the guest bathroom and flipped on the shower. Lola followed him to the door, taking a glance around as he stripped down. Then she headed for the living room and sprawled out on the plush rug in the center, letting out what sounded like a contented sigh in the process.

Levi showered and shaved, and when he

stepped out wrapped in a towel, Marcus had come in and was in the kitchen chopping an onion. Lola hadn't budged from where Levi had last seen her; she'd fallen asleep and was happily snoring away, her short legs sticking straight out in front of her.

"Guess you've always been one to push your luck." Marcus lifted a longneck beer off the counter and took a swig as Levi walked into the living room. "Thirsty?"

"I'm good, thanks, and yeah, I probably have. But then again, I suspect that's why we made easy friends."

Marcus huffed. "Well, I won't stop you from bringing her inside, so long as she doesn't crap on the floor, and when you get your own place, she goes with you."

Marcus knew he was looking at property now that he'd made the decision to stay in St. Louis. Levi figured this might help him not wear out his welcome here too fast, this and the extra work he was helping knock off around here.

"Wouldn't Lola and Arlo make a pair?" Levi joked.

Marcus lifted an eyebrow. "Guess it's getting pretty serious, then, if you're thinking about how your dogs will get along."

"A, Lola isn't my dog. B, it is."

"Then let's get clear that if you're set on making

that little hog caller someone's dog, it's yours. Otherwise, she doesn't seem to have any complaints with the life she's been living."

Levi helped himself to a beer. "Riley's coming by later. Bringing along a picnic, even. Maybe this discussion is best left for after we see how those two get along. Besides, I thought you liked her." The two dogs had sniffed noses the two times last week that Riley had brought him over, but that had been the extent of their interaction.

"Riley or Lola?" Marcus joked.

"Lola. I know you like Riley just fine, and if you didn't, you'd know better than to tell me."

"True that. And I like Lola just fine too. Only I spend twelve hours a day with dogs." He stopped chopping to draw a wide arc in the air with his chef knife. "This little thirteen hundred square feet of nothing special is my private sanctuary, and I'd like to keep it free of four-legged creatures. And kids. They're more trouble than dogs."

"Some people don't think so."

"Or we wouldn't have a global population crisis to contend with, huh?"

Levi shook his head. "You know how to ground a conversation in reality, I'll give you that." Taking his beer with him, he headed for the spare bedroom to get dressed.

"Hey, don't close that door," Marcus called thirty seconds later. "You've got company."

Sure enough, Levi turned to spy Lola shaking herself off before trotting his direction.

"Looks like Lola even thinks she's your dog now too."

Levi held open the door long enough for Lola to trot inside and glance up longingly at his bed. After a second or two of debate, he lifted her up, appreciating her squat, dense form, perpetual grin, and her short, wiggly tail, and plopped her square in the middle of it. "If you know what's good for you, girl, you'll starting using some of that charm on a much longer-legged canine than yourself."

Chapter 28

"YOU'RE FINE, BUDDY. I WON'T BE LONG," RILEY assured Arlo, who was in the backyard on the stone patio, staring at her through the bay window with a dejected look about him. Hercules sat perched on the windowsill at the far side of the bay window, ears flattened against his big orange head, periodically hissing and batting a paw at the glass. One week into dog ownership, and they weren't even close to trusting the cats and dog to roam loose in the same room. Considering Riley had been the one to mix things up by bringing Arlo here, she couldn't complain, but it was the cats, not Arlo, who went berserk anytime he was near.

Riley was at the kitchen counter, slicing a fresh baguette for the picnic she was putting together. Earlier, she'd offered as casually as possible to bring a picnic out his way tonight. Today's good news was something she wanted to relay in person. Like Megan had suggested, this position at the shelter becoming permanent was the puzzle piece helping everything come together.

It took another half hour to finish prepping the food she'd picked up earlier, wrap a few unconventional presents for Levi, one of which she'd needed her mom's help with, and get everything loaded into the trunk. She texted Levi as she left, saying she'd be there by six thirty and to look for a nice spot to eat. When she arrived, the wide front gate was shut and locked, making the hair on her arms raise on end to think how differently life might've played out had she encountered a locked gate as opposed to an open one her first time here.

They'd have found their way back to each other one way or another, even had their at-the-time humiliating meetup not spurred things along.

She was fishing her phone out from her purse to text him that she was here when Arlo whined. Following his gaze, she spotted Levi crossing the wide lawn from the small ranch at the corner of the property, his stride both easy and purposeful.

Arlo's ears perked forward abruptly, and Riley suspected he'd spotted the stocky bulldog trailing through the grass not far behind Levi. "With that sensitive sniffer of yours, you can smell far more dogs than her around here, but she's the only one who has free rein of the place."

When he reached the entrance, Levi pressed a button on the control box, and the automatic gate whirred open.

Having spotted where he was headed, Lola stopped in the grass and watched Riley's car pull in, seemingly uninterested in life on the other side of the gate. Riley rolled down her driver's-side window as the gate was closing behind her.

"Evening." Her whole body warmed happily as Levi dipped to brush his lips against hers.

"So, I know we saw each other yesterday, but it's nice seeing you again. Really nice." He was clean shaven, and he still had a fresh-from-the-shower look about him.

Cupping her hands on both sides of his face, Riley pulled him close for a second kiss. Wanting to get in on the action, Arlo crammed his head between Riley and the open window, panting contentedly and wagging his whole body enough to shake the car. Grinning, Levi scratched the top of his head.

Looking around and not spotting Levi's truck, she pointed ahead. "Want me to park up there?" There was only one area for public parking, and it was empty of vehicles, Levi's or Marcus's.

"Yeah, sure. Marcus has me park down behind his house to keep the drop off and pickup area clear in the morning, but if I can convince you to stay the night, we'll move you later."

Riley raised an eyebrow at that last part. "This week of abstinence has felt like a year, hasn't it?" When Levi agreed, she added, "Want a ride over there?"

"I'll follow, seeing as I have a shadow." He nodded toward Lola. "But first, what should I grab from the house? A blanket or two, and what else? There's a spot on the far corner of the property where there's a good view of the sunset."

Riley shook her head. "I've got blankets. All I need is your lovely self, and the little bulldog too, if she'd like to join us."

"I'm guessing she'd enjoy the company, seeing as Marcus won't let me keep her in the house while I'm not there."

"Where does she hang out at night if not at the house, then?"

Levi pointed toward the big ranch house near the parking spaces. "In there with the boarded dogs."

"Oh." She was about to pull forward but pressed down on the brake again, frowning. "Wait, how long has Lola been here now?"

"Closing in on three months, I think, and you don't have to say it. I know she deserves better."

"Yeah, she does."

He made a face. "Every time I think of blaming him, I remind myself how he's had enough loss that he's got an excuse not to handle it well."

All Riley really knew about Marcus was that he'd lost his mother while very young, and like Levi, in high school, he'd quite preferred keeping busy over sitting still.

After making sure Lola was out of the way, Riley headed off to park. By the time she'd gotten there, parked, and got out, Levi and Lola were walking up.

She opened the back door and secured Arlo's leash in her hand before pulling the door wide enough for him to step out.

Undaunted by Arlo's size, Lola trotted straight over to sniff his feet and legs, weaving underneath him as she did, her little nubbin tail wagging in welcome. Arlo leaned down for a quick sniff before ignoring her entirely. "It seems more and more like he's a people-person sort of dog."

"You think?" Levi said, grinning. "You might as well let him off leash. The property's fenced all around. Marcus gives use of the big field every weekend to a group who train SAR dogs. Even the young, eager ones who run off don't get out, and I'll bet every dollar I have Arlo's not a runner, at least not when he's not panicked."

Riley looked at Arlo, who, after appraising the place, was looking at her questioningly. "That's not a bet I'll take considering I agree with you. And search and rescue dogs? That's cool. We'll have to invite them to the friendraiser." With a touch of elaborate flair, Riley unhooked Arlo's leash and draped it over her shoulder. "There you go, buddy. Want to stretch your legs?"

Perhaps he hadn't yet realized he'd been unhooked, but Arlo didn't so much as move away an inch. Instead, he stuck by Riley as she headed for the trunk. "Maybe it'll take a bit to sink in."

Riley had packed her mom's picnic blanket in

addition to hers, knowing that Arlo would take up a full blanket by himself. She handed both to Levi and then offered him the lumpy package she'd wrapped in butcher paper, tying with raffia and accenting with a swig of greenery. "Ta da."

"What's this?"

"You'll see."

"It's lumpy." Levi had tucked the blankets under his arm and was turning the package in a circle, squeezing it with his thumbs.

"Lumpy presents are the best, aren't they?" She hoisted the loaded picnic basket and grabbed the lone bottle of bug spray in case they needed it, then closed the trunk.

"What'd I do to deserve all this? And want me to carry that basket? Looks heavy."

"I've got it for now, but thanks." She leaned up and brushed her lips against his cheek. "And in answer to your other question, everything. Fair warning though, it's kind of a figurative present."

Levi held up a hand. "No hints. I like surprises."

Riley waggled an eyebrow. "I'm still hoping you'll be surprised."

Arlo continued to stick by Riley's side as they headed across the grass toward the far end of the property, giving the picnic basket a thorough sniffing along the way. "I wonder if Arlo realizes that meal he had before we came was his dinner," she said. Lola trotted along behind at her own pace, zigzagging back and forth among the trees, rocks, and paddock fence posts to sniff them.

Levi grinned. "If it wasn't people food, I'm sure it wasn't as good. But he's walking better, not stiff, and hardly favoring the boot."

Arlo paused to sniff something in the grass but lumbered into a trot to catch up as soon as he realized he was being left behind.

"I agree. It was the afternoon walk to Megan's that did it." With the basket starting to weigh her down, Riley switched it to her other arm. This time, Levi reached for it without asking, and Riley consented, relieving him of the much lighter present and blankets in return.

"Whatever this is, we won't leave hungry. And who's Megan?"

"The shelter director. I told you about her. She lives a couple blocks from my parents. Arlo had a little playdate with her dogs this afternoon."

"Oh yeah? That's cool."

Riley looked in the direction they were headed in hopes Levi wouldn't notice the light flush warming her cheeks at keeping this afternoon's monumental news to herself a bit longer. There were other things she wanted to say first, so she nodded toward the knoll ahead. "Is that where we're headed?"

"If you like it. On the other side, it dips just enough before the fence line that there's a good view west." He looked at the western sky, still mostly clear blue with shades of pink, yellow, and orange starting to glow along the horizon.

"You're getting to know this place pretty well."

"Yeah, well, mostly it's been on the back of a John Deere. Marcus has more on his plate than he can handle, but me being here helped him realize he needs to hire a groundskeeper when I leave; nothing full time, but he's starting to make some money and can afford help."

"What about you?" Riley asked as they started to climb the small, sloping hill. "Are you going to miss it?"

"Maybe. Maybe not."

There was something in his expression that made it obvious he was holding back. "Because of what you said about looking for a place, or something else?"

They finished the climb in silence, and Riley set Levi's gift in the grass so she could spread out the blankets. The heat of this afternoon had relented, and the air was pleasantly cool against her bare arms.

Like Levi had said, from up here, the western view of the neighboring farmland was both beautiful and restorative after her packed day, and the coming sunset promised to bring its own fireworks. "Gorgeous. It really is."

After she was finished with the blankets, Riley kicked out of her sandals and stepped onto the nearest one, while Arlo stayed on the grass, watching her.

"Isn't it?" Levi replied after pausing to appreciate

the view. "And in answer to your question, if it were up to me alone, I'd get a nice piece of land. That'd be my choice."

Sinking down, she crossed her legs and opened the basket that Levi placed before her. Last night and today had been so busy, she'd hardly given any thought as to where she'd like to live with Levi, but at this admission of his, her imagination burst into overdrive, envisioning two toddler sized kids running in the grass and Arlo watching over them, a barn with a horse or two in the distance.

Like Levi said, something about it felt entirely right, but there were other things she wanted to tell him first. "You and your very own John Deere," she said with a smile as Levi kicked off his shoes and sank down next to her. She passed him a linen napkin before pulling out the various items she'd bought and prepared: sliced gouda and aged white cheddar cheese, salami, olives, hard boiled eggs, hummus, bread, crackers, and three types of berries. She'd even found a baby-food size jar of Dijon mustard that was almost too cute to open. At the bottom next to the ice pack was a bottle of Sauvignon Blanc and a large, insulated water jug. Fastened into the top lid were two light-turquoise melamine plates from her mom's outdoor dining collection, silverware, and cups. "Have at it."

"Looks amazing, and no wonder that basket was so heavy."

"No kidding. It was heavier than I'd thought. And my mom is to thank for all these perfect little containers and plates. All my kitchen things are in a storage unit in Atlanta. I figured it didn't make sense to haul everything here since I didn't know where I was headed."

"Makes sense." He reached for the wine and wine opener. "Want me to?"

"Please."

Seeing that Arlo hadn't budged an inch but was watching from the grass, hopefully wagging his tail, Riley leaned over and patted the second blanket, beckoning him but to no avail. "What's the matter, bud? Don't you like polyester fleece?"

Lola, on the other hand, was just making it up the hill after chasing a butterfly. Panting happily, she collapsed onto her belly at the edge of the blanket without waiting for an invitation, her back legs stretching behind her. She eyed the food with what looked like an eager grin on those bulldog jowls of hers. After observing her ease on the blanket, Arlo stepped tentatively onto the second blanket, taking his time stretching out, letting out a long, slow grunt as he did.

"More than any dog ever, I'd love to know what he's thinking half the time," Levi said, popping open the cork.

"He's contemplative, that's for sure."

"No kidding."

Riley passed Levi two stemless silicone wine glasses, a recent find her mom had been happy to lend her. "I'm still getting used to the fact that I could've lost him forever, both with that woman adopting him and then with him running in front of that car."

"I bet. Well, he's yours now, and he's young. He's not going anywhere for a long time." Levi handed her the first glass before pouring his own.

"I guess that's been a theme in my life. Until now, at least." She took a sip, appreciating the dry crispness waking up her taste buds.

"How's that?"

"Not holding on to the things I love most the first time around. You. Him." She shrugged. "Riding lessons, even."

"We all make mistakes, Riley. The important thing is that we figure out when we've done so."

"I know, but I've been giving a lot of thought as to the why behind those mistakes."

"And what'd you figure out?"

"That I can't blame it all on my parents, not as much as I have been. Honestly, I can't blame *most of it* on my parents."

"What was it then?"

She was quite a moment, looking out across the field and considering her words. There was an old, two-story farmhouse surrounded by a copse of trees whose white siding on one side was glowing pinkish yellow where the growing sunset was reflecting off it. Something about the property and the glowing sunset had a timelessness to it that Riley wanted to lose herself in. A place like that, she thought, would be just perfect.

"That it seemed less painful to let something I love go—or to run away and try not look back, like with you—than to risk losing it when I wanted desperately to hold on."

Levi tucked his legs into a cross-legged position as well and began turning his glass in a circle between the fingers of both hands. "I always thought—I don't know—I guess I figured if you'd felt half as much as I did, it wouldn't have been easy to leave like that."

"It was anything but easy, Levi."

He nodded. "I guess what matters is what are you going to do about it now?"

Riley lifted a finger, a smile spreading across her face. "I'm glad you asked." Raising onto her knees, she stretched out and locked Levi's gift between two fingertips, pulling it closer. "I think it's time you open this."

He nodded toward the food she'd set out that the dogs were both eyeing so intently. "Don't you want to eat first? You went to a lot of trouble."

She shook her head and passed it to him. "Nope. Besides, this won't take long."

After handing her his wine glass, Levi placed the package on his lap and worked free the raffia.

He surprised her by first taking the time to tie the greenery attached to package around the wine bottle. While Riley couldn't imagine loving him any deeper than she already did, it occurred to her that there was still a host of beautiful things she'd yet to learn about him.

Once that was done, he refocused on the gift, turning it over and working his finger underneath the tape, freeing it so that the butcher paper stayed in one piece. He blinked to spy a pair of shoes tied together inside. "Shoes?" He turned them over, his eyebrows furrowing lightly. Not only were they clearly not his size, but they were also light-blue-and-white women's running shoes. And while they still had a new look to them, they'd been worn a handful of times.

Looking at her, he shook his head.

"I bought them in Atlanta right before coming here, after my last breakup. For a couple weeks there, I was all about starting to jog again, but I've come to the realization that I *hate* jogging. I don't know how I forced myself to do those 5Ks in high school. Every block was torture."

"So, you're giving them to me?" Levi asked, a crooked smile lighting his face.

"Well, I guess you could say it's a metaphorical gift."

He leaned in and brushed his lips against hers. "Riley Leighton, are you telling me you're ready to stop running? Because if you are, that's the best gift anyone's ever given me."

"I was hoping you'd appreciate my barely broken-in athletic shoes," she said with a giggle. Closing her eyes, Riley met him for a second kiss that deepened, lasting long enough that Lola hopped to her feet and ambled over to check out the food, unaware her clomping and noisy breathing would give her away. Levi pulled away to shoo Lola back to an acceptable distance, and Arlo gave Lola a look that seemed to say, "I told you so."

"Are you wanting to talk about what this means?"

"Not quite yet; there's one more thing," Riley said. "This one is both a literal *and* a figurative gift, and I didn't want to wrap it with the shoes, so it's in here."

"Note to self, put a lot of thought into your Christmas gifts for Riley and make sure they all have a deeper meaning."

Riley laughed and leaned over to get the second gift from the bottom of the picnic basket where she'd hidden it underneath the water jug. Also wrapped in butcher paper, this one was flat, floppy, and unadorned.

Levi took the same care unwrapping this one as he had the first. The kitchen towel was from her mom's natural linen collection. After Riley designed the image on her laptop, Brenda embroidered a traditional pineapple welcome symbol on the face of the towel with "Welcome" rounded above its green top, and "to Riley & Levi's" rounded below the bottom of the pineapple.

"I couldn't decide whose name to put first," she spouted off while he was still taking it in. She was about to add that she'd ended up flipping a coin, but suddenly he was kissing her again, this time more intensely, so much so that Arlo barked loud enough to hurt Riley's eardrums.

"Tell me this means you've decided you feel good about staying." His words were soft and husky, and he pulled away enough to look her in the eye.

Riley nodded. "I'm staying. That trip to Megan's I was talking about earlier… It turns out, there's an open position at High Grove. Mine, actually. The guy who'd taken it is staying in Washington."

Levi lifted a brow. "And?"

"And it's mine. Megan's not even posting it again." Riley raised an eyebrow. "I'm staying here, Levi, and I'm taking a job at High Grove, a place where I very much would've wanted to work all along had I not started running in the first place."

Levi sat back, studying her. "Wow. That's amazing, Riley. All I can say is when it's meant to be, it's meant to be. It's what you want though, staying here in St. Louis? You're sure? Because I love you, Riley. I should've said it before today. But I do. And I'll love you the same regardless of whether you're here or somewhere else."

"I know you do."

"Good, because I've been thinking how I shouldn't have pushed you like that last week. We can take this at whatever pace you'd like."

"Rabbit fast or turtle slow?" she said with a smile. "And last week, everything you said, it was what I needed to hear." She brushed her lips against his, savoring the experience of his mouth against hers before pulling away to press her forehead against his. "If you want to know, I've loved you forever, and now that I have you, I don't want to let go. Ever."

"Neither do I."

Down on the hillside, a big red squirrel was jumping from limb to limb of a big oak and started making enough of a racket to catch the dogs' attention. Faster than Riley would've given her credit for, Lola was on her feet and dashing down to the base of the tree, barking and planting her front paws against the bark.

"She's got some spunk, hasn't she?" Riley asked before noticing Arlo had gotten to his feet and was staring at the branch where the chittering squirrel was making a racket, its tail fluffed as it heckled Lola. He took off straight from the blanket at a slow lope, heading down the sloping hill more gracefully than expected in his boot.

He joined Lola at the base of the big oak. When he raised up on his back feet, bracing his front paws against the trunk of the tree, Arlo was tall enough that the squirrel clambered up a few branches higher, chittering even louder.

It was something to see them both stretched out as much as they were able, Lola with her squat legs, and Arlo a certifiable giant beside her. They dropped to all fours at the same time, and Arlo bent down to give Lola a sniff, his tail wagging easily.

"Maybe she'll teach him how to act like a dog if they hang out long enough," Riley said with a laugh.

"Yeah, maybe. The truth is I was hoping they'd get along."

"Oh, yeah?"

He shrugged. "When I lost my dog like that not quite a year ago, I didn't think I'd ever want another one. Maybe it helps that she's nothing like him. Neither of them are, honestly."

"I wouldn't imagine either of them are much like a devoted and rowdy Lab in his prime like your dog was." When Levi gave her a questioning look, she shrugged. "I internet stalked you often enough to catch some of your posts with him in it. He looked like a character."

"He was. Quite the character. And ditto."

"Will you tell me about him sometime?"

He looked away. "Mostly I try not to think about him."

"Take it from someone who knows. When you lock a lid on the things that hurt to think about, they never stop hurting."

He smiled softly. "I suspect you're right."

With the squirrel having retreated higher, both dogs lost enough interest that they headed back up the hill. Riley didn't think it was her imagination that Arlo was waiting on Lola when he paused and looked back over his shoulder, as if seeing where she was. "Look at that. They're becoming friends already."

Levi smiled. "Sometimes the unlikely pairs are the best fits."

"Touché," she said, certain he wasn't only talking about the dogs. "And maybe it's a good thing Marcus isn't warming up to her that fast."

"You mean because she's growing on me instead?"

"If the shoe fits."

Arlo reached the picnic blanket first and this time sank right next to the food like he was ready to be served a plate, making them both laugh. Breathing hard and tongue lolling, Lola planted herself within arm's reach of her oversize playmate, her round eyes also focused on Riley and Levi's dinner.

"You'd be good with keeping her too?" There was a hopeful undertone to his words that melted Riley's heart into a puddle.

"Of course, I would," she said without having to give it a moment of thought. "It'd be nice to have a dog to balance out the dog who thinks he's a person."

Looking down at his lap, Levi lifted the towel, appraising it a second time. "You know, a couple months ago, when I woke up in the hospital feeling like my head was in a vice and hardly able to recall a moment of the last several days, I was half resigned to thinking nothing would ever be right again. I'm a bit hard-pressed to believe things could turn around so easily."

Riley offered him back his wine glass and held hers up in a toast. "Well, Mr. Duncan, if I have anything to say about it, from here on out, things are only going to get better."

Chapter 29

Just shy of three weeks later, Levi headed to the same sloping hillside at the back of Marcus's property, though this time it was chilly enough to see his breath. The sky was glowing pink and purple in the east, the stars overhead were fading, and the nearly cloudless sky promised a fair-weather day ahead. High in the trees, a few crickets were still chirping, and a handful of birds were bustling about, hunting for worms in the grass or staking off their territory in the tree branches, but the morning had a quiet stillness about it that came in fall. Lola and Arlo were keeping him company, while in the big house, all the kenneled dogs must've been still sleeping, silent as they were.

The two dogs trailed behind Levi as they headed deeper into the property, sniffing various spots in the damp morning grass. For his first night without Riley since his adoption, Arlo was being a trooper, even if he'd had a bit of trouble settling down initially.

It was "go" day in more than one way, and Levi had been awake for the last hour, his mind buzzing with the dozen different things that still needed to be done before the gates opened to the public at ten. Before tackling any of them, he was treating himself to this short morning walk.

Back when he and Riley had begun planning this friendraiser in conjunction with Marcus's open house, neither of them had realized it coincided with her thirtieth birthday. Once he'd made the connection, Levi had decided there was no excuse; it was go big, or go home. It had worked out in his favor that he'd had last night without her to get ready, thanks to Riley and Lana having a girls' night to celebrate both of them turning thirty this week.

While Riley hadn't wanted to abandon Levi the night before the big event, she'd had no idea it was by design that last night was the only night that Lana claimed to be available. Levi had needed the night without Riley to finish getting things ready and to do a quick run through with the SAR dogs, whose weekly practice session had been moved to Friday night instead of this morning thanks to today's event. Most of the group would be back here today as well, doing demonstrations in the big field that had been roped off for them yesterday.

"What do you think, Arlo?" Levi asked when the curious canine was the first to join him on top of the small hill. Standing here, Levi had the perfect view of both things he wanted Riley to see this afternoon: the SAR dogs' field and the remarkable farmhouse flanking the property to the southwest.

In the field, a ten-by-ten canvas tent had been set up in the front corner. Underneath it was a table that would serve as an information booth for the St. Louis County SAR dog group, but the tent didn't block anything important from view. From up here, the markers that had been strategically placed in the field—three tires, a portable mailbox, and two wooden pallets—looked like random practice stations for the dogs.

Arlo lingered next to him, looking up at him expectantly. The grass was too damp for him to want to lie down, and no doubt, the exceptionally perceptive dog wondered why they were standing up here doing nothing.

Levi fiddled with Arlo's new collar and its attached bone-shaped pouch meant for carrying rabies tags, keys, pet waste bags, or any small item of choice. Lola was wearing one as well. Levi had bought the new collars with a specific purpose in mind, though when they'd arrived, he told Riley that he'd bought them so that they'd always have a bag or two around when they were on the go.

Both dogs had been wearing their new collars for a week now, and the waste bags had in fact come in useful a time or two. After Riley had taken off yesterday morning for work, Levi had replaced the bags with small leather gift boxes instead. He'd wanted the dogs to get used to the pouch being weightier, and he'd wanted to test the zippers with something bulkier inside than decomposable bags. "So far, so good," he said, sliding the zipper shut, after which Arlo gave his big head and neck a shake and stared at Levi's front jeans pocket.

Chuckling, Levi pulled out a treat and gave it to him, not making him sit in the damp grass before receiving it. "Just do me a favor and be this on point when you're up here with me this afternoon, will you?"

Arlo munched the treat loudly enough that Lola realized from twenty feet away that she was missing out on something. She loped up the hill and sank into attention, not minding the wet grass one bit. Though, with her squat stature, she was mostly wet now anyway. Offering her a treat of her own, Levi crouched down. He scratched the top of her head as she munched and checked her collar.

"Who wants to give Riley what?" He smiled at himself for putting the offer out there. "What am I talking about? Unless you're on leashes, you'll be up here first, Arlo, no doubt." He scratched Lola under the chin. "Just do me a favor, girl, and don't dawdle, will you? I'm going to need you too."

Giving her a pat, he stood up. He wished Tank were here for this. No doubt, the three of them would've been like the three canine musketeers. Who was he kidding? More like Larry, Moe, and Curly. Levi was no longer trying to tamp down his memories of Tank. At first, this release had stirred up a cavern of ache inside him. It still wasn't easy, but more than once, he'd caught himself smiling at one thing or another, like the time he'd come home a couple hours late from work to find that Tank had worked open the fridge, torn apart a pizza box, and eaten every last crumb of the leftovers, or the time they'd had the beach to themselves, and Levi had made a game of hiding Tank's tennis balls in the sand, then letting him lose to sniff them out. Each time, he'd find them faster than the last.

The remarkable dog should've gotten more than three years. The buddy he lost last year in a diving accident should've gotten more than twenty-five.

But that was life. There were no guarantees, and that in itself was a big part of what made the human experience precious. Anytime he tumbled down the trail of regret as to the years he and Riley lost, he intended to remind himself that the ones stretching out before them would be even sweeter as a result. And as far as Levi was concerned, he'd be savoring each one.

———

Riley heard her best friend before she spotted her in the light crowd. Lana was with Grant and the kids over at the balloon animal tent soothing Jackson. The little guy was on the verge of a tantrum, convinced the gold kitty balloon being made was for him, not the little girl in front of him who'd asked for it.

"But I want *that* kitty." His lower lip was quivering, and his eyes were welling with tears.

"I thought you wanted a puppy," Grant chimed in, rolling his eyes playfully as Riley walked up.

"I *do* want a puppy!" This awareness proved too much. Jackson dropped to the grass and wept, a toddler-sized mound of dejection.

With Grant wearing the baby sling and swaying back and forth with a dozing Rosie, Lana was free to hoist Jackson into her arms. She patted his back and leaned her head against his as he collapsed against her. "None of them slept well last night," she said to Riley in explanation. "Go figure. They never do when I'm not there, not that our girls' night wasn't worth it, because it was."

"That includes me," Grant said, stifling a yawn, though Riley could already tell that by the dark circles under his eyes. "I'll be due for a tucking in early tonight."

"Oh, bummer. You guys didn't have to come," Riley said. "I'd have understood."

"Lana wouldn't have missed this for the world." Grant clamped his mouth shut as Lana gave him a look. "What?" he shot off.

It was Lana's turn to roll her eyes before turning to Riley. "It's your first big fundraiser. Of course, we're here."

Riley knew better than to hop in on whatever was causing that underlying tension and stuck with a far easier subject. "Friendraiser, technically. Today's more about awareness than raising funds, though whatever proceeds are made will be split between the five nonprofits that're here."

"Big of Marcus not to take a penny from this," Lana said.

"He's getting his name out there. For him, that's what matters. Hopefully he'll pick up a lot of new customers too."

Grant rolled his eyes, smirking. "Have you seen him recently? He's got a line of people fifteen deep waiting to talk to him. I'm thinking they mistook him for Idris Alba."

"Jealous much?" Lana coughed into her hand.

Riley choked back a laugh. Good friends that they were, Grant and Marcus always had a bit of competition going, but Grant was right about the line. For the bulk of each hour, Marcus was in one of the training pens, offering short training consultations with anyone who'd brought their dog along and wanted pointers. From what Riley had seen, he'd not had a dull moment all day, though mostly she'd been too busy troubleshooting to talk to him yet.

The second paddock had been turned into a scent maze for today's event, and the third into an agility course. With the property being so big and the events spread out, it was hard to estimate, but

Riley's best guess was that there had been a couple hundred families here at any one time for the last several hours. Those press releases and social media posts had done their job. Thank goodness for the extra row of parking spaces they'd marked out in the grass at the last minute this morning.

Spying that the balloon woman was finishing up, Riley called out to Jackson, who was burrowing his head closer against his mom's neck and rubbing his eyes. "Hey, buddy, it's your turn for a balloon." To Lana, she nodded toward the basket of aluminum water bottles she was carrying. "I'll catch up with you later if you don't head out first. I've got to run these to the greyhound group. They haven't used their drink coupons yet." It had been Levi's idea to make the event plastic free. Food and drinks were being served in easily recyclable or compostable packages. "Oh, and make sure you stop by High Grove's station. There's a senior yorkie here who'd be so good with the kids. Just saying..."

Before Grant could object, she headed off. Last night, Lana had confessed to wanting a dog, and Riley had made it a personal mission to see to it her friend ended up with the perfect fit for her family once Lana talked Grant into another being to care for under their roof.

Two other staff and several volunteers from High Grove were here, along with the ten dogs who'd been at the shelter longest. Riley had high hopes that all ten would get adopted today. Mrs. Reyes from the farm animal rescue out past Washington was participating as well. In addition to the two piglets Riley and Levi had dropped off who'd yet to be adopted, she had two pygmy goats, several geese, and a miniature pony, and hers had proven to be quite the popular spot today. The other two nonprofits participating in the open house today were a group who trained service dogs for veterans with PTSD and the St. Louis County SAR dog association.

For recreation, in addition to the balloon animals, maze, and agility course, there was a dog-friendly photo booth, and a cartoonist with an uncanny ability to draw people as the dogs they most closely resembled—though Riley's mom had not been that pleased with being drawn as a bulldog. There was also a cupcake and dog-treat walk, and a dance area over by the food and picnic station.

Busy as she'd been, Riley was still determined to make time to get Arlo and Lola around to a few of the activities. When her parents and Tommy had shown up an hour ago, Riley had talked Tommy into dog-sitting duty, and the last she'd checked, he was hanging out over by the picnic area with both dogs. Earlier, they'd been hanging out with Levi, who was helping with the barbeque when he wasn't troubleshooting one minor emergency or another.

Riley intended to head over there, but by the time she finished delivering the water, her walkie-talkie was going off again. Another half hour had passed, and the crowd was visibly thinning when she spotted Levi coming her way with both dogs on leashes. At the start of the event, Lola hadn't been leashed, but with all the unknown dogs on the property, they figured it was safer to keep the trustworthy canine tethered at least until the crowds died down a bit more.

"How you holding up?" Levi asked when they met in the middle. "Get anything to eat? You never came by for that hot dog."

"I'm okay for now. Adrenaline's carrying me through. It's going great, don't you think?" She brushed her lips against his before leaning down to hug Arlo, who whined like they'd been apart for days rather than hours. Lola, on the other hand, was focused on watching a sweat bee buzzing around in the clover and paid her no notice whatsoever.

"I do. Fantastic, actually," Levi said. "You know how to organize a successful event, I'll give you that. We just ran out of hot dogs and veggie dogs. The burgers will be gone soon too, beef *and* plant, though I still find it hard to believe you were right about how many people readily forgo meat when it looks, tastes, and smells so much better."

Riley collapsed against him, draping her arms around his waist. "I don't know about you, but Marcus's hot tub is calling my name. I'm betting I more than made my ten-thousand-step goal hours ago. Maybe we can make use of it tonight…assuming I have the strength to walk my butt out there."

Levi's laugh echoed in his chest against her ear. "Good thing we decided to put off celebrating your birthday until tomorrow. And you keep forgetting there's a golf cart at your disposal."

"I've been using it. Mostly."

"So, you in middle of anything right now?"

Riley stepped back from his arms and shook her head. "No, I just finished a round of emptying the donation jars. I'd love to take these two through that scent maze. Got a couple minutes to join me? The crowd's thinning out a bit."

"Yeah, sure, but I want you to see something first." He locked a hand around hers and started walking before she even agreed, heading for the back of property.

"With the search and rescue group?"

"Kind of."

Rather than heading to the SAR dog information booth as she'd anticipated, Levi led them up the sloping hillside across from it. Ever since their picnic last month, the quiet knoll had become her favorite spot to sit out and watch the stars whenever she was here at night with Levi. For the event today, no activities had been stationed up there, to keep everything accessible to all. However, it had proven to be a popular spot for kids to run around, and for some of them to roll down as well.

"Everything okay?" she asked after spying that his breathing was off more than the sloping hill warranted.

"Yeah," he said, locking a hand over her shoulder. "Never better. I just wanted an out of the way place to tell you happy birthday. If this event is any indication, you're going to have a remarkable decade."

"Thanks, but honestly, I don't see how it couldn't be. You, these two, my job at High Grove. My family showing up to support me at an event that is everything dog and nothing cat. If I had candles to blow out right now, I don't know what I'd wish for." Her thoughts flashed back to Lana and Grant a little bit ago and the sweet warmth that filled her when she was around the kids, even when they were tired and cranky. *Well, maybe one thing. But there'll be time for that.*

"Not a thing?" he asked, a smile playing on his lips.

Riley shook her head, laughing softly. "I know you, Levi. You're up to something, so you might as well tell me."

"You think?"

Arlo had also picked up on the change in energy and was looking between them inquisitively, while Lola had plopped on the grass, panting happily.

Levi stepped close and pressed his lips against her forehead. "You really can't think of anything? What about a place to call our own? With a bit of space to it. A house with some character and a lot of possibility."

Riley tucked a lock of hair behind her ear. "Well, I guess I meant something we aren't already focused on, seeing as how we're online looking every day." They'd decided on property as opposed to a house in Webster but were waiting until the right one popped up within a half hour drive to High Grove. There were a few places they'd given serious consideration to but had decided to hold out for something better.

He pressed his lips together and took a breath. "So, don't shoot the messenger, but the right thing came up a week ago, and I've been working to make it happen."

"What do you mean?"

"I'd tell you, but Arlo fought me for dibs and won."

Riley shook her head, laughing. "You're being such a Levi right now, you know that?"

"I'm totally serious."

"That Arlo wants to tell me something?" Riley leaned over and cupped her hands around Arlo's big head. He wagged his tail excitedly and licked the tip of her nose. "What is it you want to tell me, boy?" she asked, dragging the back of her hand over her nose to wipe off his doggie kiss.

After a handful of seconds of Arlo looking at her expectantly had passed, Levi said, "If this were an escape room, you'd need to be looking for a clue."

Riley looked over her shoulder at Levi. "You're serious? We're playing an escape room game? Right now?"

He shrugged. "This one is easier to solve than you might think."

Riley returned her attention to Arlo, who was clearly trying to figure out what was going on as well. Lola, on the other hand, had stretched out completely on her side and was blinking deeply like she was about to fall into a doze. Riley gave Arlo a once over, and it struck her that the small pouch on his collar was bulging more than it typically did. Either Levi had overstuffed it with pet waste bags, or he'd slipped something else in there. Shaking her head lightly, Riley unzipped the pouch. She gasped to spy the small rectangular leather box inside.

"It's not what you think," Levi interjected.

"How do you know what I think it is?"

"Doesn't every girl think the same thing when she's surprised with a jewelry box?"

"Oh my gosh, you're so not a romantic, even when you're *trying* to be romantic. Do you want me to open it, whatever it is?"

He nodded, chuckling.

Riley worked the box free from the pouch and took a steadying breath before lifting open the lid. Whatever this was, she certainly hadn't expected any birthday presents in the middle of the event.

Inside was a piece of paper that had been folded

several times. When she lifted it out, something shiny fell to the ground. Arlo dipped to sniff it, so Riley knew right where it landed. Spying a silver key lying in the grass, her pulse began to race. "Levi, are you telling me you bought a house?"

His lips were pressed flat, and he shrugged, so Riley had nothing left to do but open the folded paper. She stared in silence a few seconds at a color photocopy of a very familiar farmhouse. She turned toward the farmhouse to the southwest— the one she'd lost minutes appreciating every time they were up here—confirming they were one and the same. "Levi, are you telling me you bought that house? I thought Marcus said they wouldn't sell in a million years when you asked him about it."

He ran his tongue over his lips. "I know you haven't gotten to see inside, but we've looked at enough houses the last few weeks that I know you'll love it. It's got great bones, and whatever you don't like, we'll fix."

Swiping at a swell of tears, Riley started to pick up the key, but Levi was already dipping for it. She looked from the paper to the house again, shaking her head in disbelief. "I don't know what to say except I promise never to say you're not romantic ever again."

"That's good, because I really am trying here."

She looked back at Levi to find that after getting the key, he'd dropped to one knee. Suddenly the world was spinning wildly enough that Riley had to plant her feet not to fall backward. Was he proposing to her with a key? Even if he was, she'd take it.

Then, with zero formality, he passed her the key. "We'll go later. If you like it, it's ours. The house and all forty-two acres. The contract's negotiated, but we still have to sign."

Riley took the key in shaky hands. He was talking about the house, but he was still down on one knee. "I already know I'm going to love it."

He grinned. "You are. It's even better up close. The catch here is Lola wanted a piece of this birthday celebration too, and now she's falling asleep. In her defense, it's been a big day."

Riley bit her lip, watching as Levi slid Lola's collar in a circle until the pouch was on top and accessible. When it was obvious that Lola's pouch was crammed with more than bags too, Riley clamped a hand over her mouth.

Eyes opening again, Lola lifted her head an inch, mouth gaping open in a grin, but otherwise didn't budge an inch.

Riley's tears started flowing once more even before Levi pulled out a second small jewelry box, this one perfectly square. Without dropping her gaze, Levi nodded down the hill in the opposite direction of the farmhouse. "Riley, will you..."

Confused, she followed his gaze. A small crowd of guests over at the search and rescue station were staring up at them. Her parents and Tommy were among them, as were Marcus, Lana, Grant, and the kids, but Riley's vision was so clouded with tears it was hard to make out their expressions. Suddenly she realized Lana was pointing toward the SAR dogs.

The dogs and their handlers had spread out in the field in a specific pattern. A second later, it hit her. "Marry me," she whispered, her voice barely audible.

When she looked back at Levi, he was holding a ring, a gorgeous solitaire on a platinum band. "Yeah," he said, grinning. "Will you marry me, Riley Leighton? We didn't have enough dogs and people to spell the whole thing out."

Before he had time to stand, Riley sank to her knees and sat back on her heels, brushing away tears as Arlo gently nuzzled her hair.

"You okay?" Levi asked, concern lining his expression.

Riley nodded. "Better than okay. Just have to catch my breath. For a second there, I thought I was going to pass out in front of all these people."

Still holding the ring, Levi sank back on his heels too. "Take all the time you need."

Wiping at a few fresh tears, she laughed and shook her head. "I already did that, didn't I, and I'll never need to do it again. Yes, I'll marry you, Levi. A thousand times over, I'll marry you."

Levi closed his eyes for the space of a breath before slipping the ring on her finger, a ring that somehow fit perfectly. He brushed his lips against hers. "Riley, you taught me that some endings have new beginnings on their tails, and for that, you've made me the happiest man on the planet." He grinned and kissed her again. "Most certainly, the happiest man this side of St. Louis."

Laughing, Riley closed her eyes and rested her forehead against his, taking the experience in for a handful of seconds before the world pressed in. Unsure of what was going on but wanting to get in on the excitement, Arlo woofed loud enough that Lola hopped to her feet, startled. She pressed in alongside him, and for the moment, it was just the four of them on a hill with a view that made it seem like time could stand still.

If you love Debbie Burns's heart-warming contemporary romance, don't miss Book 6 in the Rescue Me series

TO BE LOVED BY YOU

Ava Graham pulled into the High Grove Animal Shelter a solid six minutes ahead of schedule and snagged one of the last open parking spots. With the wild morning she'd had, the handful of extra minutes was a gift. An hour ago, making it here at all—let alone on time, let alone early—had seemed next to impossible despite the promise she'd made to her sister, Olivia. Considering this afternoon's dog wash was one of the few things Ava had been looking forward to all week, she was pleased on many levels.

Ava's eleven o'clock Saturday-morning real-estate closing had gone from bad to worse when her high-profile clients had come up with a handful of nitpicky items on their final walk-through.

While waiting on hold for the front-desk assistant to reschedule the closing for Monday, Ava fished out the first three wrapped chocolates she could reach at the bottom of her purse. Finding them to be one chocolate caramel, one dark chocolate, and one milk chocolate, she smiled. Too much repetition wasn't as enjoyable as a variety. Most everyone had their vices; Ava's was chocolate—sweets in general, but chocolate always topped her list of stress-relieving indulgences.

As the assistant clicked her tongue while combing their agency's packed schedule and the sound rolled over Ava's Jeep's speakers, she glanced discreetly at the silver van immediately to her left. The passenger seat closest to her was empty, but the driver was still inside. Like her, he was on the phone. She could hear the faint, muffled voice of a woman through his speakers.

A movement through the van's middle window caught her attention. Where she'd expected to spy a kid or two, her gaze landed on a dog, a big, adorable black-and-tan one. The window was too tinted for her to be confident of the breed, but the animal was watching her attentively, head tilted thirty degrees, as its handsome owner stared off into the narrow strip of trees between the parking lot and street.

A touch guiltily, Ava popped the dark chocolate piece into her mouth. *You aren't thirteen and bingeing in your closet*, she reminded herself. Grabbing a bite of food when she'd be occupied the next several hours was nothing to be embarrassed about. Like it or not, in the wake of her short-lived marriage, the resulting sale of the condo she'd adored, and moving into her sister's one-bedroom apartment until she had a better sense of what she wanted to do next, Ava had been feeling particularly uprooted, and this had her feeling not so far removed from the teenager who'd hidden in closets and school bathrooms to binge on brownies, cupcakes, and candy bars when the world was too much to handle.

Thankfully, two things had kept her afloat these last few months—her rekindled relationship with her sister and her decision to enroll in a yoga-teacher-training program. When Ava was on her yoga mat, everything made sense.

When the assistant let out a sigh, Ava tensed, hoping for good news. "Looks like we can squeeze your clients in at eleven thirty."

"Thank heavens." Ava let her head fall back against the headrest.

When the meeting time was booked, she hung up and settled back in her seat, popping the milk chocolate piece into her mouth and promising herself a nice, healthy dinner later tonight. While her clients hadn't gotten the keys to their dream house this morning, they were getting a two-night stay at the Ritz, and most of their demands had been met. It was a good enough way to go into the second half of her Saturday.

Before heading inside, Ava savored a few seconds of silence while attempting to work some of the tension from her shoulders. Just as she was opening the driver's-side door, a new text popped up from her sister.

> Spotted you pulling in. The dogs will be here soon. Glad you're joining! Left a bag of clothes behind the counter. Find me out back when you're done with Tess.

Leaving her door ajar, Ava responded by filling one entire line with alternating soap and dog emojis before dropping her phone in her purse. She was unwrapping the last chocolate—the milk chocolate caramel—and was about to pop it into her mouth when the big dog she'd been admiring rushed right up to her, planting his front paws on her doorjamb and pressing in to greet her.

Ava jumped reflexively before looking into the most endearing brown eyes mere inches away. He must've gotten out on the other side of the van while she'd been on her call. He was a big dog, no question, maybe eighty or ninety pounds, and he took up most of the open doorway of her Jeep, so much so, she could feel his breath on her face. His mouth gaped open in a playful grin, his ears perked forward but folded at the tips, and his tail was wagging. His expression, at once playful and pleading, was priceless, and his long, silky black and brown fur invited her to bury her hands in it. Whatever assortment of breeds he was, it was a big-dog mix that blended together into a ball of perfection. "Seriously, could you be any cuter?"

"Rolo! Down, buddy." The guy had gotten out as well and was jogging over. Reaching them, he locked his hand around the dog's collar, gently pulling him down from Ava's doorjamb, causing the dog to let out what could only be described as a disappointed grunt. "Sorry!" the guy added, his tone sincere. "He's never run up to someone's car like this before. Ever."

Ava grinned at the connection between the dog's name and the chocolate caramel in her hand even before the dog was out of the way and she was able to get a good look at his owner. "It's okay. Rolo, huh?" Dang, the dog and owner were a well-matched pair. The guy was even cuter head-on, a grounded, classical kind of handsome with dark, wavy hair, broad shoulders, and a short beard. And those eyes—hazel green and piercing. They were more effective at filling her with a spurt of energy than a double shot of espresso. "Well, it was fated, I'm sure." She lifted the chocolate in her hand for him to see. "It's a Dove, not a Rolo, but it's still chocolate caramel." To the dog, Ava added, "I'm sorry, buddy, if it wasn't chocolate, it'd be all yours."

The guy raised an eyebrow. "How about that? There's some synchronicity for you."

Synchronicity. Ava had heard her yoga teacher say something similar more than once in yoga-teacher training. *"Pay attention to life's little synchronicities. They're like road signs on a trip with no map."*

Still looking at her, the dog whined and wagged his tail. Ava reached out and let him sniff her hand, his cold, wet nose tickling her knuckles. "That's for sure," she replied.

She was about to ask the guy's name when her phone rang out from inside her purse, its tone somehow considerably more jarring than normal and cutting right through the pleasant vibe hanging in the air.

The guy stepped back a foot, and his easygoing smile vanished. "Hey, I'll let you take that. Sorry again." With a glance at his dog, he clapped his hand once against the side of his thigh. "Rolo, come."

He headed off in the direction of the shelter before Ava had time to reply. *That's it? Didn't we just have a little moment there?*

Rolo obeyed his owner but glanced back longingly as they crossed the parking lot, causing Ava's disappointment to settle in deeper. She fished out her phone from her purse to see that her agency had called with a potential lead that she wasn't about to take on right now. Her schedule was already packed to the brim.

Popping the chocolate into her mouth, she watched in her rearview mirror as the two neared the shelter's front entrance, the dog trotting confidently at the man's side without a leash. After they headed in, Ava closed her eyes and rolled her neck in a few slow circles, wondering what exactly had her feeling so unexpectedly disappointed.

No dating until you're in your own place, remember? And even if his dog is adorable, he's most likely married with kids.

After a handful of calming breaths that helped wash away the lingering buzz of her chaotic morning and a quick teeth check, she chugged some water and hopped out.

The door to the shelter popped open as she was crossing the parking lot, and Tess, the shelter's lead trainer, stepped into view, a wide smile on her face. "Thanks for squeezing me in first. With as many dogs as we'll be washing this afternoon, I doubt you'll want to stick around long afterward."

"I bet you're right." Ava followed Tess into the building. It was awash with commotion and crowded with a slew of potential adopters talking to staff, watching the cats in the kitty play area, and browsing in the gift shop.

On the far side of the room, Ava spotted the guy again and immediately reminded herself she wasn't noticing guys on the other side of the room—or anywhere else, for that matter. He was listening attentively to Patrick, the quirky staff member who'd be coordinating today's large-scale dog wash, no doubt better than anyone else here could. Rolo was five feet away, standing on his back legs, front paws resting on the back counter, as he sniffed the shelter's resident senior cat, who was curled up contentedly and ignoring the giant canine checking her out.

"No doubt all this chaos makes it obvious why I'm proposing we do your class after hours." Tess motioned around the room as she led them to the only open adoption desk.

"No kidding. I'm sure the quieter it is, the better chance we'll have of getting the dogs to relax." Truth be told, in her two hundred hours of yoga-teacher training, Ava hadn't learned a single thing about introducing dogs to yoga.

"I can't tell you how pumped I am to offer this class." Tess's excitement was evident on her face and in her tone as she took a seat on the opposite side of the desk. "I figured we'd offer the first one as a pop-up class before we list the series on the website. I'm sure you know we have a loyal following who'll bring their dogs back to visit any chance they get, but I can't tell you how many requests I get for yoga with dogs. You're still good for starting this Tuesday?"

"Yep. I went ahead and blocked off Tuesday nights in my calendar for the next two months. I've found if I'm not proactive, I spend all my waking hours with my clients touring houses and at closings and such."

"That's like me and dogs. My fiancé asked me the other day if I dream in barks and whines instead of English."

Ava laughed. Having heard about Tess's skill with dogs, she could almost imagine that.

Over the next fifteen minutes, they decided on the flow of the trial class and came up with a list of poses to try. Tess would be announcing the class to the High Grove Heroes Facebook group, a group whose seasoned canine alums would hopefully be comfortable enough here to relax next to their owners. Ava decided she'd start the class with a few simple poses for the new yogis while the dogs—hopefully—hung out on their owners' mats. During the second half, Ava and Tess would help the yogis assist their canine counterparts in some beneficial poses for them.

As they were wrapping up, the drone of oversize vehicles nearly drowned them out. Through the wide front windows, Ava spotted three full-sized cargo vans and one small moving truck pulling into the parking lot. Brakes squeaking, they headed toward the back parking lot.

"Looks like it's go time," Tess said, standing up.

"It's hitting home how many dogs you guys are taking in with this rescue. That's a genuine convoy out there."

"No kidding. Between the new kennels and the two revamped trailers out back, we'll be doubling our numbers of dogs. Another twenty or so are going to be fostered by staff and volunteers. The rest will be moving through to other shelters. The plan was to expand slowly, but then this came up, and you know how it goes. On the bright side, considering the dogs' breeds, we expect they'll move right on out of here after they get out of quarantine."

Ava was having a hard time wrapping her head around how anyone could've kept upward of three hundred dogs on their property, even a for-profit venture. Growing up on her grandparents' farm, she'd found it difficult to divide her attention between the two or three dogs that were always around. "I can imagine goldendoodles and labradoodles getting snatched up fast. And what's the other breed, Maltipoos?"

"Yep. If Ewoks had dogs, they'd be Maltipoos, no question."

Ava giggled. "I can't wait to see what they look like. Speaking of which, I'd better get moving. I still need to change. I got hung up at a signing and didn't have time to run home."

Tess promised to meet her out back, and Ava headed to the counter for the bag her sister had left before locking herself in the nearest bathroom. She sifted through the tote to find pink jogging shorts, a sleeveless orange exercise tank, and flower-power flip-flops and let out a groan. *This is what I get for not having time to run home first.*

Begrudgingly, she stripped down and slipped into clothes that were markedly tighter on her than Olivia's clothes used to be. "I'm going to look like a walking sherbet cone. And an overstuffed one at that."

She reminded herself that it wasn't as if she were here to impress anyone, and her thoughts immediately flashed to Rolo's owner, whom she'd lost track of while talking to Tess. *You have no one to impress, Ava. No one.*

As she stashed her purse, phone, and the tote bag in one of the empty lockers in the shelter's break room, it occurred to her how familiar she was becoming with this place. She wasn't an official volunteer, but today's dog wash would be the third project she'd be helping with in the last few months.

"You really need to make this volunteering thing official," Olivia had said last night, and Ava couldn't deny the wisdom in it. Her hesitation was her packed real-estate schedule and hopefully expanding yoga classes. She'd been known to create time in her schedule that wasn't there, but even she had her limits.

She headed through the kennels, pausing to pet a few dogs who were pleading for attention. Her insides melted at the look an adult pit bull with silver-blue fur and matching eyes gave her. The sweet thing licked the flat of her palm and wagged her nubbin tail. Heart melting, Ava sidestepped into the break room where she knew a jar of treats was stashed and snuck a couple paw-print-shaped treats to the happy dog before heading outside through the rear exit. "Sweet girl, I hope you're snatched up quicker than those newly renovated condos in the West End."

Shielding her eyes from the bright midday sun as she stepped outside, Ava looked around at all the people and stations that had been set up.

Patrick, the newly promoted operations manager with an uncanny ability to retain facts and figures that would make him an MVP at any trivia night, was holding two orange traffic batons tucked under one arm and was over by the vehicles that had pulled in, talking to the drivers. He was dressed in a red polo and his typical cargo pants that had as many pockets as Ava had shoes.

Elsewhere, several of the staff were setting up what would soon be various washing stations.

"Hey, I was just coming to check on you. I see you found the clothes."

Acknowledgments

Writing stories reminds me of working in the garden. Some days are joyful and productive, and the harvest is plentiful. Other days, it's a bit like toiling under a hot sun, and the words are weeds with roots that won't budge. By and large, writing *You're My Home* was one of the easy days in the garden. The next sentence, paragraph, and chapter were always at the ready, so eager were Riley, Levi, Arlo, and Lola to share their stories with me.

Also like a day in the garden, life has an ebb and flow from easy to trying, but it's love that gets us through—love of family, friends, partners, and our animals. Over the years, the pet stories you've shared have warmed my heart, especially the ones by readers who've been inspired to adopt a shelter pet. Like the second-chance romance between Levi and Riley, shelter animals can find happily-ever-afters with their human counterparts too. Thank you for your part in this. Whether you're starting now or have been with me through all seven books in the Rescue Me series, I'm thankful you're here. It's been an honor to create each and every one of these novels.

In addition, I'd like to thank the amazing team at Sourcebooks Casablanca—from the cover design team to the copy editors and everyone in between—for all they do to bring these stories to light. Special thanks to my talented editor, Deb Werksman, who believed in this series from the beginning and who has helped shape each story with her keen guidance. Thanks also to Megan Records for her insightful eye and for helping me to see exactly what *You're My Home* needed to shine. Thanks to beta readers Theresa Schmidt and Sandy Thal for your valued insight as well. As always, thanks to my agent, Jessica Watterson, at Sandra Dijkstra Literary Agency, for her unwavering support. Here's to many more books together!

About the Author

Debbie Burns is the bestselling author of heart-warming women's fiction and love stories featuring both two- and four-legged stars. While her books have earned many awards and commendations, her favorite praise is from readers who've been inspired to adopt a pet in need from their local shelter.

Debbie lives in St. Louis with her family, two thoroughly spoiled rescue dogs, and a friendly but self-absorbed Maine coon cat who has made appearances in two of her stories. When she isn't writing (or reading), you can find her hiking in the Missouri woods, working in her garden, or savoring time with family and friends.

Follow Debbie online:

Facebook: /authordebbieburns

Instagram: @_debbieburns

Bookbub: @AuthorDebbieBurns